The Girl in
the Red Wig

Trigger Warnings

As the author of this book, I value the sensitivity of the reader. This is a New Adult romance book with some dark and disturbing themes. The trigger warnings are strategically placed in the back of the book (on the last page) for readers who want to avoid any potential spoilers. If you're easily triggered, I *highly* encourage you to read the trigger warnings before starting this book. Thank you.

Sincerely,

Timothy Kyle

Dedication

This book is for the person who feels different, looks different, and maybe thinks a little differently. I hope you read this book and learn to love your brand of different. That's because, as my mom taught me, we *all* deserve affection, attention, and appreciation. And most importantly, we deserve a life where we feel like we matter. That's because you do! I promise!

Other Work by Timothy Kyle

The Tree House

Prologue

David

I look out into the backyard as the water runs down our sliding glass door. The multiplying water droplets make everything outside so blurry and distorted—the full moon, the light post by our shed, even the stars look different when the water trickles down the glass in the middle of the night.

The crash of thunder has my whole body flinching. The wrenching pain in my stomach spreads upward, slowly creating a suffocating pressure over my chest and throat. It's like an incurable flesh-eating disease, devouring what's left of my insides. Luckily, there's not much left.

Everyone else is asleep. I only know because I've checked multiple times. Sleep has felt impossible lately. I can close my eyes for prolonged periods of time, but falling into a bliss of unconsciousness only feels like a fantasy.

How does a twelve-year-old boy sleep into a dream or alternate reality? That's what I want—to blink and wake up in a new life. The kind of life where people aren't unfairly taken away from you in the blink of an eye.

"The roads were slick. Six inches this way, and we're looking at a totally different outcome," the police officer said to my father.

The words keep playing back in my head. Each time, it's like barbed wire slowly scraping through the inside of my chest. Then I hear the screams of a grown man as he collapses to his knees, begging. I wasn't meant to hear those words preceding his screams, but I did. I'm glad I did. It showed me the true evils of the world.

"Twelve, twenty-one, eighteen, thirty-six. For emergencies only," my dad told me when I was younger.

The numbers to the safe click as I rotate the knob. I grab hold of the metal handle, surprised by how cold and heavy it is in my hand. I'm sure this qualifies somewhere under the umbrella of emergencies—no longer wanting to live. But if I left this world to escape the pain, would I even find her? Perhaps that's a risk worth taking, albeit selfish to Dad and Angela.

I walk back downstairs, feeling the weight of my world in my right hand. I close my eyes and lean my forehead into the sliding glass door. This sharp, cold sensation sends a shiver down my spine and may be the last feeling I experience.

The Glock 19 goes up to the side of my head. My index finger becomes clammy as it traces along the trigger. I close my eyes. Then, my countdown begins.

Five, four, three…

Our aluminum trash can clanging to the ground has my attention. I put the gun on the counter to take a closer look outside. All I can see is a shadowy figure. The figure then walks under the light post by our shed.

It's a girl!

I know this girl. I rarely ever see her, but I know her. But there's something off. She's huddled under the thin eve of our shed roof.

A white light flashes, giving me a split-second vision of the girl. Another thunderous roar from the sky follows the lightning. I watch the young girl shiver in her pajamas, soaking to the bone.

Millions of questions run through my head. The first is why a girl my age is in my backyard in the middle of the night. Or why her lips move to a conversation she could only be having with herself. But those questions are suddenly unimportant. The intriguing part is the way the light post shines down upon her fiery red hair. It's odd how it doesn't look damp despite the rain coming down harder. In fact, it has a translucent red glow that has my eyes transfixed. It's *so red*.

It takes another minute or two before I gather the courage to head outside with my umbrella. The closer I get to her, the more I feel the need to slow my approach. She's huddled against the shed siding with her back to me. All I hear is the indistinct mumbling of words and water pelting the shed.

"Hey! Hey! Are you okay?"

The wind kicks up. The rain goes sideways, pelting the shed harder. There's still no response. She won't turn around, and her shivering worsens. I take another tentative step closer while positioning the umbrella at an angle to keep her dry.

"I know who you are," I tell her as I peer around to see her face. "Can I help you?"

The girl slowly turns around, looking at me like she's lost. But she's not lost in the physical sense. She couldn't be. She's my neighbor. It's her mind. She's here in front of me, dripping wet and wide-eyed with fear. But she doesn't seem to recognize me or even see me. Her line of vision goes over my head to an alternate reality. It's like she's lost in a dream.

"I'd like to help you," I tell her again—still nothing.

I'm running out of options. Talking to her is going nowhere, and the temperature is dropping by the second. The only option is to lead her into the shed to dry her off and see what's happening.

My trembling hand slowly extends out to her shoulder. I know a boy is not allowed to touch people like her. But I just don't care. All I feel is the innate need to help her. It's what Mom would do without a second thought.

The second my hand touches the sleeve of her shirt, she flinches and lets out a loud gasp. Then, her other hand slams down on my wrist, squeezing it with an ungodly amount of strength. Her entire body begins to shake violently.

"She lives! Go find her! She lives! Go find her!" Her whisper is loud and raspy. *It's terrifying.* But more than anything, the pleading tone in her voice has my whole body chilled.

The same words keep pouring out of her. Each time, it's a more desperate plea than before. Her hand continues to dig into my wrist as I feel her panic in my chest.

The need to no longer live becomes a distant memory in this moment. And to think, I was two seconds away. Mom was only six inches away from living. It's ironic how something so small and minute can be the threshold between living and dying.

Eventually, she lets me guide her into the shed. Once we're in there, I take stock in my situation. It's the middle of the night. I have no way of helping her or understanding the meaning of her words. All I have is a gut feeling. A feeling that's overflowing with clarity. It's a resounding truth I feel in the marrow of my bones.

I will live a little bit longer. Maybe to help. Maybe to just listen. But most importantly, I'll do as Mom would have done.

Chapter One

Ellie

Four Years Later

I read it again. And again. And again.

Each time I absorb his words, I melt on the inside. The flutter in my chest is not because it's the love note I've always dreamed of getting. It's no different than the thousands of notes we've shared through the wall that separates our houses. This one is just a reminder that we're meeting up tonight. But as always, the message is sprinkled with so much *more!* The *more* is what I love most about David.

Ellie,

Don't forget, we're meeting up tonight at midnight, or I guess that would technically be tomorrow. Anyway, I'm looking forward to it. I have some new fantasy books for you. Hopefully they'll provide some escape. And I'm sorry things are getting worse. Just know I'm here for you, just like you've been there for me. And I know you already know this, but I just want to say it. <u>I'm not going</u>

<u>**anywhere.**</u> **So, the next time you feel alone or treated as less than, remember this one thing my mom would always tell me and my sister: "You matter. We <u>ALL</u> matter!"**

Sincerely,

David

Sincerely? Sincerely? Sincerely?

My teenage brain begins to over-analyze that one word. It's something I've become good at over the last couple of years: obsessing over the weirdest things. I've also gotten better at learning about cultural things that exist outside of the Jewish world. That part is due to my natural curiosity and because David is a good teacher.

Most days, I have too much time for myself. The majority of my loner life are fantasy books, Hebrew School, Temple, and the solitude of my bedroom. I don't have many friends either. Dad rarely lets me do anything outside of religious functions and holidays. It's even harder because he won't allow me to have a phone or TV.

The only minority in my world is David. He's the piece I want more of in my life. But for now, letters and late-night meetups in his shed are all I've got.

My eyes take another pass over his letter. Usually, it's just his name at the end. Occasionally, I'll get a smiley face, which is even more confusing. But he had to throw in that three-syllable salutation. Now, my brain is obsessing over that word and not over him telling me I matter. Maybe I'm losing my mind.

I chuckle to myself because it's lunacy. It was as if I needed a reminder that he sincerely cares for me. There's not a person in the world who could be more sincere and caring than David Cohen. He was there for the first night terror and he hasn't missed a single one. That's why he didn't need to write that word. But he did. And because he did, I *almost* feel like I do matter.

Almost.

After reading his letter for the twentieth time, I look at my reflection. My tabletop mirror provides a tiny picture of myself, but I like it that way. Seeing all of me is not a good thing. Typically, my mirror's only function is to ensure my hair is properly set into place.

However, today, I feel different. The constant overbearing weight in my chest feels alleviated. Not entirely, but a little. I can even feel my chest expand into natural breaths. Is it all because of his letter? I don't know. All I do know is I'm feeling courageous.

I adjust the mirror for the first time in a long time. Then, I take a few steps back to see more of myself. My hands go to my hips. It oddly feels like my figure is becoming more shapely despite my petite size. Maybe hourglass-like? It's something that no one would ever notice, considering the only clothes I'm allowed to wear cover me like a straight jacket. But today, I'm actually able to look at my body and feel a bit feminine. I say a bit because my femininity left me shortly after my mom abandoned us.

Breathe, Ellie. Remember, you matter to him.

I arch the mirror up so it reflects off my chest. My hands cradle under my breasts to feel the weight. They feel bigger than usual. Maybe it's because I'm about to get my period. But I also feel like they're just getting fuller. But are they too big? My back sure thinks so.

The critique of my body moves to my face. I lean in close to the mirror. Slowly but surely, my fingers trace their way along my chin and nose while my nails occasionally pick at the bits of acne. Then I try smiling, but it looks fake and forced. It's because my mind is too busy critiquing everything. The large shape of my nose. My droopy, almond-shaped blue eyes looking blood shot from lack of sleep. Even my chin juts out further than most people. It makes me feel like my facial features are not proportionate to my petite and curvy figure.

My body insecurities oddly make me think of David's sister, Angela. The other day, he told me he overheard her berating her body while talking on the phone with a friend. David mentioned it very matter-of-fact, but I told him to take it seriously. I explained how little compliments at unexpected times go a long way for a girl. It's ironic I had to remind him of this. I only know because David pays me little compliments all the time now. It means the world to me. I don't even think he realizes when he does it because, for some odd reason, it comes naturally to him. That has to be rare for a 16-year-old boy. Right?

Besides, it's unbelievable to hear that Angela, of all people, feels insecure. She's drop-dead gorgeous. It's only her lack of height that'll probably prevent her from becoming a model one day. She has long, voluminous, honey-brown hair that lands just above her hips. It shines in a way that has me in dire envy to just remember what it felt like to have those silky strands be a part of me. And that's just the tip of the iceberg. She has significantly more toned curves than mine and a perfectly proportionate face with teeth as pearly white as snow.

I can't help but be jealous of her and other girls my age. Insecurities are supposed to be expected for most teenage girls—maybe boys, too. But my situation feels completely different. After all, I'm the diseased one.

The commotion outside has me spying down from my second-story window. The small opening in my blinds gives me a private yet perfect, narrow view into David's backyard. He's busy scraping on his dad's grill as he talks to his sister. He's wearing just a tight black tank top and shorts.

His booming, deep belly laugh brings a smile to my face. I realize I'm giggling to myself. I can't help it. The infectious sound of his deep voice does it every time. He's no longer the unsure little boy I met four years ago in the middle of the night. That version of David was skin and bones with shaggy hair to his shoulders. This version of David has sprouted up to almost six feet tall with a sturdy, broad frame of a body.

He attributes his hulk-ness to taking his first weightlifting class at his high school. I have no complaints about what it's done to his body—especially his biceps and shoulders. The ripples in every muscle from forearm to shoulder become more defined as he scrubs harder along the grill. It's a sight to behold!

Everything about him is more brawny and manly. His cheekbones jut out, giving him a more chiseled jawline. Even his voice is husky and more confident. And the long, shaggy hair draped down to his shoulders is now a modern crew cut paired with a bit of stubble on his chin.

His booming laugh gets louder, and now I'm laughing with him while he's unbeknownst to my stalking gaze. It's amazing how his laugh resonates into the deeper parts of me. It's like a wave of goodness that washes over me to make my whole body feel lighter and freer.

It makes me slightly envious, too. David can express this natural emotion so easily. He has this intrinsic happiness and sunny disposition despite all the hardship and trauma he and his sister have endured. Seeing his beauty and natural smile in this form is like seeing a picturesque purplish-pink sunset—the kind I wish I could freeze in time. David is more than just a beautiful boy I've been crushing on for years. He's the *only* light in my world that can penetrate my darkness.

Only him!

However, one problem remains: My beliefs and stringent upbringing will always cast a shadow on what I want and what I can never have. But religion aside, I don't even know if he likes me in a way other than friendship. But if all I can get is friendship, I'll take it in a heartbeat.

"Ellie! Ellie! Get your tuchus down here!"

The shouting command echoes from downstairs, reverberating in my head like a dark cloud descending over my mood.

I head downstairs, unsure of what I'm walking into. Did I mess up the lunch I made him? Maybe there were too many pickles? The wrong kind of matza? Not enough food? Too much food? Or maybe it's all of the above. It's usually something unavoidable.

After a couple of deep breaths, I turn the corner and walk into the dimly lit kitchen. The blinds are drawn. They're always shut in this part of the house. Nevertheless, it's the middle of the day in Phoenix where the sun always finds its way through the cracks.

I pass the kitchen counter, noticing the prescription pill bottles that are still full. I'm surprised they're not collecting dust. He stops taking them every now and then for reasons I'll never understand. When he goes off them, it's a slow transition into his worser self. I can't explain my dad's behavior because it becomes a roller coaster of highs and lows. But lately, it's just been predominantly low.

A black plastic bag catches my attention as I turn the corner into the dining room. I glance in both directions to see that Dad isn't around. Barely poking out of the bag is a thick wad of envelopes. All I can see is a postage stamp with a person holding a baseball bat and the name Roberto Clemente.

I know not to look into my dad's stuff, but I'm drawn to this bag for some reason. There are so *many* envelopes. I step closer to peak inside. The second I see who the envelope is for, a hand slams down on my wrist.

"Ow!" I jump back, pulling my arm from his grasp.

"What do you think you're doing!" Dad screams.

He steps closer. I cower from him, feeling the rage in his eyes as he stares down at me.

"Nothing," I mutter, clearing the dryness in my throat. "I, uh, I was just trying to see what was in the bag. I swear. I'm sorry, Dad. I thought I saw—"

The full glass cups on the counter are slapped into the adjacent wall quicker than I can blink my eyes. They hit with such velocity the shards flew into the side of my face. Instinctually, I flinch my body away from the glass as his hand goes into the air, balled into a fist. My eyes squint shut as I wait for him to hit me.

It's never happened before. But for some demented reason, I want it to happen. A prodigious swing across my face that'll leave a mark. Maybe I want it because it'll give me the ticket I need out of here. Or maybe it's because it'll be a reprieve from the verbal abuse that hurts worse, sticking to my insides like tumorous scars. But nothing happens.

I slowly open my eyes as he lowers his fist, still breathing heavily. The look is still that of a man who wants to hurt me. But he can't—at least not physically.

"This is my business! You hear me! Don't you ever go through my mail! Do you hear me!"

His face vibrates as he leans in closer to my face. I step back, instantly slipping into shards of glass on the wet floor. I look at my arms and hands, already stinging with little specks of blood slowly seeping out of me. Then I look at my dad. He smirks down on me like I'm worthless. It's nothing new. I see variations of this look most days. But this time, in this moment, I truly feel it.

I am worthless. And I'm stuck.

I don't know what to do as he grabs the black bag and heads upstairs. All I can do is begin the process of pulling out the shards that feel invisible and prickly all over. Physically, I know I'll be fine. But mentally, I am my mother. *Again!*

I flinch when the hydrogen peroxide and tweezers land at my side. My dad looks down at me with exasperated breaths.

"Don't you think we're going to the doctor. You'll pull those out on your own and clean them up properly. And if you ever…" he pauses to bow his head down, shaking it from side-to-side. Then his eyes burn back into mine with gritting teeth. "If you ever speak of tonight or snoop through my stuff, I'll hit you so hard you'll see stars. Don't test me on this, Ellie. You're just like your mother. A pathetic bitch!"

My body recoils to his last two words as he walks away. The tears should come next, but for some reason, I'm too sad to cry. It's an odd feeling to have so much bottled-up sadness and have it feel stuck inside me—like there's no escape from these demons.

That night, it takes a good couple of hours to pick out all of the glass and clean each prickly little wound. Then, I find myself waiting in the desolate solitude of my room. It's still a couple hours until midnight and my chance to be with David. I wonder if I should tell him what happened. I probably won't. It'll only make him feel more helpless.

Time moves slowly when I need him the most. I contemplate taking a mini nap and setting my alarm for midnight. However, my brain is racing like crazy over that one thing. The black bag. I didn't get to look at it long enough to see who the envelopes were from. I only recognized one thing. Who they were addressed to. And that person was me.

Chapter Two

David

Two Years Later

The clattering in my head won't go away. I toss and turn, fighting the internal angst to wake up. Then, the sudden sound of glass shattering has me awake and on the edge of my bed.

"Fuck!" I grunt, picking up the rock at my feet. I wait a moment to see if Dad or Angela are awake, but I hear nothing.

I quickly make my way to the window. This isn't the first time I've looked below my second-story window to see a shivering young redhead pacing in my backyard.

My internal autopilot takes over. The routine of grabbing a fresh blanket and pulling on my gloves in the middle of the night is done without a second thought. I've repeated these steps a thousand times over the past few years.

My toes glide along the carpet as I rush downstairs. When I slide the back door open and see her face, I instantly know. She's fully awake but nowhere close to living in reality.

"Are you—" I stop, trying to swallow away the tension in my voice. "Oh, Ellie," I sigh, wrapping her up in my blanket.

I'm careful that our skin doesn't touch. It never has since that fateful first night.

She's mumbling unintelligible things, like usual. But it's the fear in her teary eyes that gets to me. Maybe it would feel different if she'd make a sound when she cries, but it's nothing—only mute tears—the worst kind. No matter how many times I see it, it always kills me on the inside. Everything terrible in her mind is living behind those blue eyes. It's like she's stuck behind that stormy ocean in the same nightmare, each one progressively worse than the last.

"Let's go to the shed," I tell her, guiding her towards her makeshift home, which is our eight-by-eight-foot storage shed.

I never knew what a night terror was until I met my next-door neighbor, Ellie Merkowitz. Initially, I thought it was just a horrific nightmare. But it's much worse than that. It's when a person wakes up in the most heightened state of panic. They're inconsolable for a short time and either screaming or talking in ways that make no sense. People who have them will typically sleepwalk and can even become violent towards themselves and others. However, the most unique aspect of night terrors is the amnesia that follows. Ellie *never remembers* anything about what happened or why she says the things she does in this panicked state of mind.

Her night terrors are the singular reason our paths crossed six years ago. But they're not the only thing that makes Ellie unique. The bigger piece to her story is her devout beliefs as an Orthodox Jewish woman. She's proud to be a part of this religion, which is also a conservative, stricter form of Judaism that closes her off to mainstream society.

Our neighborhood in north-central Phoenix is home to a large congregation of Orthodox Jews like Ellie and her father, Jacob Merkowitz. We typically see droves of Orthodox Jewish families walking the streets on Fridays and Saturdays to celebrate their weekly celebration of Shabbat, or Shabbos, as most call it. When spoken to, they're a friendly group. However, they typically keep to themselves and only interact with other Orthodox families.

In Jewish vernacular, I'd consider myself part of the tribe, or at least I used to be a Reform Jew. It's the most liberal form of Judaism and nothing like being Orthodox. Some Orthodox Jews don't even see it as a legitimate form of Judaism because it's so lax in its requirements.

They may have a point. After all, I never had my bar mitzvah. I haven't even set foot in a temple in over six years. If anything, I'm Jew-*ish*.

Those days of going to Temple felt like a different life. I can barely remember it, even though it was my life a few years ago. But maybe I've blocked it out because I don't want to remember it. It was my other life when my mom *was* around.

It takes quite a while for Ellie's breathing to level out. Her eyes are still a running faucet, but I think she's slowly starting to come back to me.

"There you go, Ellie. Squeeze my hands as tight as you can. And release with a deep breath. That's it. That's it. Keep going."

It's four in the morning, but everything is already set up in the shed for Ellie. I have snacks, my Kindle, and a Bluetooth speaker playing the Nutcracker album.

"Zit-zit. Bloody strings. Keep pulling. Keep digging. Zit-zit. Bloody strings. Keep pulling. Keep digging." Ellie keeps repeating the words, but each time she says it, it gets more desperate.

I grab our notebook to quickly jot down these words and anything else I remember her saying in the last few minutes.

"He chased me. I swerved. I'm sorry. He chased me. I swerved. I'm sorry," she says with a feeble whimper.

I give my hands back to her because the panic is revving up. My knuckles begin to crack as her grip tightens. Then it happens, quicker than I can blink my eyes. Her hands fly into my chest, putting me flat on my back. Ellie falls backward, slamming into the aluminum siding of the shed. Time freezes all at once. It all happened so fast. The air getting knocked out of me. Her eyes coming back to full consciousness. And her hair. Oh, I love that stunning strawberry hair with subtle hints of blonde streaks. But it must've caught the corner shelf above her head, causing her wig to disconnect from her head completely.

Her gasping breath leaves us both speechless. "Look away!" she shouts.

I quickly turn away from her. "I'm so sorry, Ellie."

"Oh no! I need a mirror!"

The panic in her voice leaves no doubt that she's finally awake. Even the embarrassment is palpable in this tiny, enclosed space. She doesn't know I know—or at least I've never brought it up.

Ellie may only be eighteen years old, but until she gets married in a couple of years, it's not necessary for her to wear a wig. She only wears it out of necessity.

"You can turn around now," she whispers.

I slowly turn around. Her eyes are lost, staring only at her feet. Meanwhile, my heart still feels lodged in my throat. And I wonder, hopelessly. What can a seventeen-year-old boy say in this impossible situation? There's got to be a way to rid her of the embarrassment that has my insides agonizing.

"It's okay—"

"Shut up. Shut up. I changed my mind. Please stop. Don't even look at me right now," Ellie demands coldly.

My eyes fall to my feet while my hands fidget in my pockets. The deafening silence carries on until I can't take it any longer. "I got new fantasy books on my Kindle for you. I also stole some of Angela's nail polish. If you, um, you know…"

I clear my throat. Maybe the best thing I can do is let her be. But usually, she wants to talk about it.

"I'll head back to my—"

"David! Please don't go!"

The electrical current in my body has nothing to do with the begging cadence in her voice. It has everything to do with her touch. All I can do is stare at her hand, squeezing tight over my wrist—*my bare wrist*—*her bare hand*—desperately clinging until she knows I'll stay.

I can barely stammer out the words, "Okay. I'll, uh, I'll stay longer."

Ellie lets go. She takes a few more wipes at her eyes before blowing her nose. We both take a seat in our usual spots on the blanket. I'm typically a good foot or two from her, but tonight, our knees are inches from touching.

"How bad was it?" she asks, slowly looking up to meet my eyes.

"About ten minutes. It was one of the longer ones. Not to mention, you just put another hole in my window."

Ellie gasps loudly as her hands clasp together by her lips. "I'm so—"

"It's okay. It's okay. My dad's CPAP machine is like a revving engine. He and Angela slept right through it. Besides, I can tape over it and keep the blinds closed."

My copacetic response does little to rid the embarrassment. I don't like seeing shame on an angelic face like hers; it kills me.

"I've known for a long time, Ellie. It's okay."

I watch as her throat goes inward. Somehow, I can feel the same tension in my throat. But I don't know what else I can say.

"I need a distraction. Give me your hands. I don't care tonight. We can touch. Just give me your hands," she begs, looking even more desperate.

"I don't understand…" I pause as she reaches for the nail polish. "I'm not going to let you paint—"

"Relax! I'll wipe it off! Besides, I'm tired of painting my nails only to wipe them off fifteen minutes later. Dad could smell the acetone on my hands the other day. I don't like making him more suspicious than he already is."

All I can do is scoff at her. She can't be serious.

"Oy vey, David!"

"Fine," I giggle nervously under my breath.

She pulls my right hand onto her thigh. It's not her bare thigh. But I can't help it. The way my breathing becomes erratic. My heart is beating so fast I hear it like it's lodged between my ears.

"Relax, David," she says, her voice calmer. "This stays just between us."

Daveed! Daveed! Daveed!

I love the way she says my name. Everyone else says it the boring way. But every time Ellie says it, she accentuates the long "e" sound in her sexy Israeli accent. My stomach flutters away in happiness every time I hear it.

It's one of many things that drives me the good kind of crazy. It also makes Ellie unique and different from any other girl my age. But I love her brand of unique and different, *a lot.*

To any other person, Ellie Merkowitz may seem beyond ordinary. But not to me. She is the absolute opposite of that word. She's extraordinary in every way imaginable.

Most people would first see the modest way she's always dressed. It's typically long skirts to her ankles and turtleneck sweaters—even in Phoenix's worst summer days. But this is how she's been conditioned since a young age in her religion. She must hide her body from the male gaze as it's something that will only be sacred to her future husband. But these things only make Ellie more intriguing and different from all the other girls.

Ellie is also unlike most subservient Orthodox Jewish women. She's searching for more out of life, learning to speak her mind. Ellie wants more rights as a woman, and more say in her future. She's always been eager to learn about culture and different ways of thinking and believing. Over the years we've shared many late-night conversations about such topics. It's a testament to her willingness to break free from the shackles of a sheltered life cast down by her controlling, narcissistic father.

It's a never-ending conundrum with Ellie because she's not fighting against her beliefs. She's proud of her Jewish roots and her religion. She's just innately curious. But her natural curiosity only scratches the surface of who she is. She's a talented artist who can create masterpieces with multiple mediums. She also aspires to be a counselor one day, hoping to specialize in helping children heal from past traumas.

"Be curious. Not judgmental."

The words of Walt Whitman keep playing in my head while my eyes fixate on each brush of pink. It puts me in a hypnotic, Zen-like state of mind. Those four words were from a great poet, but to me, it's the most memorable thing I always remember my mom telling me.

Everything that hurts in my memory gives way to this moment of quiet relaxation. Not to mention, it feels good—the way her non-painting hand deftly glides along my skin. It has every hormone in my body coming to life.

I wonder if she's feeling the same things I'm feeling. She'll give me little hints sometimes, but other times, I can't tell if she really does like me. For me, these feelings have been here for quite some time now. And while the fantasy of being with the girl you can never have feels like a dream, I can't stop how she makes me feel.

I discreetly move my arm across my lap, hoping she doesn't see what I'm trying to cover up under my pants. But I may have been too late.

Her brow furrows as her eyes meet mine. "You…o-kay?"

"Yeah, why?" I swear my voice just squeaked like a prepubescent little boy. I try clearing my throat, but it feels fake and forced.

"Hmmm," Ellie sighs, shrugging. Her eyes return to my hand as she finishes the last fingernail. "So, what did I say this time?"

I read back everything I've written in our shared notebook. Our typical routine is documenting the date, time, and notes on what Ellie said during her night terror. It's integral because Ellie never remembers anything about her night terrors.

"Wait." She stops me. "Say that word again."

"What? You mean zit, like pimples?"

Ellie shakes her head as she pulls the notebook out of my hands. "You spelled it wrong. I think I was trying to say Tzizit. It's spelled t-z-i-z-i-t. You know, the white strings that Orthodox men wear at their hip."

I look at her, feeling a bit dumbfounded. I see Orthodox men wearing them all the time. "I forget, what's the point of them wearing those?"

"There are exactly 613 threads when men wear them on their clothes. It represents the 613 commandments in the Torah," she explains as if I should already know this. "Anyways." She shrugs again. Maybe she's just as confused as I am.

Ellie goes back to reading through the notebook on her own. It's less of a notebook and more like a chronological journal of her night terrors. She scrolls back and forth, muttering frustrations every few seconds. The notebook is over 100 pages thick, with notes from the last few years of night terrors. She typically has one a week, but they've been more frequent lately. We don't know why.

The frustrating part for Ellie and myself is we never fully understand why she says what she does. It's like she falls into this weird psychosis or alternate personality. And all it leaves us with are thousands of clues and puzzle pieces. But they never seem to connect with one another fully.

"What is it?" Ellie asks, breaking me from my meandering thoughts.

"Nothing, I just…I don't get it—any of it. The things you said today don't make any sense, like usual."

"I know," she agrees. "Let's not talk about it tonight. Tell me how your dad's doing."

"He's okay." I look down, staring mindlessly in my lap. There's nothing more to be said because things are the same— never better, only ever so slowly getting worse.

"I'm sorry, David. You know what we need is something to look forward to. Isn't that the key to life, finding something to look forward to? My Rabbi said that the other day."

"Well, aside from graduating in a few days, all I have is my road trip coming up."

My trip to New York is something I'm genuinely excited for. I'm being honored for a movie script I wrote a few months back called *The Tree House.* The whole reason I'm being honored is because of my sister. Angela fell in love with my story after reading it. Then, without my knowledge, she submitted my script for a prestigious scholarship given out every year by The Young Writer's Guild of America.

I found out two months ago that my story was selected as a finalist. If my script is chosen at the ceremony in New York, I'll get all my tuition paid for to any film school in the United States. There's also the chance a film studio could choose to buy the rights to my script and make a movie out of it. This would all be quite an upgrade to my current plan. All that includes is attending a local community college and knocking out my prerequisite classes.

It's a long shot I'll win. There are nine other honorees for the award. But even if I don't win, the trip itself with my best friend, Scotty, should be memorable.

I watch as Ellie's face begins to light up. Her smile stretches up to her eyes as she seems to be lost in her imagination. She's obviously not going, but it's like she's vicariously living through me as the most excited person for my trip.

"Oh, David," she marvels, tilting her eyes to the sky. "If I ever went on a road trip, I'd go everywhere. I can see every little town, every big town, and every random site. Oh! It would be something else!"

"That's no trouble. I'll just ask your dad. I'm sure he'd be cool with you being gone for a week with two boys and driving a thousand miles away from home. We'll tell him we're getting matching tattoos and celebrating Shabbos with some bacon cheeseburgers."

We both chuckle for a moment. The lunacy of an Orthodox girl doing those things is blatant sacrilege to Judaism. But even as her smile fades, I can tell her mind is still transfixed on this idea. A cross-country road trip is most definitely a pipe dream for Ellie, but it feels like something more. It's symbolic of her dream of breaking free from a life of ultra-conformity and rigidity. A free spirit is who she is—or at least who she wants to be. All I can hope is she finds that side of her one day.

It's just been Ellie and her dad for some time now. Her mom ran away when Ellie was just twelve years old. No one knows where she went or if she's alive or dead. I remember when it happened because it was only a couple days later when my mom died. Ellie doesn't know why she left without saying a word to her. What I do know is that her mom, Leah Merkowitz, wasn't much of a mom to begin with.

Leah had some form of severe clinical depression most of her life. She also had many extended stays at psychiatric hospitals when her depressive episodes were at their worst. Ellie claims that her dad never disclosed what her mental illness was. But she does tell me how her mom would fluctuate quickly from being herself one moment then the next, she's hallucinating and going through a manic-depressive episode. I've always felt like Ellie's known more about what's happened to her mother. However, I also believe it was such a traumatic time in her life that it's still hard to talk about.

Her dad is an even worse human being. He doesn't acknowledge the mom's existence and has always adamantly refused to give Ellie any explanation. He barely even acknowledges Ellie's existence. When he does talk to her, he's verbally abusive and constantly degrading to her. It's all done with the intent of being manipulative and extremely controlling. He's created the most sheltered life imaginable and uses religion as justification for his ways. There's no phone, limited internet, no friends outside her temple, and no life of enjoyment.

Sometimes, I tell her things about my dad, and I think she's envious. But my dad isn't the same person either. It's not his fault. He's still a lovely man. But the loss of my mom, followed by his Parkinson's diagnosis and worsening dementia, has been too much for him and our family.

"You, okay?" Ellie asks.

I clear my throat. The sensitivity in her voice somehow ameliorates the tension in my chest. Then I get lost in her eyes. They're a glossier shade of aqua blue that reminds me of the most picturesque ocean.

"I'll be fine. How about you? Tell me something you're looking forward to."

She vigorously shakes her head. "I got nothing."

"Oh, come on, Ellie. You have to give me something."

Ellie takes a long, stressful breath. I watch as her eyes tilt up. It's like she's searching for an answer that may not exist.

"Well, I should be excited now that I've graduated high school and turned 18. But it's scary. Things are getting real. Certain things will be expected of me in the next couple of years—you know, marriage, having kids, things like that. But I don't know." Ellie pauses, shaking her head as she takes another arduous looking breath. "It's not that I don't want to do all those things. I just don't want to rush into it. You wouldn't be able to understand the lack of choice. The lack of control over my own destiny. It's complicated."

The stagnant feeling in the air is her words sucking the breath out of me. I clear my throat and take a deep breath. "I know I can't relate to all the shit you go through. But I can always try to be there for you. I mean, I think we know each other pretty well…for neighbors.”

I don’t know what I’m trying to tell her. We’re way more than just neighbors. We’ve been leaving notes for each other in the wall that separates our house for years. And most nights, we secretly meet up in the shed to just talk and enjoy one another’s company.

If anything, I just don’t want her ever to feel alone. Her life, like mine, is full of trauma. But the traumas of our pasts are also what unites us. We have one another to talk about grief and the struggles of living without a mom. It’s why I take privilege in our chance encounter six years ago by the shed. And I care for her, *deeply*. I can’t help it because, without Ellie, I wouldn’t be alive. She’s the only one that gives me hope. *Only her.*

Her eyes come back to mine. The corner of her lip barely perks up into a half-smile. Then I watch as her hands brush through the tips of her hair. It’s one of her nervous twitches. When she does it, it’s impossible not to be mesmerized by her natural beauty. But as she runs her fingers through the tips of her wig, I feel tension in the air.

“It’s called alopecia,” Ellie says, keeping her gaze intense on mine.

“I’m sorry. What?”

“The reason I have no hair. It’s a disease. The doctors don’t know why I have it. I mean, they have their theories. But it’s likely my real hair will never grow back.”

“Oh, um…okay.”

Wow! “Oh, okay.” That’s the best you got?

I clear my throat. “I mean, I’ve known for a while now. I didn’t know what it was called, but I knew you didn’t have any hair.”

“Really?”

“Yeah. A couple of times, you’ve come over with your wig not fully on. But I’ve always been able to adjust it for you. But don’t worry, I always had gloves on.”

Ellie's lips part. A sudden discomfort washes over her face. I can't imagine many people knowing it's a wig because it looks so real. I didn't even know what alopecia was until now.

"Are you upset that I know? I swear it's never been something that scared me. I mean, the first time, I was surprised. But it's okay. I mean, I love your wig. Red really looks good on you."

Ellie lets out a confused giggle. "You love my wig? Thank you…I guess. I like red as well. It was the color of my mom's hair. She also wore sheitels that were different variations of red." Ellie pauses to clear her throat. "You know, I think you know too many secrets about me—even though most of them make no sense. But let's even things out between us. Tell me a secret. Something big."

I ponder her question, not knowing what I can give her. It's not that I don't have secrets. But my secrets are few and so different from hers. Her secrets feel like they lie somewhere in the alternate reality of her night terrors.

"Come on, give me anything," Ellie begs. "If you can't think of a secret, at least try and get something off your chest."

My mind veers to the night I almost ended my life. It's a dark place to go, but it's my deepest secret. And it's a secret I can't share with Ellie—at least not yet.

"I didn't cry when my mom died…not one tear. There's that…and my dad will be dead at some point in the next few years. Maybe sooner. How's that?"

A piercing tension has my stomach swimming in a sludge of anxiety. I'm instantly regretting what I've said.

"I'm sorry, David. I know it must be hard. But I'm thankful you still have him in your life."

"Right now, I do. But it will only get worse for him over the next couple of years, not better. He basically has no short-term memory, and soon, he's going to be suffering even more. There's only so much Angela, our caretakers, and I can do for him. Eventually, he'll need around-the-clock help with everything, and we don't have the money or resources to help him—especially since he can't work. And when he dies, what do I do next? And how will Angela take it? It'll ruin us. It's just…"

A cold shiver jolts through my body, leaving me speechless. I glance down, seeing the smoothness of her bare hand caressing over mine. It has me stunned into a paralyzing silence.

"David, look at me."

I do as I'm told. But seeing the sanguine look in her eyes puts intense pressure behind my own eyes.

"You'll find a way, David. I'll help you. I don't know how. But maybe things will find a way to just work out. Adonai is good to all of us."

There's conviction in the way she says Adonai. It's a reference to *her* god. But how can she believe in something that's been so cruel to her? How can she have faith for me and my life but not always believe in her own? It's like we're each a crutch to stand on. But crutches aren't meant to be permanent or shared between people. Eventually, we have to support ourselves.

The blaring sound of my alarm startles us. It's 5 a.m. *Fuck!* I hate it when the clock strikes 5 a.m. Her dad will be up in twenty minutes, and he'd have a heart attack if he knew where Ellie was right now.

I walk her to her back door, a routine I've done with her thousands of times. She puts her hand on the doorknob, hesitating for a moment.

"David?"

"Yes, Ellie?"

She turns to look at me over her shoulder. Her eyes somehow glow through the darkness. Her mouth starts to move, but nothing comes out.

"What is it?" I beg.

"I just want to thank you…for everything. I, uh, I have a lot of things wrong with me. I know that. But I'm glad you know about my alopecia. It's such a relief that you know. It's like I can breathe easier now. So, um…thank you."

And before I can respond, Ellie lunges towards me. Her arms come tight around my body. For a moment, I'm paralyzed. Then the reflex for something I've always wanted and always dreamed of comes out as I hug her with everything I've got.

I'm feeling so much in this moment of sensory overload. Her lavender scent. Her warm breath along my neck as she squeezes tighter. And her strength. Someone as tiny as her shouldn't be able to hug like this. But it's a desperate hug.

The reality is we've both been desperate for this moment of touch. But my happiness is overshadowed by sadness. I'm thinking how she'll only be allowed to hug one other man for the rest of her life. And that man can never be me for a long list of reasons. It's why I refuse to let go of her or this moment.

The faint squeaking noise comes so suddenly and stealth-like. Our embrace disconnects faster than I can blink my eyes. The air leaves everyone's lungs as her ultra-conservative father, Joshua Merkowitz, stands tall in the doorway, staring a look into me that can kill.

Oh, fuck!

Chapter Three

David

My Cheerios stare back at me from my bowl. They're already soggy and breaking apart into little puffed-up pieces. There's no way I can take another bite. If I do, I'll probably vomit all over the table.

"Why are your nails pink?" Angela asks in a sour tone.

"Don't worry about it."

"No, I'm serious—"

"Angela!" I stop myself from exploding on my sister because I hear my dad shuffling in on his walker. "I'll explain it all later," I quietly mutter, giving my best don't-fuck-with-me stare.

Angela lets out a loud huff, shaking her head. "Whatever."

"Oh my! What a beautiful day! Good morning, my wonderful blessings!" Dad announces in his usual chipper tone.

He slowly slides his way to each of us, then delicately leans down to plant kisses on our heads. It's the same way our dad has woken us up every single day since birth. The only difference is the tremors in his hands and the slow-moving pace in his body.

"All of your pills are ready," Angela says, pointing to his sixteen pills neatly arranged by his spot at the table. "And David made you some fresh oatmeal with blueberries and raspberries."

Dad clears his throat. "Oh, no bacon and cheese omelet today?"

He asks us that same question every morning, even though we always eat oatmeal. We've gotten used to him repeating questions and looking confused by all the medicine he has to take. But this is just the life we live with our dad. It's never easy, but we're getting used to his deteriorating short-term memory.

"It's brain food, Dad. You need the antioxidants in the berries and the oatmeal for strong digestion," I explain.

"Right. Right," he tries to convince himself. "You two are too good to me. Thank you."

Breakfast carries on like it would on any other morning. Dad intently listens to everything going on in our lives. He's always enthralled by what we share because he rarely remembers us telling him these things. Angela's doing most of the talking. She's boasting on and on about her new boyfriend, Sam. They've been an item for four months, but they're going to separate colleges. I worry that her heart is going to be broken in the coming weeks.

I want to talk seriously with her about the topic, but her head is just too much in the clouds. After all, she's more than just my sister. She's my twin sister. But now isn't the time. My mind is still stuck in the murkiness of last night.

The doorbell rings and my body is a human pogo stick, springing off the chair.

"I got it!"

"Are we expecting someone over this morning?" Dad mutters to Angela.

I'm quickly at the door. Luckily, everyone stayed at the table. My already clammy hand grabs the doorknob. The hesitation and fear of what awaits on the other side freezes my hand. I have no plan, no explanation, and only Ellie to protect.

The second I open the door, his glaring eyes tell me everything. They're dilated to the point where I wonder if his eyeballs can literally fall out of his face. Even his look is snarling, to the point where I can hear his raspy breathing.

"Good morning, Mr. Merkowitz."

"Step outside, boy. We need to talk."

I close the door behind me and look up at his tall presence. His fedora hat makes him look closer to seven feet tall. And the grimace he's wearing looks like it's permanently etched on his face.

"Tell me what happened," Joshua says in his thick Israeli accent.

"I was just helping her."

"With what?"

"She had a bad dream. She has those quite a bit. I swear, she came to my backyard. And I just gave her a blanket and talked to her. Then I walked her back to your door."

So far, so good.

I watch as he bites down on his bottom lip and stares off in the distance, shaking his head.

"So, you're saying my Eliana came to you," he says, his tone disbelieving.

I nod my head, barely. The silence between us feels deafening. I don't know what else I can say to pacify his concerns because it's the truth. *She comes to me for help—not him. Never him!*

"How many times?"

Oh, fuck me!

"Um, I'm not sure. But she's been having bad dreams for a while now." I stop to clear the nervousness from my throat. "Sometimes it takes her awhile to snap out of her dreams. There's some uh…things going on in her head. Maybe it's things from her memory that she doesn't understand. And it's really scary for her."

"Has she mentioned names when she's like this?"

"Names?"

"Yes, you heard me," he persists with an intense stare. "Does she mention names?"

I hesitate again as he takes a step closer. "No, there's no names. She gets stuck in these dreams and typically says things that make no sense."

Ellie's dad begins tracing his hands through his long, straggly salt and pepper beard. He's deep in thought, but he's suddenly perturbed by something else—something that feels much bigger than my hugging his virgin daughter. And I find it odd that one of the first things he asks me about is names. *Why?*

"These night terrors, I know what they are. You don't think I've seen them before, do you? She had them for a short period of time after her mother left us. I thought they stopped. But none of this matters because you'll have no business with my daughter. You won't stare at her. You won't acknowledge her. I don't even want you to ever speak her name again. And she won't ever sneak over…*ever again*. That I can promise. You hear me. You are nothing but a pathetic sheygetz. That's all you'll ever be."

It feels like he just spit those words into my face. I want to ask him what a "sheygetz" is, but judging by his condescending, accusatory tone, it's some type of slur.

I want to be strong-willed and stand up for myself. He needs to know that his daughter needs real help—not the tough it out kind. But I know anything I say in this moment will be the wrong thing. I'm only an outsider to him. That's all I'll ever be. So, I settle on nodding and turning to head inside with my tail in between my legs.

"One other thing, sheygetz. If I ever find out that my daughter has been touched by you again, I'll hurt you. Don't test me on this. I will hurt you. That's a guarantee."

Mr. Merkowitz turns away and marches back home. I head inside. Angela's practically blocking my path back into the house. It's clear she's been eavesdropping.

"Why was Ellie's dad here?" she whispers, visibly concerned.

"He uh, he wanted to pick some of our lemons from our tree," I explain, giving a quick wink as Dad slides his way into the hallway.

Angela just stands in the hallway, looking worried. It's probably the pale, deer in headlights look I feel in my own face.

Then she mouths the words, *"Tell me later."*

Once Dad goes down for his mid-morning nap, Angela drags me into her room for the inevitable interrogation.

"Tell me everything," she quickly demands.

I don't keep anything from my sister—not even my secret rendezvous in the middle of the night with Ellie. The only thing I've kept from Angela is Ellie's wig.

"It's complicated. I don't even know where to start."

"Try me," she says, getting comfy on her bed.

I hesitate for a moment. But all I can do is just come out and say it. "Ellie gave me a hug last night by her back door. Then her dad opened the door and saw us…we were mid hug."

I grit my teeth as Angela's eyes widen. Her mouth falls open, looking at me like I'm lucky to be alive.

"Say something, fuck!" I shout.

Angela gives me a disbelieving chuckle as she shakes her head. Then she chucks a pillow at me.

"This isn't funny, Angela. I'm in some deep shit. Her dad just found out about us. I need your help."

"You're really not kidding. Are you?"

"No!"

"Okay, okay," she sighs. "Did you guys do anything else?"

"No, of course not. It was just a hug."

"Hhhmm. Sure, David," Angela mocks me.

"It's not what you think. You know she'll only ever be with a real Jewish guy. But I don't regret doing it. Besides, she initiated the hug on me."

My mind transports to our warm embrace last night. I can't help it. There was a desire in her eyes that I can't get out of my mind. And I don't want it to ever leave my memory. I can still feel what it was like to have her wig brush over my face. Even though it's not her actual hair, to me, it's such an intriguing part of her beauty.

"Okay. Well, clearly you two don't like each other. Sure. I believe you." Angela's eye roll and disbelieving tone apparently aren't enough to mock me. She blows raspberries to add a little extra salt to the wound.

"Whatever, the point is she needs me—now more than ever. And now that her dad knows about us, there's no way I can get anywhere near her, especially at night."

"Okay, but I don't know what you want me to do. I can't stop her night terrors. Her dad won't let me near her either since I'm not Orthodox. But I'll help. Just tell me what you need."

I close my eyes to take a few deep breaths. The frustration and lack of control is agonizing. The truth is, I don't know how Angela can help me.

She puts her hand on my shoulder. I open my eyes, seeing the worry all over her face. "What else is going on here? Are her night terrors getting weirder?"

I tell Angela how they've been lasting longer than usual lately. Then I pull out the journal that Ellie and I have been keeping. It's nice having a fresh set of eyes and ears to analyze all the weird things Ellie's been saying.

"What if you guys are looking at this the wrong way?" she asks.

"What do you mean?"

"Well, what if all this has nothing to do with her mom running away? I mean, I know the night terrors started after she ran away, but…" Angela scoots closer to the edge of the bed. She runs her hands through her long, honey brown hair. Her squinting eyes have her deep in thought. "I forget, does she have any family at all?"

"No. Not really. Most of them are dead. She has a half-brother named Yosef. But he's married and quite a bit older than her. She also has an aunt from her mom's side. But they don't have a relationship with her because she quit Judaism a long time ago."

"How long has her mom been gone?" Angela asks.

"She left when Ellie was twelve. It's been about six years now. I think she's given up hope on reconciling with her. More than anything, she just wants to know why she left."

"This is all so weird," Angela says, rubbing her temples.

"I know."

"So, what do you need me to do?" Angela sits up taller. She looks ready to run through a brick wall for me.

We slowly start to hash out a plan. I'm going to get a kosher phone from my best friend, Scotty, who works at a phone store. Then I'm going to give it to Angela. She'll see Ellie walking by the restaurant she works at while she's on her way to temple for Shabbat. Hopefully she'll be able to give the phone to her.

Shabbat, or Shabbos, is the holy day for Jews where they celebrate the Sabbath. It starts at sundown every Friday and goes on until sundown on Saturday evening. It's a day of worship and a day of rest and reflection on the week with family. But it's also a day where the use of electronic devices of any kind are strictly prohibited. It's so strictly adhered to that Orthodox families can't even flip on a light switch.

I know she'll be apprehensive about calling me on a holy day. But she may need me in case there's an emergency. I want her to know that I'll always be there for her. There's nothing that can separate us.

Later that night, I lay in bed unable to slow my racing mind. I can't stop imagining Ellie having a night terror and me not being there for her. It sounds like a worser nightmare within a nightmare.

On the bright side, thanks to Angela, everything went to plan with getting Ellie the phone. It's just a matter of waiting to see if she'll call or text me.

It's a little past midnight now. Each minute ticks by and I get more anxious. I've already texted her to get in touch with me once her dad goes to bed, but she never responded.

After a while, I feel myself drifting away. The anxiety is still heavy in my heart. However, I'm relieved in knowing that typically her night terrors don't happen on consecutive nights.

Then, I feel a blanket of relief wash over me. I imagine the five seconds where I got to hold her in my arms last night. It was so unexpected, so perfect, and yet, even now it doesn't feel real. But it was real, and there's no way I could ever forget it.

The buzzing noise in my head feels like static in my brain. I'm trying to fight it away, but it keeps coming back.

Wake Up!

"Ellie!"

I'm quickly upright, lunging toward my nightstand while my phone dances its way to the edge.

"Ellie! Ellie! Are you okay?"

"Oh, David—"

Her words give way to the most hopeless, pathetic, muffled crying. My heart sinks, knowing instantly how alone she feels. Our rooms may be twenty yards apart, but it feels like she's on the opposite end of the earth. It takes her a couple minutes to calm down and collect her breath.

"He's installed special locks on my windows and my doors—like a prison. I mean, what if…what if I panic in my dreams and hurt myself?"

"Don't say that, Ellie. Don't even put that thought in your head. We'll figure this out. Just breathe with me and talk to me. I'm here for you—all night if that's what it takes. You're not alone. It'll be like…like I'm sleeping right next to you."

There's a brief awkward silence. I don't know why I made the comment like I did. Maybe it was a Freudian slip. *"I'm sleeping right next to you."*

"It just feels good to hear your voice," Ellie says, letting out a deep exhale. "I'm sorry it took so long to call you. I could hear him pacing outside my door every few minutes. But he's asleep now."

"Are you sure?"

"Yeah, I'm sure."

A loud silence infiltrates our conversation. The frog in my throat is the realization that this is the first time I've ever talked to Ellie on the phone. *Ever!*

She's always been easy to talk to in person. But for some reason everything feels off. It's like the paradigm in our worlds has shifted in opposite directions. The cracks in the foundation, *our foundation*, are widening by the second. And I have no control over any of it. All because of her father.

Our history is more than me being there for her night terrors. It's the late-night talks in my shed. The notes we leave for each other in our shared wall. These things *are*, or *were*, the foundation we built together. It's redefined our friendship and even aged us in a way. And while she's barely 18 years old, and I'm still 17, I feel like our complicated histories made both of us adults a long time ago.

"Tell me something good, David."

"What do you mean?"

"I'm spiraling. Just uh, just tell me anything. Please."

"Um, okay." I take a moment to stall by clearing my throat a couple times. Then I remember something completely random.

"Did you know Koala bears sleep 22 hours a day?"

Ellie goes silent on the other end. I stop breathing for a second because I feel like the biggest idiot. Then her booming laugh comes to life. I join with her because it feels natural.

"Why are you telling me this?" Ellie asks, still giggling under her breath.

"I don't know. My mind went blank. Then, for some reason I pictured Angela's old stuffy when she was younger. It was a Koala named Marty. She had an obsession with Koala Bears. She thought they were super cute and was constantly begging my mom and dad to get her one as a pet for her birthday. Weird, right?"

"Not really. I think it's cute. Every girl gets obsessed with cute animals. I used to pretend to be the mother to all of my dolls and stuffies as a kid. But my obsession was with penguins. I loved how they walked. My mom used to call me her little penguin because she said I walked like one when I first learned how to walk."

Ellie quietly laughs to herself. Then I hear her let out a deep exhale. She sounds relieved. Maybe it's because she's remembering something happy with her mom, which would be a rarity.

"David, can I ask you something?"

"Of course."

"Well, I don't want to make you uncomfortable. But it's about last night when I was painting your nails. You see, you kind of moved your arm over your groin in a funny way. Is it because you were, um…you know."

My throat locks up. It feels like I've suddenly forgotten how to breathe. I mean, what can I say?

Yes, Ellie. You gave me a rock-hard erection from barely touching my wrist.

Yes, Ellie. I was picturing you naked and taking your virginity.

Yes, Ellie. I probably was pitching a tent in my pants after you hugged me in front of your dad, too.

"David, are you there?"

"Yeah, sorry. I just…I just—"

"David, just because I believe in waiting doesn't mean I don't think about it all the time."

Think about *it*. What does she mean. I mean, I know what she means by *it*. But our conversations rarely go down this road. It feels so out of the blue. Out of the norm of possibilities. Something that could never ever be a reality. And yet, here we are.

"Ellie, is this really what you what to talk about?"

"Well, it's helping to distract my racing brain. So yes, just answer my question."

"Then yes—what you thought happened really did happen. I couldn't help it."

"And it's probably not the first time that's happened…around me…right?"

"That's right."

"How long have you been attracted to me…like in that way?"

Her question hangs in the air feeling like the most rhetorical thing on earth. But for some reason, the embarrassment is starting to fade. Maybe it's the way her voice sounded so innocent and curious. It's as if this moment, and my answer, suddenly means everything to her.

"Since the first day we met. I can't help it. It's how I feel. What about you? Are you—"

"Yes," she quickly interjects. "I don't know if it was that first night we met, but I've felt this way for a while now."

My mind begins to wander. I'm imagining the enchanting beauty of her smile. It has me thinking of how my whole world transformed into a greater purpose because of Ellie.

"What's going on in that brain of yours, David?"

"I'm thinking about that first night we met. You were so scared. But I don't blame you. Waking up in your neighbor's shed was probably terrifying. But you calmed down and you talked to me. I couldn't do much to help you. I was scared to talk to girls back then. I also didn't know what was going on with you. But I just listened. And I was happy I could help you, even though you just needed someone to talk to. It felt good to just keep you warm…and safe."

I clear my throat and take a deep breath, trying to come back to reality. But nights like those are hard to forget. It's even harder to believe how close I was to ending it all. And to think, Ellie still doesn't know that she saved my life that night.

It makes me introspective and thankful for all that I do have in my life. Ellie's always been appreciative of my help, but I'm infinitely more thankful because she's given me back my life…and *more*.

"Keep talking," she delicately whispers.

My mind is trying to catch up on so many things that have just been said. It's hard to slow my thoughts and find a starting point on what to say. "I guess I'm glad that we're finally talking about these kinds of things," I admit.

"I know. It feels good to be honest like this. Because I know I'm not perfect. God knows you sure put up with a lot of my craziness."

"Don't put yourself down like that," I quickly contradict her. "You are the way you are. And none of it is your fault. Besides, I like you the way you are. You give me hope. On days I'm feeling low, sometimes all I need is a note from you, or a nighttime meet-up and I instantly feel better."

"Me, too. But things are going to be different. My dad is on to us. Which reminds me, what did he say to you this morning?"

"Well, he said a lot of things I'm sure you can imagine. Threatened me a little. I don't want to upset you. Let's just say it ended with him threatening me and calling me a sheygetz. What is that by the way?"

"It's Yiddish for being a non-Jew. It's not a compliment. I'm sorry. That's such a terrible thing for him to say. But let's not talk about him anymore. Talk to me about something else. Tell me something good. I need to get out of my own head and stop worrying."

We spend the next couple hours talking about anything and everything. I tell her more about my upcoming trip to New York. She tells me about her dream of traveling through Europe and becoming a counselor one day. I can feel her whole spirit lighting up when she talks about these things.

When we run out of things to say we just lay in silence. I play all her favorite songs in the background. When the playlist plays its last song, all I can hear is her faint breath in the background. Every now and again she'll ask me if I'm still awake, begging me to not fall asleep before her. And even when I feel myself drifting, every time I hear her voice, I'm suddenly wide awake to give her the assurance she desperately needs.

I don't know what time it is when we fall asleep. All I know is she feels safe with me on the other line. And all I can imagine is one thing: sharing this night as I'd hoped—right next to her in bed.

Chapter Four

David

The coffee mug slowly goes up to his mouth. I don't mean to stare out the corner of my eye, but it's impossible to not notice his worsening tremors. The coffee probably doesn't help things either. However, coffee and morning chats with me and Angela is what my dad lives for. He loves telling us the same stories and having us repeat what's going on in our lives. It's a little annoying some days, but we've gotten used to it.

"Can I tell you guys one more quick story?" Dad asks, slowly lowering his mug as his coffee continues to slosh around.

I glance at the clock. "Make it quick, Dad. I need to be out of here in five minutes. I only have four more hours before I'm free from prison—I mean high school."

Angela chimes in. "Yeah, Dad. Sam will be pulling up any minute now."

The three loud honks signify that Sam is already out front.

Angela plants a goodbye kiss on Dad's forehead. "Love you, Dad."

"Bye, sweetheart." Dad turns to me. "Okay, just you and me, David."

I let out a huffing exhale because I need to drop off my note for Ellie before Scotty picks me up.

"Oh, come on, you still have time. This is a good one. It's about the day we moved into this house. Did you know we bought it from Joshua?"

"Wait, you bought this house from Joshua Merkowitz?"

"Yeah, his wife Leah was pregnant at the time. They were looking to upgrade their house, so they bought the house next door and sold this house to us. Your mom was so happy the day we closed. It wasn't easy because Joshua sure was a stickler on the price. But it all worked out."

My dad goes on to tell a story about my mom. It's about how they had no running water the first three days they lived here. I was so young at the time I don't remember it. I have a hard time concentrating on his story because my mind begins to wander.

"Wait, Dad," I interrupt him. "What year did we buy this house?"

"We bought it on your fifth birthday. Why do you ask?"

"Oh, nothing."

My dad goes on to finish his story, but my mind is completely checked out. Then I realize something.

"Wait, Dad. Ellie doesn't have any younger siblings."

"I know. It was really sad. Your mom found out shortly after it happened…miscarriage," Dad pauses, bowing his head down. "That poor Leah never seemed happy to begin with. But after that, she was a shell of herself."

"Did you and Mom ever get to know the Merkowitzes very well?"

"Joshua never gave me the time of day after he sold us the house. But your mom got to know Leah Merkowitz really well since the two of them weren't working at the time. They used to bake challah for each other every Shabbat. Your mom also had tea with her a couple of times a week. It was all kept secret from Joshua since we aren't Orthodox. I didn't get to know her very well because I was working too much. But poor Leah. She struggled with her mental health. Mom did what she could to be there for her, but she needed professional help. And she wasn't getting it. But they were good friends for quite a while. Then Leah left. It felt very out of the blue. Mom was really concerned for her welfare…and Ellie's."

My stomach begins to churn. Something feels off. I feel it in the marrow of my bones. Ellie's never mentioned anything about a miscarriage. I wonder if she even knows about it.

"Did Mom ever tell you why Leah left?"

"I have a hard time remembering. But I think Leah had to go look for someone. I just remember it really bothered your mom. It's one thing Maya was always good at—worrying and caring about others. There wasn't a more caring soul on this earth. It could be the most random stranger or her worst enemy—it didn't matter. She was put on this earth to help others. But…"

I watch as my dad's eyes glaze over. His mind is in another time. It's a time where he loved a woman with everything left in his heart.

The honking horn startles us. I give Dad a quick peck on the head. "Bye, Dad. Love you."

"Love you, too. Hey, David. Why are you so curious about the Merkowitzes?"

"I don't know. I guess I just feel bad for them."

"So, it has nothing to do with the cute redhead that lives over there."

I take a deep swallow inward, feeling completely tongue tied.

"There's no shame in looking, son. She's a beautiful girl. Just be careful. I don't trust her father. Never have."

"Um, okay, Dad. I got to go."

I bolt out the front door. I quickly make my way around to the side of the house and plant my note for Ellie in the opening of our shared wall. Then I head off for my last day of school.

"Earth to David!" Scotty shouts.

"Sorry, what?"

"Bro, what's wrong with you? I just asked you like three times about when we're leaving on Friday."

My mind comes back to reality. "Sorry. We'll leave first thing in the morning. Maybe around seven. We should be able to easily get to Amarillo by nightfall."

Scotty pops another fry in his mouth, chewing it over with a curious glance. "What happened? Something's up. We got ninety more minutes of high school and a weeklong road trip to New York. You look like your puppy just got ran over."

"I don't have a puppy."

"It's a saying, jackass. Did something happen with your ginger princess?" Scotty asks in a chastising tone.

I chuck a fry that hits him right in the eyeball. He knows I hate when he calls Ellie that.

"Hey, fucker! That hurt!"

After I have a quick chuckle, I tell Scotty about my two encounters with Ellie's dad.

"Wait! He caught her hugging you?"

"Yep."

"Wait, wait, wait." Scotty raises his hands in the air. "*She…hugged…you*?"

"Yeah. Then her dad opened that back door. He didn't even say anything. Just that murderous stare. I still can't get it out of my head. Then the next day he came over and tore me a new one."

Scotty's eyes go wider. "Oh fuck!"

Scotty and I attended the same reform temple growing up. He's had his Bar Mitzvah and done a little bit of Hebrew school, but aside from that does little practice in the religion. But Scotty knows enough about my situation with Ellie over the years to know this is crazy. And he knows that while I have a crush on Ellie, I also have no chance in hell because she's an Orthodox Jew.

I go on to tell Scotty the extent of the lock down that Ellie's currently under.

"So, what're you going to do?"

"Fuck if I know. She has the phone you got me. We spoke for a long time the last couple nights. But she's still worried she'll have one of her dreams and hurt herself. It's just hard because I'm basically all she has."

Scotty shakes his head. He already knows how fucked up her dad is. But what's even worse is Ellie feels estranged from everyone. Her own congregation has done little to support the Merkowitz family since her mother left. Ellie thinks the temple leadership sees her family as some type of pariah.

"You know what that girl needs?" Scotty asks.

"What?"

"A fresh fucking start. I mean, she recently turned 18, right?"

"Yeah. She's legally an adult now."

"Good. She needs to get away from that prick of a dad. Does she have any other family?"

"She has her half-brother, Yosef. He lives in New York. But I get the feeling from Ellie that he doesn't give two shits about her. Then she has her aunt. But that's her mom's sister. She stopped being Jewish a while ago so her dad has been sure to keep her out of Ellie's life."

My mind begins to resonate with Scotty's remarks—"*a fresh start*." After all, he's right. Ellie needs a do-over. She's too good a person to deserve the family she's been given. A mother that abandoned her. A detached, narcissistic father that's verbally abusive. And no one else to look after her— *except for me*.

Ellie has told me on multiple occasions how she doesn't like holding on to the hate she feels constantly on the inside. Sometimes she'll even reference lines from the Torah about forgiveness. But I don't agree with her. Someone in her circumstances should be allowed to unleash all the hate she's bottled up over the years—without a shred of regret. And she deserves real answers on what caused her mom to abandon her. It would help her move forward with her own life and find belief in herself. But she's stuck in this fucked up situation, which means I'm stuck, too.

Later that night, I continue to wait for her call. When midnight rolls around, I head outside to see if she left a note in the wall. It would be her only other way of communicating with me if her dad somehow got her phone. But there's nothing there.

I look up to her second story bedroom window from the side of my house, but there's no lights on. It's odd. She usually has her bedroom lamp on, even when she falls asleep.

Fuck it!

The first couple of rocks I hurl barely miss the window. Luckily, they don't make too loud a sound hitting the stucco exterior. Then, my next three rocks hit dead center on her window. The sounds should have woken her up by now. I contemplate throwing a couple more, but I begin to worry that she may not even be in her room. But that wouldn't make sense either.

I decide to head back inside to see if I can reach her on the phone. Then, as I put my hand on the doorknob, I hear it. The blood curdling scream to *stop!* It echoes out two more times from Ellie's house, sounding even more perilous.

Everything becomes instinctual. The adrenalin coursing through my veins has me over the side wall in a split second. I stagger my way up to her back door, jiggling the doorknob that's securely locked. I run around to the side of the house, finding another door that's locked. Then another scream echoes inside from Ellie, this one more dire than the rest.

I grab a boulder by my feet. My heart is pounding out of my chest as I sprint my way around to the back door. After smashing the glass, I reach inside to undo the deadbolt. Once inside, the silence becomes so eerie and unexpected. All the lights are off except for a faint hint of light coming from the top of the stairs. I slow my movements as I grab the railing of the staircase.

"Sasha! Sasha! Sasha!" Ellie screams hysterically.

I sprint my way upstairs. The second my foot hits the top of the staircase, I feel a blunt force whipping my head forwards. My body goes lifeless in an instant. My vision becomes a dark abyss. The ringing in my ears is getting louder. All I can see are the white spots. Then a cold shiver takes over my body. I feel myself drifting further and further away—helpless to do anything. Helpless in saving *my* Ellie.

Chapter Five

David

The intense pressure on the back of my head makes the pain worse. It also doesn't help that my hands are still cuffed behind my back.

"Fuck, man! Take it easy, will ya?"

"Sorry about that," the paramedic says, reaching for more gauze. "You have a good size gash here. I'm guessing this'll be about five stitches."

He wraps the bandage tightly around my head while I wait for the investigator to come back. I've already told the investigator the same fucking story twice. But he keeps heading back in the house—like he's trying to corroborate what's really going on here.

I let out a loud sigh, trying to will my brain to remember anything about the last thirty minutes. Everything feels crystal clear until I made it to the top of that staircase.

The police officer still hasn't told me if Ellie is okay. My mind doesn't want to expect the worst. But when her screams for help play back in my head, I can't help the dreadful thoughts.

"Please, sir. Just tell me if the girl inside is okay. Her name is Ellie—I mean Eliana Merkowitz. That's M-E-R-K—"

"Listen to me! You are the only person with any reported injuries. I assure you, there are at least six cops inside that house. If someone was hurt, they'd be out here, and we would tend to them. Do you understand? If that girl is in the house, I assure you that aside from being shaken up, she's fine."

I begin grinding my teeth so hard that I feel my jaw cramping. If I wasn't already bleeding out of my head, I'd contemplate head butting this dumbass paramedic.

I look out across the lawn and see Angela walking back with the bottle of water I requested. Once she gets to where I'm sitting, she feeds me the water.

"Thanks."

Angela rubs my shoulder. "Are you sure you're okay?" she asks, furrowing her brow.

"Yeah, I'll be fine. They just said a few stitches. Is Dad still asleep?"

"Yeah."

"Angela, you have to promise to not tell him anything about this. It'll only stress him out and make his symptoms worse. You hear me? Promise me."

"Okay. Okay. Just relax. It's just between me and you. But I don't see how Dad doesn't find out about this at some point. Don't forget…" Angela pauses, leaning down to my ear to whisper. "We're still seventeen for another day."

Angela leans back as I notice the same cop walking back out of the house and up to me.

"Turn around, David," he demands, his tone still ass hole-ish but calmer than earlier.

It's then I feel the release of tension in my wrist and back as my handcuffs are undone.

"I apologize for this. We were unsure who the suspect was when we came onto the scene. But apparently the man inside just admitted to this being a mix-up."

A mix-up?

"What the fuck do you mean?" I holler. "This was no mix-up!"

"Relax, David," Angela tries to calm me down. "What happened, officer?"

"Mr. Merkowitz had forgotten to lock the front door. That's where they heard the intruder enter the house. Unfortunately, since it wasn't locked, the camera at the front door entry was not recording. But when the intruder came through the front door, he and his daughter retreated to his room, locked their door, and called 911. We think that's about when you broke in through the back door. You likely spooked the intruder. At which point we think you got knocked unconscious by the intruder and that person got spooked and ran off. If anything, I think you helped in resolving the situation."

I scoff, shaking my head in disbelief. "What? Are you kidding me? That's bullshit. I'm telling you, Ellie was being harmed. She was screaming for help. Did you not question her at all?"

"We did. The father spoke on her behalf, and she corroborated the story. Aside from being shaken up, she's fine. I didn't notice any physical harm done to her."

"You're wrong. There's no way they'd keep their front door unlocked. You don't know that guy," I raise my voice, pointing towards their house. "He's a paranoid asshole. Something happened inside between him and Ellie. You have to believe me."

"Son, listen to me! The intruder came to rob them. We found Joshua Merkowitz's wallet just a few minutes ago. It was a couple houses down the street with missing credit cards and cash. We also got a call three minutes ago. We may have caught the guy already just a few blocks from here."

I sigh. Something still feels fishy. I rub my eyes vigorously until my vision gets blurry. The blurriness feels like a metaphor for my life. I can't see things clearly and nothing makes sense.

"Whatever," I concede.

I stand up, ready to head home and avoid this douchebag. He hands me his card to let me know he'll be in touch. Then I lie to the paramedic, telling him that I'm eighteen. The lie gets me out of a huge ambulance bill as Angela agrees to take me to the hospital to get stitched up.

The next day I wake up feeling groggy. My headache somehow feels worse than it did last night. We didn't get home from the emergency room until 4 a.m. And as much as I want to sleep in, I know I need to get up, so Dad doesn't get an inkling of anything stressful going on.

Before heading downstairs, I check my phone. Still nothing from Ellie. I walk out front and notice the Merkowitz's car isn't in the driveway. I even check our shared wall for a note, but still nothing.

It's hard to act normal during breakfast. My dad's in his usual jolly mood. Angela looks exhausted, but she's doing a better job of hiding it.

"What are you two up to today?" Dad asks.

"I'm packing and just vegging out," I tell Dad.

"Sam and I are going to the movies and grabbing dessert later," Angela says. "But he's been acting weird since yesterday. Why are boys so weird?"

"So are girls," I quickly shoot back.

"What do you know? You've had like half a girlfriend in your life."

I itch the side of my face with only my middle finger extended in her direction.

"You two settle down," Dad butts in. "You both have one more day as kids. Tomorrow you're both adults. I just can't believe I forgot you two will be eighteen tomorrow. It's funny how fast time flies by."

Dad's thoughts about the future get me to thinking. I worry about his health every day. It's only a matter of time before he'll need a live-in nurse. It could be our reality in the next year or the next few years. Parkinson's and dementia are weird in the way they attack the mind and body.

Dad clears his throat to get our attention. "Hey, I got an idea. Since David will be gone on his actual birthday tomorrow, how about we barbecue and celebrate this afternoon—just the three of us. You two can help me a bit on the grill if I need it, but it'll be just like old times. Come on, what do you say?"

"Fine with me," Angela quickly replies.

"Me too," I mutter.

My dad's glare lingers on me. "Hey, what's wrong with you?"

"I'm fine. I just didn't sleep well."

The events of last night play out in my head. I try to shake them away, but it's impossible. The ironic part is it has nothing to do with getting knocked unconscious. I'd get knocked out a hundred times if it would rid me of the memory of her screams. And it was more than just a cry for help. She screamed out for Sasha. *Who is Sasha?*

Angela kicks my shin under the table. I realize dad is still giving me a worried look.

"You know you're a terrible liar, David." He chuckles softly. "Maybe not as bad as your mom. That woman couldn't hide an expression or emotion if her life depended on it."

I want to be honest with my dad. I really do. But if I do it, I'll need to water it down quite a bit.

"Sorry for spacing out. I'm just a little stuck. Maybe it's the realization that I'm basically an adult and need to figure out what I'm doing with my life. You ever feel like no matter what you do, no matter how bad you want something, there's some things you just can't have?"

Dad takes a slow swig of his coffee. Then he tilts his head the slightest bit as his forehead crinkles and his eyes gaze deeper into mine. His tremors suddenly look non-existent—like he's my younger dad for a fleeting moment.

"Well, David. I'd ask 'why?' Why do you feel stuck? If it's because you're afraid to take a risk—or maybe do the wrong thing…I'd say who cares? Go out there and fuck up. I mean it. Lord knows, I've fucked up plenty in my life. And I can wallow in regret, or I can move forward, knowing I tried. But if you fuck up by doing what'll make you happy…then go out there and fuck up a thousand times."

I try to breathe in my dad's wisdom. It was full of expletives, but somehow so eloquently put. And I believe him. He's *so right.* But putting it into action is hard without direction, or a starting point on what to do first.

The day moves forward like any other day with no school. I check my phone all day long for any updates. But after a while, I realize Ellie's phone is nowhere near her. She would've called me or at least texted me by now.

When nighttime rolls around, there's still no car out front. There's not even a light on in the house or a single peep of a sound. It's clearly vacant. But for how much longer? And why?

I'm not able to eat much for supper. I am, however, able to put on a face to fake my way through a birthday dinner. But even after dinner, my mind is still a mess.

Angela keeps telling me not to worry. Scotty has told me the same thing. I've told them both every detail of what happened last night. But even they don't have an inclination of what could've happened. They've only told me to keep faith that Ellie's okay.

But I know better. I know her dad. She's not okay.

The next morning, I wake up from another sleepless night. When my phone rings I dive across the bed to my nightstand. I'm disappointed when I see the name on the screen.

"What up, Scotty?"

The next thing I hear is the sound of gagging. It's followed by the sound of a viscous liquid splashing onto porcelain. After a few more seconds, I hear his labored breathing.

"Oh fuck, dude," Scotty groans. "I'm sick as fuck. I went out and got some Taco Dell last night. Holy shit, man. It has to be food poisoning. I've been puking and shitting my guts out all night. There's no way I can go. You're going to have to fly solo to New York."

"Seriously? Of all days, you're telling me you got food poisoning last night."

"I'm really sorry. Look, man, I need to go."

"Okay. Feel better."

"Hey, David. One more thing. Happy eighteenth birthday. I hope you have a good trip. And whether you win the scholarship or not, I'm super proud of you. I mean that, bro."

"Thanks, man. You'll be missed. But don't worry, I'll keep in touch."

I end the call, realizing I forgot today is my birthday. I wonder if this trip is even worth doing. The whole point was doing the road trip with my best friend. I already know I have a very slim chance of winning the scholarship. But I've already invested close to a thousand dollars in this trip—half of which was contributed by my dad.

After a quick breakfast, I say goodbye to Angela and Dad.

"Can we walk you out to the car?" Dad asks.

"No, Dad. It's okay. I don't need a long goodbye. Besides, I'll be back in a week. And I'll be texting you every day, so don't worry."

After quick hugs, I head out to my car. I chuck my luggage into the back seat and quickly pull out of the driveway. I have a full tank of gas in my Maxima and a lonely eight hours of driving until I get to Amarillo, Texas.

Then I hear my phone ring. It's a text from Ellie!

Don't leave yet. I need to come with you. PLEASE!

I quickly turn around. My heart feels like it's about to implode as I drive the two blocks back to my house. When I turn down my street all I can see is the color red. But as I pull up next to her, I know instantly that things are not okay.

Her eyes are pink from either hours of crying or not sleeping. Her lips are a perfectly straight line of uncertainty and fear. Even the tension in her jaw is palpable, like her mouth is wired shut. I can read her like a book because I've seen the fear in this beautiful face too many times.

So many questions play out in my mind as she walks around the hood of my car, hugging a sheet of paper to her chest. She opens the passenger-side door, chucking her luggage into the back seat. She slams the door shut and keeps her eyes glued straight ahead.

"Ellie."

I can barely muster that one word as I try to swallow the tension in my throat. And all my one word can do is make her eyes well up. Then the first tear pours quickly down her face. She hands over the sheet of paper while her eyes stare straight ahead. She seems lost in her own depressive hypnosis.

Can't talk. Please drive me away from here. NOW!

Chapter Six

David

I've been on the highway for almost an hour now. It's so hard to concentrate. Keeping my car between the lane lines is even a struggle. I keep glancing out of the corner of my eye. Aside from the occasional wiping of her eyes, her expression continues to look lifeless. Her body feels so still next to mine, like she's hardly breathing.

I need her to say something. I don't even know where I'm taking her. Is she just coming with me to New York? That doesn't seem logical. But she's here, living a fantasy we were joking about just the other day.

She needs to at least tell me what's going on. There must be something I can do for her. But I feel like driving away from Phoenix is the only thing she needs—at least for now.

I suddenly notice what's coming up on the next freeway exit. It ignites the spark of inspiration I need. It feels like a long shot, but it's the least I can do for now.

I park in the first open spot I see in front of the grocery store.

"I'll be right back in five minutes. I promise. I'm just grabbing a couple things."

Her eyes continue to gaze away in their forward-facing trance. But I'm not leaving until she gives me some type of response.

Then her eyes shut so tightly the corners begin to squint. It looks agonizing. I can even feel the pressure in my own eyes. Then she slowly nods her head up and down.

Five minutes later I'm back with two paper bags containing everything I need. I'm not ready for her to see what's in one of the bags so I put it in the backseat. I open the other bag as she takes her first full glance in my direction. I pull out the dark chocolate and the potato chips first.

"Don't worry, I checked. They're all kosher. Perfectly safe for you to eat."

Next, I pull out the nail polish. Then I pull out the cylinder vase, wedging it into my center console.

"These are for you. I know the white ones are your favorite," I tell her, forcing an uncertain smile on my face.

My hands shake nervously. I delicately place the white roses into the vase. Once the last rose is in, I feel the warmth of her hand on mine.

Her blue eyes come to life for the first time today. They're still welled up, but there's a glimmer of shine in them. It's not the first time my eyes have gotten lost in Ellie's. But everything is redefined in this moment. It's a brand-new way of experiencing her beauty because I can't breathe. I can't think. I can only *feel*. And all I feel is her soul slowly coming back to life.

"It's okay, Ellie. Just know, when you're ready to talk…I'm ready to listen…to help…or just listen…to do anything for you. You hear me…*anything.*"

The tears pour down her face as she nods her head. We pull away from the grocery store with my right hand still holding tightly onto hers. Then I turn on her favorite song from my playlist. It's a song called "One Day" by her favorite musician,

Matisyahu. The lyrics and the rhythm of the music fill the car with hope. And for the first time since seeing her this morning, I can feel the change in her demeanor. She may still be scared by something I don't understand, but at least she has me. And most importantly, we have each other.

"I need to use the restroom," she quietly says.

We've just crossed the border into New Mexico and it's the first sound of her voice. It has me shocked and feeling like I've forgotten how to talk.

"Um, of course. No problem."

We pull into the first rest stop. While I wait for her to come back, I text Angela and Scotty about what's going on. After I send the text, I realize quickly that I'm in over my head. Both of their replies are to turn around and bring her back. I decide not to respond, for now. If I continue the conversations, they'll scare me into turning around.

The second she returns and shuts the car door, I seize my opportunity.

"I know you don't want to talk. But can I just ask a couple clarifying questions...Please, Ellie?"

Ellie turns her body fully in my direction, barely nodding as she bites down on her lip.

"Okay. Well, does your dad—"

"He doesn't know," Ellie interrupts. "He doesn't know I'm with you. No one does. That part's taken care of. My alibi is good for the next few days. What else do you need to know?"

"Well, where are we going? Are you just coming with me to New York?"

Her brow furrows. I can see her mind chewing over my question, like she herself doesn't even know the answer.

"Well, I'm still figuring everything out. But yeah...I want to come support you in New York. But I also need your help. And I can't explain what's going on because I'm still figuring that part out. But we'll likely need to stop along the way to see someone in Pennsylvania. That is…if you're willing to help me. I know I'm not making sense, but—"

"I'll help you. Whatever you need, Ellie. I'm here for you. When I said anything, I meant it. Don't forget that."

My strong-willed reply has a confidence that even surprises myself. But I can't help it. Helping her feels like the only thing that matters.

"I just need one thing from you, Ellie."

"What's that?"

"This," I say, reaching to grab her hand. "I don't want to hesitate anymore when I touch you. This feels natural. Don't you think?"

Ellie's smile comes to life for the first time today. "I do. And you're right. It's just like you said…*natural*."

We get back on the freeway with a lightness in the air. I'm relieved by more than just her words. It's her touch. The one thing I've never been able to have. And it's so small—just taking her hand. But it's hard to not wonder how many days lie ahead and the options that exist before us.

Ellie may be only holding my hand, but she's violating the tenets of strict Orthodox Jewish laws, the biggest being I'm not Orthodox. It's beliefs she strictly believes in and wants to adhere to. But she can't help it. And neither can I.

The drive progresses and my mind wanders to memories of my mom. I only had twelve years with her, and the older I get, the more I feel like the memories fade away—except for one that's been my constant.

Our tuck-ins were the best when I was young. I can still feel her putting her hand on my bare chest. Then she'd bow her head and be completely silent and still for such long periods of time. Sometimes it would last until I fall asleep. It would be easy for me to believe that she was praying or giving thanks to God. And who knows, I'm sure that was part of it. But I always *felt* something more in those tuck-ins.

It's the one memory I wish I could re-live. However, as I glance down at me and Ellie holding hands, something feels so similar and reminiscent. And yet, Ellie's sharing something with me that's forbidden: her own need for touch.

"How close are we to the next city?" Ellie asks, taking a deep yawn.

"Albuquerque is about twenty minutes away. Should we stop to stretch our legs and get some food?"

Ellie's whole face lights up. "Yes! Yes! Let's do it. I've never been there. Albuquerque. Albuquerque," she repeats under her breath with astonishment.

"How many places have you been to outside of Phoenix?" I ask.

"Nowhere really. I mean, I went to Brooklyn to see my aunt on my mom's side. But that's when she was still practicing Judaism. I was just an infant, so I don't remember anything."

"Does she have kids?"

"No. I Don't think so. I remember my dad saying one time that my aunt wasn't able to have children."

"Why?"

A silence passes as Ellie thinks about my question. It's a question I had no business asking, making the silence feel awkward.

"I honestly don't know. I know she was married, but other than that I don't know why she couldn't have kids."

"My aunt and uncle couldn't have kids either. It seems more common nowadays. But his issue was a low sperm count."

I quickly glance at Ellie. Her eyes tilt up, lost in thought. "I wish I knew more about my aunt. All I know is she left Judaism and my dad said we can never speak of her again.

And that was it. But it would be nice to know if I have cousins."

An uneasy feeling suddenly washes over my chest. I remember my dad telling me how Ellie's mom had a miscarriage. The miscarriage by itself is incredibly unsettling. But what's worse is wondering if Ellie even knows about it.

"David?'

I realize I'm spacing out.

"Yeah. Sorry, what?"

"I'm going to paint my nails and maybe read for a bit. You mind if I…" She nods at our hands.

"Oh, of course."

Ellie reaches into the back seat for the grocery bags. Then I realize she's grabbing the wrong one.

"Wait—"

"What's this? Oh!" Ellie's voice squeaks with surprise.

She's already busy analyzing the pads I purchased for her.

"Is this…for me?" she asks, unable to hide the surprise in her tone.

I feel my face go flush. My throat constricts like there's a noose tightening around my neck.

"Why did you…um, thanks," she says, her voice polite, but still unsure.

I clear my throat before speaking. "I'm sorry. I know this is awkward. But when I started driving my dad made me carry pads in my glove compartment. He wanted me to have it on hand in case I was ever with Angela and…you know. So, when I was in line at the grocery store, I remembered I didn't have any more in this car. And I thought maybe with everything you have going on in your life that you could've forgot. It's ridiculous, I know."

"It's not, David. It's sweet of you to be considerate. It's just not what I'd expect from a…boy. The boys I know don't even speak of things like this. I mean, I only learned what a mikvah was a few years ago."

"What's a mikvah?" I ask.

"It's all part of the Halakah—you know, Jewish laws. When a woman has her period, the husband can never touch her during that time. They even have to sleep in separate beds. The no touching goes on for even a week after her menstrual cycle ends. Then the woman goes to a special place called a mikvah where they cleanse themselves in the cleanest of water. What? Why are you looking at me like that?"

"What? How am I looking at you?"

Ellie chuckles to herself. "Well, for starters, your face is as red as the paint I'm about to put on my nails."

I know this is a topic that shouldn't embarrass me or shock me. After all, I've gotten used to Angela mentioning it a couple times each month when she's dealing with cramps. But this idea of marrying someone and then not being able to touch them for almost half the month blows my mind. Lord knows, I'm touching myself at least once every couple days.

"I just, I don't know. If I'm married to a girl, I'd want to be touching her all the time. And I don't mean just as in having sex all the time. But just showing affection and making the other person feel desired seems important."

I see Ellie's lips part out of the corner of my eye. But nothing comes out of her mouth.

"What is it?" I ask.

"Nothing," Ellie says, shaking her head.

"Well, I guess absence makes the heart grow fonder. Right?"

"Maybe. But can I ask you something, David?"

"Sure."

"Earlier, when you were talking about your aunt and uncle you said the word sperm count. What did you mean by that?"

I take a deep swallow at her question. The tension in my throat is strangling my ability to respond. I can't help it. I just feel so bad for Ellie. How is it an eighteen-year-old girl can be this naïve and lack any form of basic sex education?

"Um, okay. Well, it's what's in the semen, you know, when a guy orgasms or cums. It's what fertilizes the egg to maybe get a girl pregnant."

My words felt so awkward and unsure. And now the weight in my chest is the discomfort radiating from Ellie. She's embarrassed. Plain and simple. She knows these are things she should have a more than basic understanding of as an adult. But she doesn't. She feels shameful for something that is not her fault.

"Do you need me to explain—"

"Nope! Stop, David!" Her hand goes up in the air to deflect this conversation. "This is just stupid. I shouldn't have asked."

I quickly glance over to see her arms tightly crossed over her chest. She stares out the passenger-side window sniffling like she's on the brink of tears.

Do something! Say something to her!

My emergency flashers go on. I quickly pull over to the side of the road.

"Let's talk more about this," I tell her.

She shakes her head emphatically. "No, David. Keep driving. I don't want to talk about this! Please! Please! Keep driving!" she screams before letting her face fall into her hands.

Before I can put my car in park, she's already crying, *hysterically*! I put my hand on her shoulder as she flinches. There's nothing I can do or say that will change how she feels right now.

Angela has often told me that sometimes a girl needs a good cry. Maybe this is that time. I want to solve Ellie's problems and let her know this isn't her fault. Or at least help her see the intrinsically kind, beautiful soul that I see. But I know that's not possible—at least not right now.

I can't forget that her home and who's allowed into her life is so closely guarded by her father. She has no family and so few lasting friendships in her world outside of me. Even the congregation at her temple sees Ellie as less than.

She has little understanding of culture and ways of living outside in the real world. Sure, I've given her a broadened perspective of the world over my years of knowing her. But it can't undo the years her father has taken from her—hiding her like stealing sunlight from a blossom ready to bloom.

Despite her onslaught of tears, I feel a sense of calm slowly settle over me. Seeing her release these pent-up emotions may be the best thing for her. And it's not just her being embarrassed about her lack of knowledge on sex. That part was perhaps just the straw that broke the camel's back.

"I'm really sorry, Ellie. This isn't your fault. You hear me? This is not your fault."

I hand her a tissue as her breathing starts to calm. Her body seems less tense as I watch her take three deep breaths. Then her dampened eyes come up to meet mine.

"Okay. We can talk about it."

Then, the unthinkable happens. We spend the next ten minutes talking about sex. Ellie knows most of everything based on books she's read at the library. More than anything, my role is to clarify and answer her questions as they organically come up in conversation.

The longer the conversation goes the more Ellie begins referencing aspects of the Torah. She reminds me that there's nothing in the Torah that outlaws premarital sex. If anything, she references aspects of the Torah that mention the importance of pleasure for both man and woman. It's only the Orthodox Jews that teach abstinence until marriage.

One thing I do speak up on is the importance of consent. I tell her that she should never feel pressured to do something she's not fully comfortable doing. It feels odd, echoing these sentiments that I was taught by my own parents. But I'm glad I'm able to be there for Ellie in this way. These are things she *needs* to know.

Eventually, our conversation steers towards the concept of foreplay.

"So, um…you have experience…doing these things with other girls?"

I watch as her jaw clenches and her throat goes inward. It's impossible not to feel the discomfort and jealousy radiating from her question.

"Yes, but um, just one…girl," I stammer. "But that was a while ago."

"What was her…actually, never mind. I don't, um…should we get going?"

I've clearly admitted too much.

"Yeah, good idea. Let's get going," I say, starting the car back up. "But, if you have more questions, I'm happy to answer them. Really, it's no big deal at all."

Ellie nods back with a hopeful smile. It gives me a momentary sense of relief. The last thing I want is for her to feel embarrassed. And as weird as it felt at first, it oddly became a bit of a turn on to talk about these things.

"Thanks, David. You know, the books you let me borrow are helping too. I'm only fifty pages into the last one, but I can tell it's going to have romantic scenes."

I chuckle to myself, reaching for my water bottle. "Don't worry. I assure you Harry Potter is not going to get steamy. It's basically a children's book."

"I'm not talking about that book. I'm talking about the other one you gave to me about a week ago. It's called…oh what was it called?" Ellie mutters to herself as she digs into her backpack. "This one. *Loaded Cowboy.*"

The water halfway down my esophagus suddenly sprays everywhere. I'm coughing up a lung and laughing at the same time. I've never read the book in her hand, but I know the loaded reference has nothing to do with a big gun.

"Are you okay? What is it?" Ellie laughs.

I clear my throat a few times. "That's an erotic book. I've never read it. It's my sister's. Oh my god. I can't believe I did that. I thought I was giving you the first three Harry Potter books. I'm so sorry. I feel like an idiot."

My sincerity is meant as an apology. But when I look at her unmoved expression, I realize her confusion.

"David, it's okay. I really like the book so far. I know I'm not allowed to read these books. But I don't care about that stuff anymore. I want to know things. And not just sexual things. I want to know about…so…many…*things*. Do you understand what I'm saying?"

I tentatively nod my head. "I think I understand what you're saying. I've just never read that book—or those kinds of books."

"So, what then? Are you saying I shouldn't read books like this?"

"I'm not saying that. You can read what you want. I just don't know if that's the best way to learn more about sex. I mean, I guess you can read it if you're enjoying it. But many times, the things in those books are probably just fantasies."

"How do you know?" Ellie challenges. "You said it yourself that you never read the book. I mean, I know it's fiction. But it's written by a woman—a real woman. If it's sexual fantasies that women want, then there's still things to be learned…right?"

This whole conversation is incredibly ironic, and in a weird way funny. I remember needling Angela about her addiction to romance books and calling them book porn just the other day. She could care less; she's always liked the books with covers dawning super models with six-pack abs.

I chew over Ellie's words, carefully wondering how I can respond. Her logic is sound, but it still feels weird. It's a very weird way to learn about sex when you have such a blank slate to begin with. But then again, this probably wouldn't make her the first girl to learn more about sex through an erotic book.

"You know what, you're right. I've never read the book so I shouldn't judge it. Maybe we can read it together."

"Really?"

"Sure, why not?"

"I'd like that," Ellie says, reaching for my hand. "I'd like that a lot."

And that's how my eighteenth birthday started:

A birds and bees conversation with an eighteen-year-old Orthodox Jewish girl.

My commitment to reading my first erotic novel with Ellie.

And road-tripping with Ellie to destinations still unknown.

Today will go down as the weirdest birthday experience of my life. But I wouldn't want it any other way. Today and the next few days have so much in store for us. We're both unsure about what comes next, but we're doing it together—holding hands on an adventure—never wanting to let go.

Chapter Seven

David

Downtown Albuquerque is a first for Ellie and me. There's so much to see and experience. But as we walk hand in hand, the best part is seeing the curiosity in her face. It's like she's seeing a new world for the first time.

I may not know what's going on in the deeper parts of her brain. We still haven't clarified exactly where I'm taking her and how I can help her. Nor have we spoken about the night I got knocked unconscious after hearing her pleading screams for Sasha. Getting to these topics is important. But the selfish part of me wants to bask in the present moments where she's happy.

We walk through a street fair full of southwestern art and different types of cuisines. Once our feet get tired, we take a seat at a fountain to enjoy some frozen yogurt. I notice a police officer walking by who gives us a lingering stare. I know I'm just being paranoid. After all, I didn't force Ellie to come with me. And Ellie assured me she has an alibi. I believe her. But I can't help to wonder what her dad would do if he found out.

"Are you okay, David?"

"I'm fine. I just…I don't mean to spoil things. But can you at least tell me where your dad thinks you are?"

Ellie stabs her spoon back into her yogurt and stares off in the distance. She keeps her gaze away from me as she talks.

"He thinks I flew to New York to see my half-brother, Yosef. He took me to the airport this morning and dropped me off. He was flying somewhere as well but in a completely different terminal. He wouldn't tell me where he was going."

"I don't understand. Isn't Yosef going to freak out when he doesn't see you get off the plane?"

"No, I've already spoken to Yosef. He knows I'm not coming. And it's okay. He owes me a great debt. He and his wife do. It's hard to explain, but I need these next few days with you to figure things out."

"What are we figuring out? I mean, aside from driving myself to New York, I don't even know where I'm taking you in Pennsylvania."

Ellie turns to face me. The sudden intensity in her eyes sends a shivering chill up the back of my neck. Then she places her hand on top of mine.

"I should know more soon. But I'm sure we'll need to stop in a small suburb outside Pittsburgh. But it shouldn't delay us getting to your award ceremony on time. It's important to me that I'm there to support you."

Ellie's eyes linger over mine. My mind debates whether I should dig for more details. But the stress is everywhere on that gorgeous face. I can see the tightness in her jaw, like she's grinding her teeth. Even her eyes begin to glaze over. It's like her mind is racing to a place she wants to avoid. It's a sadness I've seen too often in her, so I decide to not press further. Getting to the bottom of this will have to be gradual.

"Okay, Ellie. Should we get back on the road?"

Ellie just nods her head.

We make our way across New Mexico with time flying by. After Ellie reads for a couple hours, we get back to chatting. She quickly comes back to her talkative and inquisitive self.

Ellie tells me how one day she hopes to backpack through Europe visiting all the famous landmarks and every art museum along the way. Upon finishing her trip, she wants to get a master's degree in either social work or counseling. She hopes to have children one day but doesn't want to do these things until she's traveled and given time to finish her education. She keeps reiterating how she wants time to find herself.

The smile on her face as she talks about her hopes and dreams becomes infectious. Happiness like this makes me want to open that path for her—make it all possible. But the more she talks about it, the more she tells me how it doesn't seem possible for these things to happen on her terms.

"My purpose is to marry and bear children. That's first and foremost along with being a good wife and mother. And I want to be those things—I really do. But I want to do it when I'm ready. I want to experience a life of my own first."

I glance at her face just in time to see the corner of her lip perk up. She's lost in this daydream. But to me, it's no dream.

"You can do these things, Ellie. You'll find a way," I say, squeezing tighter through her hand. "I just know it. Just have hope. My dad always told me…well, actually I think he got this from my mom. But he said that hope is the life force of the soul. You got to feed it."

"Feed it?" Ellie asks.

"Yeah. You have to feed it with positive affirmations. You have to feed it with belief. You know, visualize the path." I chuckle at my own words. "Oh my god, I sound like my dad."

"I like that, David. I like that a lot. Feed the life force," Ellie says, smiling brighter. Her smile becomes extraordinary. It reaches so high up on her face I want to pull over and let my eyes bask in her happy thoughts. I want to freeze time and live in that smile. *It's my life force.*

I feel Ellie scoot closer to the center console of my car. Her hand squeezes tighter through mine. Then I feel her other hand come onto my wrist. She glides the tips of her fingers with a deft, delicate touch. It tickles a little, but it's also very relaxing and almost hypnotic in a way.

"Tell me about your dreams of becoming a great writer?"

I shrug and then clear my throat, trying to level out my breathing. It's hard to concentrate because her touch has every hormone in my body screaming.

"Come on, David. Feed the life force," Ellie says with a soft chuckle.

"I don't know. I'm not sure yet how it'll look. Maybe I'll be writing screenplays for movies or maybe my focus will only be on books. But it would be cool to become a part of the movie-making process. Not the acting part. But definitely the writing part, and maybe even the directing role in making movies. But whatever it is, I want my stories to leave an impression on the world. It would be like my own kind of *Good Will Hunting*."

"Good Will Hunting?" Ellie repeats, looking befuddled.

"Yeah, that's a famous movie. It made me want to become a writer. It was written by Matt Damon and Ben Affleck. They're super famous actors now, but when they wrote the screenplay to that movie, they were just ordinary college students with a story to share. I can relate because I always have stories in my head. That's why I love writing. Getting those couple hours to put those thoughts living in my head onto my laptop…oh man…it's the best."

"So, how can we make it happen?"

Ellie's question hangs in the foggy area of my brain. I don't want to be pessimistic about my chances of getting to my dream, but I can't deny that it feels like a long shot.

"It's not that simple. My dad—"

"No, no, no," Ellie interrupts. "We're not allowed to make excuses. I know your dad is going to needs lots of help. But what if all of that was being handled. How are you going to become a famous writer or director?"

"Well, I'd need to get into a good film school. That's where winning first place and getting this scholarship would help."

"Then what?"

"Well, graduate and move to L.A. I'd need an agent to represent me. Then I'd need to start submitting scripts and setting up meetings with producers and learn how to network with others in the film industry. But I don't know…all of this feels like a one-in-a-million shot."

"No, no, no. Don't say that. Remember, we're feeding the life force."

I chuckle under my breath while Ellie continues to give me an encouraging smile. She won't let me doubt myself—not even for a second. I appreciate her belief in me. I only wish I could manufacture that belief on my own and maintain that confidence.

I take a deep breath to regather my thoughts. "Well, if we could afford the around-the-clock care that my dad will need in a couple of years, then I can think about USC. They have one of the most renowned film schools in the country. It's also relatively close to home. But I'd probably need a lot more scholarship money, even if I win in New York. Cost of living and tuition for an out-of-state school is crazy in L.A."

"Okay, let's do it. Let's find some more scholarship money today," Ellie suggests with a tone of exuberance.

I chuckle. I can't help it. She's ready to make my dream come true this very second.

"Why are you laughing? You said you'll need lots of scholarship money, so let's apply for more scholarships. Come on, David. Don't libraries have programs that help with this?"

"Well, we may have to start on that tomorrow. For now, we need to grab dinner and get to our hotel in Amarillo first."

"Where's Amarillo again?" she asks.

"It's a city in Texas."

"Oh, Texas. Wow," Ellie marvels, glancing out her window. "I can't believe we've made it this far already.

I glance over at Ellie. She's getting lost in the barren views outside that would look plain to anyone else. Then it occurs to me. We'll be staying in the same room tonight. Yes, there'll be two beds in the room, but it's hard to not let my imagination run wild.

"So, what are we doing for the celebration tonight?" Ellie asks, breaking me from my reverie.

I glance over to see her eyes glistening and a giddy smile dance across her face.

"What celebration?" I mutter, trying to play dumb.

Ellie's look becomes taunting and playful. "Oy vey, David! Don't make me sing it?"

All I can do is shake my head. "I don't know what you're talking about," I tell her, trying to fight off the full-of-shit grin probably painted on my face. And before I can beg her to not do it, it happens.

"Hayom Yom Huledet! Hayom Yom Huledet! Hayom Yom Huledet le David!"

I feel the flush of heat in my face. Hearing Ellie sing Happy Birthday in Hebrew in the tiny confines of my car is something to experience. I can't decide if I'm more embarrassed or taken aback by the beauty in her voice. I never knew she could sing. When she gets to the end of the song, I don't want it to end. The happiness radiating from her means everything.

"Oh, you are so cute when you're embarrassed. Your dimples are so big and adorable I just want to…" Ellie hesitates.

Then I look at her. "What? You want to what?"

Ellie just shakes her head with an ear-to-ear grin. But this smile has something playful and different to it. It makes me wonder what she was just reading about.

"But really, David. We have to do something for your birthday. You only turn eighteen once."

I imagine most eighteen-year-olds are excited for their birthday. But not me. My birthday always reminds me of what happened to my mom. She died so close to my birthday I can't help it. And some years it hurts just as bad on my birthday than it does on the actual anniversary date.

I take a deep breath so my mind can wade its way through these dark thoughts. Then I glance over at Ellie, still patiently awaiting my response. Her smile is still so enchanting. Everything about that face speaks of hope and belief in me. It makes me want to reciprocate the sentiment and make her world as bright as it can be.

"Okay, let's do something fun tonight. How about you come up with the idea when we get there and surprise me? What do you say?"

"Sounds lovely," Ellies says, reaching over to me. This time she puts both hands over mine to squeeze tighter. Then she traces her fingers along my wrist to lightly caress my skin. It's more than just a show of affection. It's feeding my soul with feelings so perfect, so hopeful, and *so Ellie*.

Chapter Eight

David

When we get to the hotel in Amarillo, Ellie spends a few extra minutes chatting with the guy at the front desk. She decides on a restaurant and then a trip to a place called Cadillac Ranch. She won't tell me what Cadillac Ranch is. She only keeps telling me that it's going to light up my day.

After a hot shower, I get ready in the bathroom. I spend a little extra time brushing my teeth and styling my hair. Then I put on an extra layer of deodorant to make sure I'm extra clean and tidy for tonight. I'm nervous, but I feel like I shouldn't be. It's not like this is a date...or is it?

When I'm all done, I take a long look into the mirror. Then I quietly chuckle to myself. It feels like there are two different people or some type of impostor syndrome going on. The one on the inside feels unsure about a lot of things—whether it be my future, this trip, or what awaits at my ceremony in New York. While the person in the mirror actually looks nice and well put together—dare I say confident, too.

Confidence has been an up and down journey for me. When my mom died, it took so long for my dad and my sister to grieve. It's not that I've ever been an extrovert, but I became even more introverted. If not for Ellie and my love of writing, I don't know how I would have ever coped with the pain of losing a parent.

Ellie's waiting by the bathroom door when I come out.

"Excuse me," I say, walking around her in the tight confines of our room.

"David, I'm going to look a little different when I come out of the bathroom. Can you do me a favor?"

"Sure."

"I don't want you to say anything or make a big deal out of it. I still don't even know if I feel comfortable, but I'm going to wear something that's…*different*. Do you understand?"

I nod my head, unsure on how I should respond. The door starts to close behind her until I speak. "Wait, Ellie. Um, I don't know how to say this. But I don't care what you wear if that's what you mean by looking different. That part doesn't matter. It's never mattered to me. I just want you to feel comfortable in your own skin. That's all."

Ellie hesitates by the doorway. I don't know if I've said the wrong thing or the right thing, but at least I spoke the truth.

"Thanks, David. I'll be out in a few minutes. By the way, you look really nice." Ellie flashes a bright smile as she closes the door.

Thirty minutes pass by and I'm still waiting. I wish I could have said more to her—like how beautiful she looks even when she wears her typical Orthodox attire. How the little things she does that have nothing to do with physical attributes take my breath away. The way she says my name—*Daveed!* Or the way her smile pierces into me—like an injection of the purest happiness.

Then, I hear the door slowly squeak open. My eyes look up from my laptop and everything in my world stops. I don't recognize this gorgeous woman. But it's the same Ellie, just more of *her*. It's the her that she's been conditioned to hide for so long, until now.

My heart rate continues to spike. I feel my throat lock up, fighting back the hundreds of compliments I want to pay her so badly. My eyes try their best to divert from her, but I can't help it. Even my mouth is salivating.

Holy fuck!

I notice her smile come to life a little when she steps in front of the full-length mirror. She still looks a little unsure. It's hard to imagine how weird it must feel to wear different clothes.

She admires her pink and white floral sun dress. It's paired with a cream-colored fedora hat. I saw her eyeing the outfit in Albuquerque, but I didn't know she bought it.

The dress is still modest. The sleeves go down to the midpoint between her elbow and shoulder. The tiered skirt goes a couple inches below her knees, showing off her legs. And the top of the dress has a boat neckline design that subtly shows some of her collarbone and accentuates her bustiness.

She finally rotates around to look at me. I quickly take my eyes back to my laptop, pretending to work on my screenplay. But all I'm doing is fighting the hard-on below my computer.

My mind is busy replaying everything I've now seen for the first time. The little bit of makeup on her face. Her wig styled into wavy curls. And her curves, especially her hips and ass, have me fantasizing about how they'd feel in my bare hands.

I want to look up at her and tell her with sincerity that she is the most stunning woman I've ever laid eyes on. And that even if she was wearing her typical clothes, I'd still feel the exact same way. Then I'd beg her to let my hands explore every part of her body with the tenderness she deserves. But I also need to understand how new this is to her. She's never shown these parts of her to anyone—until me.

I'm the first!

Maybe that's what makes it more special. It's an honor she's bestowing on me. Which makes me wonder, is she doing this as a birthday gift, or is this more for her? Is it her way of breaking free to find the person she wants to be? I can only hope it's more of the latter.

"Are you ready?" she asks in a delicate tone.

I clear my throat. "Um, yeah. Let's get going..." I hesitate for a moment. I just can't do it. It's too hard. "But, Ellie. Wait, please. You said I can't say anything about your new look. I can't *say,* anything. Right?"

"Um, well—"

"Stop," I interrupt with my hand in the air. I quickly pull a blank sheet of paper from my bag. Then I walk over to the tiny desk in our room.

"I just need a few minutes."

I feel Ellie's confused stare over my shoulder. But I'm on a mission. A mission to do something—to do what she rightfully deserves.

When I'm done writing my note, I fold it up, put it in a purple envelope, and hand it over to her.

"This is for you. You said I can't say anything. But you never said I couldn't write anything. And this..." I pause to gesture my hand towards her, looking her up and down. "This has me at a loss. I've never seen these parts of you. And I'm honored, Ellie. I'm honored and speechless. You look...well, it's all in the note. I hope you read it...when the time is right."

Ellie takes the note. She places her hand over her chest, staring in disbelief at the note in her hand. Then her eyes slowly tilt up to mine, emitting a tenderness I feel heavy in my chest. I'm suddenly fantasizing over things that once felt impossible. Because all I want in this moment is to lean down and taste those lusciously plump lips. I want to hold her hourglass hips in my hands. I want her body pressed tightly into mine—making the mere thought of ever letting go feel impossible.

"Thank you," she whispers, looking lost for words. "I want to read it, but maybe I'll wait a bit—for the right time."

"Of course. Let's go," I say, extending my hand to her.

Dinner in Amarillo is another brand-new cultural experience for Ellie. She's been people watching all night long, noticing everything that's new and different. The people here dress in Western wear. The guys wear tight jeans and cowboy hats. The girls wear boots. Some even wear Daisy Duke shorts. But everyone is so cordial, from the strangers we meet while waiting for our table to the waitstaff showing us the meaning behind Southern hospitality.

It still feels surreal to be sharing this adventure with her. But the predominant feeling is that I'm the luckiest man on earth. I get to stare into this new set of blue eyes—still as beautiful as before but alive with wonderment. A girl with a new smile on her face that's been stuck on her all night. She's just loving life, loving my company, and living in *this* moment.

Our conversations are all over the place, like usual. But we're also a bit silly with our humor. At one point I make her laugh so hard she chokes on her water. She almost does the same to me when she tries to convince me that I'd look cute in tight jeans and a cowboy hat.

"I don't know, Ellie. I just wouldn't be comfortable. The pants are so tight. Things have a tendency to stick."

Her mouth opens as her eyes squint. "But…oh, o-kay." Her befuddled look slowly transforms into a curious looking smile. "Does that happen often with boys?"

"I don't know. We don't really talk about our balls being strangled by our jeans."

We share a laugh. Then I watch closely as those plump, pink lips, take a long, tantalizing suck from her straw. It has all the blood in my body rushing to one spot. Then, Ellie leans forward, tilting her head the slightest bit.

"Are you really going to read the book that I'm reading right now?"

"Of course. I'm a man of my word. Am I a little nervous? Yes. I've never read a raunchy romance novel."

"Raunchy?"

"Yeah. I mean, it's probably cheesy and overly graphic with the sex parts?"

Ellie quietly chuckles as I notice her cheeks start to pinken. "Um, yeah. But technically they haven't had sex yet. Just other things have happened."

Other things?

Ellie clears her throat. "Speaking of which, can I ask you something? It has to do with things I've read in the book."

"Sure."

"Well, in the book the main characters haven't touched each other yet. But they've…" Ellie pauses, looking a little out of breath. Then she leans in closer, lowering her voice to a whisper. "Well, they're touching themselves…*a lot*."

It's suddenly hard to breathe, but in a good way. I'm still waiting for her to ask a question. But is there even a question coming?

"Okay." I clear my throat, trying to slow my breathing. "Is there something you want me to explain?"

"I'm just curious," she whispers, leaning in a bit closer. "Do you, um, do those kind of things…to yourself?"

My whole body heats up. But for some reason, I'm not the least bit embarrassed by the question. It's the complete opposite. All I feel is completely, and utterly, *aroused!*

"I do it all the time. It's normal for guys. It's also perfectly normal for girls." I pause for a moment to catch my breath. Then a question pops into my head. It's a question I could never imagine asking her—not in a million years. But my opening is here. "Do you ever touch yourself? Maybe…like the way the girl does in your book?"

"Yes," she answers without any hesitation. "But we're not allowed to. I can't help it though. Some nights I lie in bed thinking about things. And it feels right when my mind goes there. And the next thing I know, it's happening. But it also feels wrong when I'm done. I don't know. It's hard to explain."

Her candor has me taken aback. Seeing her question something that is so natural, so normal, hurts me in a way I could have never expected. After all, I know how important it is for Ellie to comply to the Torah. I get it. She's been conditioned to believe something since birth. It's all she knows. And now I get the sense that she feels a bit shameful. But it's not fair. She's an adult. Her desire for touch and need for sexual gratification should never make her feel like less of a person.

"I'm sorry you feel that way, Ellie. But I think it's great that you're listening to your needs. I mean, we all have hormones. It's nothing to be embarrassed by."

"Can I ask you one more thing?"

"Of course. You can ask me anything you want," I say, trying to make her feel encouraged.

"Well, when you, um…do that to yourself. What do you think about?"

"Would you like any boxes or refills?" the server asks, appearing out of nowhere.

Fucking cockblocker!

"No thanks. Just a check when you have time. But no rush."

"Where's your bathroom?" Ellie asks, looking out of breath.

The server explains as Ellie stands up to head to the restroom. As she walks away, she glances over her shoulder, flashing an intoxicating smile while she moves a lock of hair behind her ear.

Being with Ellie only ever felt like a childhood fantasy. But tonight, I know our fantasies are a shared place we visit often in the nighttime. And tonight, I can't help but feel like anything is possible.

Chapter Nine

David

When we pull up to Cadillac Ranch, I become even more confused. The sign says we're here. However, all I see is a pitch-dark field of dirt.

Ellie had us pick up painting supplies on our way here. She wouldn't tell me why, only giving me a sly chuckle any time I'd try prying for a clue.

"Are you sure this is the right place?" I ask as we both get out of the car.

Ellie cranes her head in every direction, searching for something. "I think so."

We start walking as she keeps looking around. I quietly chuckle under my breath because this place feels more like a scene out of a horror movie with the big cornfield behind us. The one where a person gets coerced into going out into the middle of nowhere before they're gruesome death.

We're the only ones out here. All we can hear is the crunching dirt beneath our feet and the faint noise of the highway a few hundred yards away. It's oddly calming to be out in a place so far away from home, yet next to Ellie I feel more at home than I could ever dream.

"Oh my god! I see it! I see it!" Ellie shouts, pointing at more dark nothingness. "Come on! Follow me!"

Ellie grabs my hand, towing me into the dark. Then I finally see it. It's a silhouette of something. It looks more like large hunks of metal impaled into the dirt. Some look as tall as fifteen feet in the air. But there's more than just one. There's a long line of them, one after the other.

"Wait! What is this?" I ask, stopping in front of the first one.

It looks like half of a car planted vertically with the front half buried in the dirt. But it's not any ordinary car, it's my dream car—well, kind of. It's half of a 1960's Cadillac.

"Wait right here. I have a surprise for you," Ellie says, walking down the line of half-eaten cars. She's counting out loud until she gets to the seventh car.

"Stay where you are!" she shouts, scampering around the Cadillac.

Then I hear a grumbling noise. It sounds like a generator. It's followed by a loud click. Darkness suddenly gives way to blinding lights. The Cadillacs light up like Christmas Trees, one by one down the line like a domino effect. There must be hundreds of light strands, each multicolored and bright, lighting up the night sky.

Ellie backs her way up to me, staring in awe. She hooks her arm around my waist, leaning into my side. Then she rests her head on top of my shoulder.

"Wow," I marvel. "How did you—"

"Gary helped me," she chimes in. "He works at the front desk of our hotel. He just graduated high school. His senior project was doing an act of community service, so he decorated this place with all the lights. People used to only come here during the day. Now, they can experience it at night. He said it's so new that most people don't know about it yet. Pretty crazy, right?"

"This is my dream car, Ellie. What are the chances the one place we go to has my dream car? I can't believe this."

We walk up and down the row of Cadillacs. Each one is not only lit up, but painted with splashes of every color imaginable. It creates a thick resin over the frame of the car because these Cadillacs have been painted over thousands of times. There's also notes written on almost every square inch of each car. There are messages of love, remembrance, and so many messages of hope. It's clear now why we have a bag full of painting supplies.

"Are you ready?" Ellie asks, digging right into the bag.

"I don't know what to write…or paint. What're you going to do?"

"I don't know." Ellie takes her hand to her chin, drifting into deep thought. Then her smile stretches wide as her eyes look up to the stars. "Ah! That's it!"

Ellie gets right to work. My moment of inspiration takes a little longer. We pick spots on opposite sides armed with our paint supplies. I'm not much of an artist like Ellie is. My artistic skills are in my writing and ability to be creative in my stories.

Ellie, on the other hand, is an artist. She can sculpt, paint, and do pretty much anything no matter the medium she uses. One year she even made me a small sculpture of the statue of David. I never asked why she chose to emulate that statue, but I loved it.

Once I'm done, I lay down on a blanket close to Ellie. She's still diligently working away with her brush and intense focus. It's cute to see her working so hard when it's something that could easily get painted over tomorrow.

I'm eager to see what she's painting, but she wants to keep it a surprise. So, I take my gaze into the night sky. The stars are so bright and visible. The beauty of everything tonight puts me in a relaxed, meditative state of mind.

It has me reflecting on so many things with Ellie. For one, we never finished our conversation at the restaurant. Ellie got back from the bathroom and was eager to get going. I thought about continuing the conversation on the ride to Cadillac Ranch, but I figured there was plenty of time to wait until the moment is right.

The conversations we've shared today are only the tip of the iceberg. The bigger miracle is that we're here together on this adventure. And it's going better than I could have ever imagined. Especially when you consider what's happened in the last few days.

But I shouldn't be surprised. Ever since I saw her on that stormy night six years ago, things have changed for me. I feel a connection with Ellie that's bigger than just friendship. I want to tell her that, but I don't know how to. It's why I chose to do what I did on my side of the Cadillac.

"All done!" Ellie shouts. "What do you think?"

I get up, seeing Ellie's teeth already chattering for my approval. Then I stand front and center to what she's done—instantly blown away. It's a masterpiece.

It takes a second to realize the symbolism behind what she did. "Oh! Is this from Genesis? Noah's Ark?" I ask.

Her eyes light up with impressive shock. "Wow, David! You got that fast. It looks like someone paid attention in Hebrew school," she playfully taunts.

Ellie's drawn an immaculate looking bird. It's a white dove with an olive branch coming out of its beak. The olive branch leads up to a brightly colored sun. Inside the sun is a message in Hebrew.

Seeing what she's done brings me back to Hebrew school when I was younger. Most days were utter agony because Angela and I dreaded hours of more school after getting out of public school. Nevertheless, it's hard to forget the story of Noah's Ark and the significance of that dove.

The dove is Ellie. It's symbolic of a girl on a journey. In the Torah, the dove sought vegetation and habitable land after the great flood. I may still be learning about Ellie's purpose, but for now it's more about experiencing the journey and moments like these.

"Ellie, it's just incredible. I don't know what else I can say. I love it. What does it say inside the sun?" I ask, taking a step closer. "Oh! You wrote my name in Hebrew."

"Well, a little more than just your name. It says David's hope."

I glance over my shoulder, seeing her face illuminate. The reflection of multi-colored lights amplifies her bright smile. Everything about this effortlessly gorgeous face means the world to me. It's unreal how her beauty can do what it does. It extracts all the darkness from me, replacing it with happiness—*her happiness!*

Ellie grabs my hand. "Can I see mine?" she begs, bobbing up and down.

Before I can respond, she's dragging me by my hand around the Cadillac.

"It's right here," I say, pointing to my poem.

She starts reading it aloud. **"Meeting as beauty flashed through darkness. Like lightning's brief glimmer of light. But only one brings a lightness to my dark, and it's a shimmering palette of red. That's my ray of hope, always red, always bright, even in my darkest of days and nights. She sees the me I aspire to be. Her beauty, her courage, her blue eyes, suddenly so free. So, experience the awakening. Experience first touch, to feel her skin, like lover's first lust. Like the need to breathe. The need to thirst. The need to feel. All the same, forever Ellie, my life force of hope."**

I turn around, seeing Ellie's hand over her mouth. Her eyes are already glossy with emotion. The silence passing between us feels cathartic.

"So, what do you—"

Ellie's arms quickly lasso around my body, taking my breath away. I feel so many new things all at once. Her breasts pressed tightly into my abdomen. Her red wig in my face. Ellie's mouth breathing heavily and warm over my neck. And her hands rubbing up and down my back, squeezing through my shirt like talons refusing to let go.

It all feels instantly sensual. My hands begin rubbing over her back and then down to her hourglass hips. Then, the first whimper of her voice has me leaning back.

"Are you okay?" I ask, seeing her eyes well over with tears. Her lips quiver as she tries to speak, but she suddenly can't.

"Ellie? Ellie? What's wrong? Was it something I wrote?"

Ellie shakes her head vigorously. Then her hand goes over my lips. She holds it there, taking me over with her saddened, droopy eyes.

"No…it's the most beautifully written thing I've ever read. And I just want to touch more of you—to see what your lips feel like. They look so smooth, so plush, so warm, but…"

Ellie reluctantly pulls her hand off my mouth. Her head falls onto my chest. She's fighting against her own desires. I wish I could just pull her lips into mine and not worry about the consequences. But her crying heaves make my heart feel dejected.

I wonder how a moment of touch can feel so good and so sad all at the same time. But all I can do, all I can control, is holding her tightly in my arms.

For the next five minutes Ellie's tears soak my collar. I shush and whisper words of encouragement. And I keep telling her the only thing I feel when I hold her in my arms.

"It's okay to feel this way."

New lights suddenly begin flashing all around. We release our hug to see a car driving up to us.

"Should we get going?" I ask.

Ellie nods, still sniffling a bit.

Once we have everything, we walk by a couple of people, minding our business.

"Ellie! Ellie!" a man's voice shouts.

Ellie furrows her brow at the man walking up to her like they know each other. The protective side of me pulls Ellie closer to my side.

"Oh, Gary. Gary! Hi!" she shouts, suddenly recognizing the strange man. "Hey, it's so good to see you. This is David. You know, the one I told you about earlier—the birthday boy!" Ellie's proud smile gazes up at me. I pull her tighter into my side, sharing a smile with her.

Gary slaps my shoulder, giving it a quick shake. "Happy birthday, bud. This is my girlfriend Sarah and her cousin Charlie," he says, pointing at the third person walking up from behind them.

They end up talking us into sticking around a little longer. They brought an igloo full of hard seltzers and extra painting supplies. I'm initially apprehensive about staying, but Ellie seems up for it.

Together, we all build a bonfire with the wood they brought. Then Gary's cousin, Charlie, ends up talking Ellie and Sarah into an impromptu painting project.

I sit next to Gary after throwing a couple more logs on the fire. Then I pop open a hard seltzer. I'm not a big drinker, so this'll be my only one since I'm driving. However, I am surprised to see Ellie take the drink when they offer it to her.

Gary and I get to know one another while the other three paint something together. It turns out that Sarah and Charlie are actual artists like Ellie. They won't tell Gary and me what the painting will be. They only advised us to sit to the side so it can be a surprise.

It doesn't take long to get everyone's story on how we all ended up out here tonight. For them, it was just a random idea after plans fell through to come out here and do a bonfire. They're all recent high school graduates like us. They went to a high school just a couple miles down the road.

Ellie tells them about our New York trip and the award I'm up for. We don't share other details about where our road trip is going because I still don't even know. But we tell them about the places we've driven through and how we spent some time in Albuquerque.

"Where are you guys going to college?" Gary asks.

When Ellie doesn't respond, I jump in to tell them my plans. "I'm going to Scottsdale Community College. It's just a little junior college in Phoenix. I'll just be working on prerequisites for the first year while I save up for film school."

"But what if you win your scholarship?" Gary asks.

I feel the need to downplay my chances. "Well, it's pretty slim. There's ten candidates from all over the United States. And even if I win, I'd probably just apply the scholarship money to the following school year. It's a long story, but me and my sister kind of have to look after my dad."

"What about you, Ellie?" Charlie asks, still diligently painting.

"Not sure," Ellie quietly mutters. "I'm trying to get some things straightened out with my life first."

A loud silence settles over our group. We all heard the discomfort and tension in her tone.

"Like a gap year?" Sarah asks, her tone hopeful.

Ellie turns to Sarah with a look of curiosity. "A gap year. What's that?"

"It's what me and Charlie are doing. I'm taking the whole year off for myself. I mean, don't get me wrong, I'll be working. But I just need a break from school. A break from all the useless bullshit. You know…" Sara pauses, putting her brush down to give Ellie her full attention. "I'm really excited for this next year. My parents think it's a mistake to take a whole year off. But I'll be living on my own. I'll travel a bit. I'll be making my own decisions. Eating what I want. Doing what I want. And going wherever…the fuck…I want to go!" she shouts in celebration with her hands in the air.

Everyone starts to laugh and cheer for her, especially Ellie, who's clearly interested in Sarah's story.

After Sarah offers Ellie a second hard seltzer, I debate saying something. But she's clearly enjoying the friends she's made. Ellie also gets along well with Charlie. But I can tell she's intrigued by Charlie more than anything else.

Charlie has a manly-looking face with high cheekbones and a huge Adam's apple. He's also wearing eye liner and a white dress with fishnet stockings.

Gary and I hit it off well, too. He's a big movie buff, and he's intrigued to learn more about my writing. We share about our favorite directors and underrated movies of our generation. His taste and vast knowledge of films of the last thirty-plus years impressed me.

Once we're done talking about movies, he changes the subject when Ellie and Sarah go to look at some of the other paintings. "So, what's the deal with you and Ellie?"

"She's got some family stuff we're trying to figure out. That's why she came with me. To be honest, I don't even know the full story. But I'm going to do whatever I can to help her get it all sorted out."

Gary sighs, taking a long swig of his hard seltzer. "Hhhmm. Sarah's no different. Her parents are super hard on her. They're as southern conservative Baptist as they come— the super evangelical Bible thumper types. And Sarah's not having it anymore. It's hard when you're thrown in the middle of it all and her best friend is trans. I just want to be with that girl for as long as I can," Gary says, taking a long glance at Sarah.

"Boys! Boys! We're all done!" Ellie shouts, her speech slurring the slightest bit.

We walk over to see Charlie and Sarah suddenly laughing hysterically.

"*Hard* seltzer. *Hard*, Ellie! *Hard* means there's alcohol in it," Charlie explains, still laughing it up with Sarah.

I reach over to grab Ellie's drink, but she pulls it away from my grasp. "Uh, uh. uh. This'll be my last one. I only have one sip left anyways."

She quickly takes her last drink, but it looks more like she's chugging the last half. I wonder if that's number two or three. Either way, it's going to make this night a little extra interesting.

Ellie gives me a scandalous looking smile once her hard seltzer is drained. "Don't worry about me. Look what we did," she says, pointing to the mural size cake painted on the car. Above the candlelit cake is a note saying, **"Happy 18th birthday Gary and David."**

I quickly turn to Gary. "It's your birthday, too?"

"Tomorrow it is," he says, trying to downplay it with his tone.

"Uh, uh," Sarah chastises him with her finger wagging. She comes right up to him, planting a long smooch as she wraps her arms around his waist. "It's 12:06, sweetie. Happy birthday," she whispers, her lips inches from his. They share another long kiss as Charlie groans.

I jump a little as two arms wrap around my waist from behind me. Then I look down at the redhead coiling around my body and staring up into me. Ellie is clearly drunk. It's hard to believe she was crying so hard in my arms an hour or two ago.

But there's something about this look. It's smoldering with excitement and possibilities. It's free of insecurities and worry. And her lips! Oh my *fucking god!* They have a glimmering shine with the light reflecting from the bonfire. It makes them look pinker—and somehow, even more plump and juicy.

Ellie's also seen how Sarah aggressively came on to Gary. I know she's thinking about doing the same. It's written all over her smile and those emotive blue eyes.

For now, she's holding back, and so am I. But I still worry about what kind of self-control we'll both have as the evening wears on. And I'm unsure about stealing her first kiss when she's this drunk. If it were to happen, I'd want her to remember every part of it.

"Let's get going," I tell her with a nod towards the car.

Ellie gives me an eager nod.

We all exchange contact information before saying goodbye. I doubt we'll ever see these three again. But it was still fun making friends. Moreso, it was fun just giving Ellie another experience she may never have again.

Once we head back to the hotel, I feel my body shivering on the inside with excitement. However, Ellie's been extra quiet for the last few minutes. I keep giving her side glances to see if she's okay. She's either super buzzed or lost in her own thoughts like I am.

I put the car in park. Then I take a deep swallow before I speak.

"Are you doing okay?"

"When I close my eyes, it feels like I'm floating. Is that normal?"

"How many did you have?"

"Three…I think…is that a lot?"

"Yeah. If you've never drank alcohol that can be a lot. Plus, you drank them over an hour and a half. That's pretty fast…for your first time."

"How did you know it was my first time?" she delicately asks, giving me an unsure look.

I crack a smile. Then a soft chuckle slips out under my breath.

"Right," Ellie mumbles. "Hard seltzer. I just thought I'd be able to taste it. I mean, I've had red wine before and Manishevitz on the High Holidays. But that was good. If I ever do it again, I'll drink it slower. But I don't know what got into me. Was I touching you too much? I was, wasn't I? It just felt good to be free on the inside and not always worrying about what I can and can't do. And why do I keep talking so much. Oh…" Ellie pauses, giving me a curious smile while she rubs her temples. "Why are you smirking at me like that?"

I don't want her to be embarrassed, but this situation is a little funny. She's definitely drunk, but at least I know I can help her.

"Nothing's funny. Here, let me take care of you tonight so you're not hungover tomorrow with a killer headache. Scotty has taught me a few tricks over the years. I can almost guarantee that one of my activated charcoal tablets and some headache medicine will have you feeling a lot better in the morning."

"Okay, David. Thanks. But I must warn you, it feels like things are starting to spin everywhere—even when my eyes are open."

I grab Ellie's hand, sensing her concern. "You'll be okay. That's normal. Look, we got this. I'll help you out of the car. Then I'll get you tucked into bed. And if you feel like you need to throw up, I'll help you to the bathroom. I'll even hold your hair back if you need me too."

I watch as her whole face suddenly wilts into a pale white. *Hair.* It should've been obvious why. She doesn't have real hair—only her red wig. It's in this moment, more so than in my shed, I realize her alopecia is something bigger. I want to tell her again how I don't care that she has no hair. To me it's not even a problem. Hell, I'd shave my own head if it helped her come to grips with the disease. But now may not be the time, nor the place.

I walk her into the hotel with my arm tightly wrapped around her. She clings onto my hip the whole way to the bed. Once she lies down, I help in removing her shoes. Then I pull the blanket snugly up to her neck.

"How's that?" I whisper.

Ellie takes a deep breath. On the release of air, she flashes me a heartwarming smile. But her smile quickly fades away.

"Is everything okay?" I ask.

Her extended silence tells me everything. The room is mostly dark. The only light is from the reading lamp on the opposite wall. But that light provides enough of this face for me to know that something is still very wrong.

"What is it? Please tell me," I plead.

"I can't sleep just yet," she whispers.

"Why?"

"I...I uh..." Ellie looks away, already sniffling. Then her eyes come back to mine, welling up like a dam ready to burst. "David, I just need you to not see something. It's something I have to do. I do it most nights before bed. Otherwise, it's hard to sleep because I'm so itchy and hot. Can you just shut off all the lights?"

The tears start to trickle down the sides of her face. I begin chewing over her choice of words, said so carefully and yet, unsure.

Itchy and hot! Oh my god—of course!

"Oh, okay," I mutter, feeling embarrassed.

I get up from the bed to go shut off the lamp light.

"There's a full moon out there. Can you shut the curtains, too?" she whispers loudly.

I shut the curtains for her. It ends up making the room even darker. But it's what she wants—to hide her true self in the darkness. That's how she's been conditioned to live her life— ignoring desires and needs—hiding her truths. And despite the alcohol and our touching tonight, she still wants to hide certain parts of herself—her *true* self.

I climb into the other bed, realizing this is not the way this day should end. It makes it hard to believe that moments ago I was fantasizing about all the things we could experience tonight. But not now.

After only a minute, the frustration becomes too much. I sit up in bed, scooting to the edge to face her. It's so dark in our room I can barely see my hand in front of my face. But it doesn't have to be like this.

"What is it, David?"

"I don't want our night to end like this," I say, raising my voice with confidence.

"What do you mean?"

"I mean, I don't want it to end…period. This time with you is like a dream come true. I know that sounds corny, but it's the truth. The way you looked at me tonight. The way we hugged, the way we held each other, it's so…"

I pause to catch my breath. My mind races to every perfect thought and memory playing on repeat.

"I just really like you…as more than just a friend…a lot more…and I have to do something. It's something you may not like. But Ellie, I have to do it."

Ellie says nothing. I get up and walk to the lamp by her bed.

"No, David! Please don't!"

I flip on the light and sit down next to her. She's already pulled the covers over her head.

"I've seen it before, Ellie. I don't care. And you don't need to hide who you are. Not with me. Not tonight. Not ever." I pause for a moment as the pressure builds behind my eyes. Then I take a deep breath. *"I want you…the way you are."*

The emotion in my words hangs in the air, sucking away any sound left in our worlds. Then her blanket slowly inches down. The pale roundness of her head gives way to enchanting blue eyes—so unsure, yet exquisitely beautiful. Then comes the rest of her face. Her expression is so unsure. It's like she's waiting for a reaction. But all I can do is smile.

I slowly caress her cheeks. Her tears quickly spill over as my fingertips glide deftly along her smooth skin. I touch every part of her face, wiping away her tears. Then I let my hand lightly caress the top of her head, touching what's never been touched by another person.

I don't know how long the touching carries on. All I know is I'm lost in her beauty. It's a place I feel eternally grateful to get lost in. Her insecurities and imperfections become mine to eradicate—and mine to cherish. The moment is transcendent. But there's still something missing.

I slowly lean my face down to her. Her eyes widen. But I don't go down to her lips. Not yet. That moment can wait. Instead, I go to the place where she needs me the most. A spot where I want her to feel the deepest parts of my connection.

Then it happens. My lips delicately press into the very top of her forehead. I feel her body tense at first, then relax. The intimacy of the moment becomes ours to bask in, and ours to never forget. It's unlike any kiss I've ever given—or will ever give. And more than anything, it's addicting. So, I let my lips explore every part of her bald head—planting kiss after kiss—each one with deeper meaning than the last.

When I'm done, I slowly lay back on her bed, pulling her into my arms. Her head rests over my heart as her arms wrap tight around my torso. I feel so much gratitude because she's mine to hold all night long. But with gratitude comes sadness.

I won't be kissing Ellie's lips tonight. My first real kiss with her will have to wait another day. For now, Ellie is mine to hold. She's mine to kiss an endless number of times on the bareness of her head. But more than anything, she's finding her truest self and, most importantly, letting me in.

Chapter Ten

Ellie

I can feel it taking over my insides. It's like my whole body is alive with a thousand beating hearts—each beat progressively faster, awaiting his touch. I'm out of breath. I'm confused by so many things. But I don't care anymore. All I know is the heat in my body is going to one place. And the wetness in this place is overwhelming—like it's dripping out of my insides, craving his taste, his touch, his lust.

What I want most is forbidden and maybe wrong. But what if certain transgressions were mine to choose? What if they were mine to own up to, and mine to bask in for my *own* enjoyment?

I feel him under the covers, like a warm wave of euphoria, ready to wash all over my body. His hands grip tightly around my ankles. They slide up slowly past the inner part of my calves to my thighs. Then it happens. I feel his hands glide further and further up the inside of my thighs until he spreads my legs open.

I refuse to open my eyes. I'm still scared. I'm terrified at how good this may feel. And what if these new feelings become my addiction—and his addiction, too.

His lips brush along my inner thighs, sending a new tingle of electricity through my body. My legs spread wider, inviting him in. Each kiss and each taste of his tongue down my thigh is like a new jolt of happiness. Even the roughness of his thick stubble feels overwhelmingly good as it brushes closer to where I need him.

All these new feelings are too much pleasure at once. But I don't care. My invitation is for his mouth to overtake my bundle of nerves. And I can feel him getting closer as his warm breath hovers directly over my spot. He's ready to taste me, but he's waiting. *Why* is he waiting? I *want* this! I *need* this!

"Please! Please do it!" I beg, arching my wetness into his lips.

Then my mind melts away to a new happy place. It's a place I'll never forget as his tongue barely dips into my insides. But he's not just tasting me. He's delicate and intentional in how he does it, sometimes teasing me and sometimes desperate to suction his mouth over my clit.

Then his tongue lightly goes over my clit. He starts at the base of my hood, lightly brushing up against it before suctioning over it. It creates so much pleasure I lose control of my limbs. I suddenly realize how I'm moaning and pulling his face tighter into my vagina.

Eventually, I hear the sound of him tasting me. Then he starts to moan. It's so arousing to hear him satisfy his hunger. It makes me want more of him. But it's like his thoughts can hear my need for more. I feel the girth of his finger slowly slide inside me. It barely goes an inch inside as his tongue continues its magic over my clit.

The sensation of his finger being inside me takes me to a new forbidden place. It's the one where I'll be forever changed—no longer a naïve young girl, but the slow becoming of a woman. But not just any woman. I'm assured of who I am, giving in to a need that *feels* so natural, so perfect, and so loving.

The pleasure continues to ebb and flow until new feelings blanket over me—building to something new, something better. It's a different kind of warmth. It's like all the pleasure has steamed its way up to a new peak with nowhere left to go.

Then my legs clench over his face, vibrating uncontrollably. My vision goes from darkness to flashes of white light. His mouth and tongue continue to lay perfectly over my swollen clit as I fall into a new reality. It's a place where the pleasure comes out of me in joyous shrieks as my whole-body spasms.

Hanging onto this moment is everything. It's as if I'm another person that's been found within myself, finally finding a way out—like an awakening to a new me—a better me.

A thudding sound grows louder until it's reverberating inside my head. The pleasure still hovers in every part of me, but I feel it slowly melting away to a new place. But this feeling is too good to part from. I'm not ready to leave such a profound level of ecstasy.

My eyes flash open to our hotel room. My face slowly lifts and lowers to the rhythm of his breathing. I delicately lift my head off his chest. Then I take a moment to watch him look so peaceful and content in his slumber.

The events of last night play back in my mind. I take stock in my situation. We're both fully clothed. But one thing feels off—really off! I reach down to my panties, feeling nothing but soaked fabric. Panic begins to take over.

There's no doubt what I've just experienced was only a dream. But why did it feel so real? Did it really happen? Did he taste my insides just like the man did in my book? Did I feel the orgasm that my heroine felt in the book?

Oy vey! Oy vey! Oy vey!

My hand goes over my mouth. The shock of everything hits me all at once. I remember the bonfire at Cadillac Ranch. Then we hung out with Sarah, Charlie, and Gary. Then we got back to the hotel and I wasn't feeling well. But he took care of me and made me feel safe. Now, here I am waking up after snuggling all night long in David's arms. I'm fully clothed, but my panties are absolutely drenched in my own happy juices.

The last thing I remember is falling asleep in his arms, wishing he'd kiss my lips. But he never did. Instead, he did the unthinkable. The impossible. He rained kiss after kiss on the top of my head. But wait…*my head! My wig!*

My whole body convulses into panic. I get out of bed and frantically search the room for my wig. Then I grab it off the bottom of the nightstand and scamper my way into the bathroom. The door lightly slams shut as my back slides down. I let my body fold into the fetal position on the ice-cold tile.

He saw me! He saw me!

David saw the flawed part of me that no man was ever supposed to see. Why would he want to do that? Why would he kiss me there? Why would I let him do it? And why would it feel so right last night, and yet, this morning it feels so wrong?

I grab the nearest towel and bury my face in it. The pain and tears roll out of me in heavy, muffled heaves. I try wading through the emotions of what I'm feeling. But it all feels like an endless maze. Every justification, every thread of logic left in my brain leads me to the same place: *nowhere.*

After a few minutes of letting my emotions go through this muck-filled merry-go-round, I start to slowly calm down. The underlying truth I can't deny is how everything felt right, even in my inebriated state. Everything also felt natural, including my dream. I can keep denying these truths or I can accept them. But one thing sticks out more than anything else: the unforgettable power in his words last night.

"I want you the way you are."

His words were so kind. But it's the way he said it. The way his eyes lit up with emotion as the words left his mouth. Even the tone was so full of conviction and acceptance. It made me feel what I've always dreamt of—him wanting me just as I am.

My hair fell out right after my mom left us. It was at that time my red wig became my mask to make me feel feminine. It was my way of hiding the ugliness I felt on the inside. But even before the wig I've never felt truly pretty, until last night.

The knock on the door startles me. "Ellie! Are you okay in there?"

"I'm fine! Give me a minute!"

I stand up to analyze my reflection in the mirror. My hands slowly rub over the smoothness of my head. Each time I try remembering what it felt like. The roots of hair. The silkiness. The sensation of fingers delicately brushing through threads of endless strands. But it's all a fantasy. That's all it'll ever be.

After putting my wig in place and collecting my breath, I walk out into a cone of awkward silence. He's busy working with his eyes intently focused on his laptop. It's either that or he's pretending to work. I can only glance at him for a brief second. I still feel mortified by everything that happened last night.

He closes his laptop. I turn away from him but feel his eyes lingering in my direction.

"Can we talk about—"

"No, David. Not now," I quickly bark back.

"Um, okay. How about I give you a minute to yourself? We can talk about everything later. I'll just go down to the lobby to work for a bit while you get ready. That is…if that's okay with you?"

I turn to face him. But his worried look overwhelms me. It makes me feel guilty as I pensively nod my head. "That's fine."

My attention goes to my backpack as I mindlessly shuffle through clothes I no longer want to wear. Meanwhile, his presence is still hovering behind me, not ready to leave. It's only a few seconds but it feels like forever until the door finally shuts. However, his absence only makes the pain worse. So, I do what I know best. I drown away in my tears.

The silence in the car has been overwhelming for the past hour. I still don't know what to say to David as my mind begins to stew over memories of my mom. She was never very present for the twelve years she was in my life. I guess being in and out of hospitals for severe depression and at times being on suicide watch didn't help. I don't think I ever understood the full depths of her sadness.

Looking back, I blame most of it on my dad. All he'd ever do is belittle her for always feeling sad.

"Leah, you're pathetic."

"Leah, you're a disgrace of a wife."

"You'll never do anything with your life."

"All you're good at is being sad all the time."

I look back on the verbal abuse wishing I stood up for her more. But when I was younger, I was so frightened of my dad. I still am. All I could do was go hug my mom after my father finished his tirades. I got good at comforting her. My comforting was always followed by her profusely apologizing to me for being a bad mother. And to make her feel better, I'd always forgive her, even if I didn't truly mean it.

My mom didn't work because my dad wouldn't allow her to. All she did was read, sleep, and occasionally take care of me. But usually it was the other way around—me taking care of her. Helping her get out of bed. Making sure she would eat and drink water. And making sure she took her medication for her depression. But I never liked how the medicine would turn her into a zombie. She would be able to function better, but she never seemed like herself.

Life with my mom wasn't always bad. I would occasionally get small glimpses of a naturally beautiful woman. And she was a beauty when she tried to be. I remember her wigs were so elegant. She had so many different variations of red. My favorite was her ombre wigs. They went from black on the top to a wavy merlot that went just past her mid back. I can still picture it in my mind with her bright smile.

My younger years produced the best memories. It sounds odd, but I loved how she took care of me anytime I got hurt as a kid. I loved it so much that sometimes I would fake injuries to get her undivided attention. Her reaction was always so tender, and she'd always say things that I could never forget. She'd look at a scuff on my knee or a cut on my hand and always tell me the same exact thing.

"These wounds heal," she'd calmly say after fixing me up with a Band-Aid. Then she'd place her hand over my heart. "This is the most important part to protect. Always keep loving yourself. Always be brave."

In those moments it sometimes felt like she was talking to herself more than she was talking to me. But her words of encouragement apparently never took hold. I don't know how to love myself. Bravery is a feeling I rarely experience. My own reflection is even hard to see on most days. Perhaps it's all the result of her leaving me high and dry in my most vulnerable years.

I've never felt truly brave until I went on this road trip with David. But here I am, vacillating between the old Ellie and the new. One second, I'm drinking alcohol and socializing with people who aren't Jewish. The next second, I'm learning more about sex and foreplay. Then I'm cuddling with a boy, falling asleep in his arms, and wanting to kiss him for hours on end.

But now it's a new day. I'm living in a new storm of confusion and regret. The past is not a safe place for me to live in. I need to look forward to the opportunities ahead—the good, the bad, and even the scary unknown.

I'm still unclear about my destination and my purpose for going on this trip. But the one thing I don't regret is doing this journey with David. For once, I feel close to answering why

my mom left me. And its answers I know I can no longer
avoid, which is why I must do something drastic.

"Always keep loving yourself. Always be brave."

We pass a sign that tells me a Target is only one mile away.
It gives me a moment of inspiration. I don't want to be the
same subservient, scared Ellie. I want to be bold and
courageous. But it's more than just wanting to do it for myself.
I want to do it for David—to show him I'm courageous. I want
to see that look on his face, the same one where he was
overwhelmed by my beauty after I put on that dress.

"Can we stop off at Target?" I ask, swallowing back the
tension in my throat.

David takes a couple of quick glances, looking unsure.
"Um, of course. Do you need me to pick something up for
you?"

"No. I need to get something for myself. I don't need your
help. Just twenty or so minutes to go in there alone. I need
Sarah's number, too. It doesn't look like it saved in my
phone."

"Um, of course," he says, swiping at his phone and handing
it over.

"I need something else, David."

David veers onto the shoulder, slowing to a quick stop.

"What are you doing?" I ask.

He puts the car in park. Then he shifts his hips to give me
his full attention. Right away I notice the smoldering intensity
in his green eyes. The sun is hitting them in just the right way
to give them a tinge of hazel and shine. It takes his beauty to a
profound new level.

"Ellie…anything you need right now…I'll give it to you. I
mean that. Anything I can do to help you. Just say
it…*Anything!*"

His words flow through me, igniting a brightness to my
dark mood. He means what he's saying. But is there an even
deeper meaning to that one word: *anything!*

I take a deep breath, thinking about the long list of things I want to try and experience for the first time. Some I'm not ready to tell him—at least not yet. But maybe I can start with the easy stuff.

"I need you to teach me how to drive a car. It's not fair that you do all the driving. Plus, I've always wanted to learn. My dad always refused to teach me…or even allow me to drive."

David starts to chuckle. "Really? I mean, yes! Of course! I'll teach you how to drive. What else can I do?"

I feel my cheeks rise up to my eyes. His smile is so infectious. I may not know how he'll react to the other thoughts hovering around in my mind, but I can't worry about that. I need to love myself. I need to be brave.

I want to practice what's about to come out of my mouth. But I don't even know how to verbalize it in my own head. It's too wild. It's illogical. It's not me. It's the new Ellie.

Be brave!

I grab his hands for reassurance. "David, when I come out of this Target, I'd like to try something…like an experiment. I know that sounds weird. I don't even know how to say this, but…" I pause to catch my breath. "When I come out of the store, I'm no longer the old Ellie. I mean, I'm the same person. I'd just like to try not being Orthodox for the next few days. I'm not giving up my faith. I just want to see how it feels…to take a break. I want to experience things with you and not regret it. Do you understand what I'm saying?"

My eyes notice his large Adam's apple go inward. He's trying to look composed, but my request has shocked him to the core.

"Um, are you sure this is what you want? You know, you don't have to do this."

"I know. It's just something I need to do for myself. And I need you to trust me."

"Okay. I trust you. But can you explain what you mean by wanting to experience things with me? I mean…is it what I'm thinking? Because if it is, I don't want to force the issue on anything. I know—"

"Stop! Please, David," I beg. "Just listen to me. Yes, I want to experience things with you. I figured while I'm driving you can catch up with reading. I know it sounds weird, but I'd like to experience some of the things I've been reading…with you. And you're not forcing anything. I promise. This is my choice. I want this. Don't you want this, too?"

David suddenly looks out of breath. His face flushes with a bright pink color. He looks like he's forgotten how to breathe.

I pull my hands out of his to feel the heat radiating from his cheeks. "Are you okay?" I whisper.

He reassures me by nodding his head, but he still looks nervous and lost for words. But maybe he's just overwhelmed with excitement. I just wish he'd tell me what's going on in his head.

Does he not want me like that?

"Talk to me? Please, David." I feel my own voice shuddering in panic. "If you don't want me, just say—"

His lips are on mine before I utter another word. The desperate nature of his kiss, *my first kiss*, is surreal. The way he's pulling me into him. The way his tongue slides into my mouth, shocking me at first. But it only gets better as my tongue goes into him, finding the perfect rhythm.

Everything has me entranced. The sound of our mouths, moving in perfect harmony. His scent. His lips. His tongue. But more than anything, it's his passion.

We kiss each other in ways I could have only ever imagined. But this is better, far better than any book or fantasy could ever be. Until better redefines itself. Our rhythm slows, becoming even more sensual. The arousal courses through every part of me.

I can't believe this is happening. I'm making out with a boy in the middle of nowhere, on the side of the road, somewhere in Texas. And I don't want it to end. I won't let it end. He's all mine.

Finally!

Chapter Eleven

David

I've been sitting in the Target parking lot for over an hour now. It's impossible not to worry. Then my phone finally vibrates.

Taking a little longer than I thought. But Sarah's a lifesaver. I'll be there in five mins. She had to leave to get back home but says hi.

I'm relieved she's okay. I was about to go in and check on her. Besides, it should be illegal to have a twenty-minute make-out session and leave me only to my fantasies and permanent erection for the next hour.

However, I need to put myself in her shoes. She's never purchased regular clothes before. It's probably like learning a new language with sizes, styles, and new types of bras and undergarments.

What's also amazing is Sarah agreed to make a two hour-long round trip to come help Ellie. She hasn't even known her for more than a couple of hours. Perhaps they share a connection as two girls finding their own journey, a journey that would be seen as sacrilege to those in their religious inner circles. But to me, it's two women finding their strength, breaking free of their shackles, and feeding a life force that's starving for life experiences.

The tapping on the window has me suddenly choking a bit on my water. I look like a coughing buffoon to Ellie's eager smile and request to unlock the door. After catching my breath, I jog around the car to get her door. Then my body halts, suddenly frozen to her enamoring presence.

Ellie's a new person—no longer pensive in her body language. She's confident in her jeans and a tight-fitting white tank top. I instantly realize how curvy and voluptuous she truly is. And the clothes do something more than just highlight her body. It does something to her face. She has this glow in her smile that radiates nothing but newfound happiness.

The old me would've done a subtle compliment to the old Ellie. But as Ellie shows the courage to evolve, so will I. After taking a moment to catch my breath and not drool, I choose not to say anything. Instead, I confidently march up to her, taking hold of those hourglass hips to make her lips a part of mine.

We share slow kisses. It's the way she likes it. Occasionally, I'll taste the tip of her tongue. But I restrain myself a bit since we're out in public. The only thing I can't restrain is my erection that's poking her as I pull her in closer.

I lean back to catch my breath. "Wow. You look just…wow." All I can do is smile. Words don't exist for this level of beauty.

"I could never get tired of the look on your face right now," she marvels. Then she swoops in for another urgent taste of my lips.

Ellie took well to my hour-long driving course in the mall parking lot. She's now well past the border of Oklahoma on Interstate 40. She drove the first two-hour leg. Then we stopped off at a library where she helped me research more scholarship opportunities. After that we got a quick bite to eat before getting back on the road. She refused to let me take over the next driving shift because she wanted me to catch up with reading her book.

"What page are you on?"

I start laughing again. It's the tenth time she's asked me that question in the last five minutes. I'm a quick reader, but she's dying for me to get to page 150.

"Oy vey, David! The page number! Please!" she playfully shouts with a hint of annoyance in her tone.

"Page 128," I say, rubbing her shoulder. "Don't worry. I'll get there."

My fingers brush along the edge of her bare collarbone. Her tank top doesn't have a steep v-cut to show off her cleavage, but it's tight. And holy fuck, does it look good to see how large and perky her breasts are.

What's even better is seeing her let go and melt on the inside anytime our skin touches. I've yet to make any dramatic under-the-clothes type of moves. But we both know it's probably coming soon. I just want her to be fully comfortable if things go a step further.

My phone vibrates again. I recently texted Scotty and Angela the Cliff's Notes version of what's gone down with me and Ellie in the last twenty-four hours. Their responses are so different. Scotty is blowing me up for more details. Angela's response was three simple words: **CALL ME TONIGHT!**

My phone vibrates again.

Do you know where you're taking her yet?

I ponder how to respond to Scotty's text. All I can do is be honest.

Not sure yet. But somewhere in Pittsburgh. She's still figuring things out. It's a sensitive subject. I have to tread lightly...for now.

Scotty's question has me thinking. Should I have asked for more details by now? I've been treading lightly this whole trip.

I get there's things she may not know yet. But I feel like there are also things she's holding back from telling me. For now, I'm going to continue to trust her intentions and be as patient as possible.

I get back to reading. The plot is decent so far. It's a forbidden lover's story. It's about two people falling in love at sixteen until the heroine moves a thousand miles away. Then they happen to both meet again twenty years later on a business trip after not speaking for two decades. They're both happily married with children and seem like good people. But I know the types of books my sister reads. She sometimes calls it smut. I'm not sure I know exactly what that means. All I know is that the angsty tension is building towards the main characters getting freaky here in the next fifteen pages.

The story has me briefly thinking of the one time I had sex in my life. Her name was Grace. It happened at a summer camp when I was sixteen. I didn't last long, and it was a very spur-of-the-moment thing I did with a fellow camp counselor who was my age. It's something I didn't regret doing, but afterwards I felt weird about it because all I could think about was Ellie.

Reading this book with Ellie really has my mind racing. After all, she couldn't expect me to emulate some fantasy in a book as our first time together. It's not that I wouldn't want to do it with her. But I value her virginity and how important that is to her.

Nevertheless, I power through with the book. I keep reading…and reading…and reading…and *holy mother of fuck!*

After flipping to page 151, I stop to catch my breath, already feeling flush and pink on the outside. It suddenly makes sense, but it should've been obvious based on our conversation at dinner. I realize that it's not about taking her virginity—at least not yet.

"What page are you on now?" she asks.

I clear my throat and take my gaze out the window. I'm praying she doesn't somehow see that my face is probably redder than a strawberry.

"Um, I'm on 140," I lie.

"Can I ask you something, David?"

"Sure."

"How come you don't let me read your screenplays or your books?"

"I don't know. Maybe because most of them probably aren't that good."

"I doubt that. Is it because you're scared I won't like them?"

"I don't know…maybe. I just think writing takes time. It's not something you're just good at right away. You have to find your niche and hone your skills until you feel ready to share it with the world."

"How do you know when you're ready?" Ellie asks, rubbing her hand along my forearm.

"I don't know."

"What if you're never fully ready? I mean, you're always going to be your own worst critic. I bet they're wonderful. But no pressure. Just know that when you're ready to share your stories with me, I truly want to read them."

Ellie smiles my way. She's being sweet, like usual. But it doesn't change the discomfort I sometimes feel when discussing my work as a writer. It always leads down the path of people wanting to read my work. But usually that response feels more like an obligation than it does genuine interest. And that *always* makes me uneasy—even though I know that's not the case with Ellie. She genuinely wants to read my stories and be my number-one fan. I'm just worried she won't like it.

"Think of it this way, Ellie. You and me, we're both artists, right? You create with different tools, and I create a story with words on a laptop and my own imagination. Some people will think our art is shit, others will think it's gold. It's just hard to be vulnerable. I'm the kind of person who doesn't do well with compliments or criticism, so I'm screwed either way. But I guess that's just something I'll have to get over. Right?"

"Yeah, but you're doing it right now. You're nominated for this award because you were willing to be vulnerable and share your story. It's exciting. I'm proud of you for putting yourself out there. It's a huge baby step."

"Thanks. But it's only because Angela read it without my knowing. Then she went behind my back and entered me into this contest. Otherwise, I wouldn't be where I am right now. Funny how things work."

"So, this is all because of your sister?"

"Yeah. Angela's pretty amazing.

"What's this story about?" she asks.

"It's a romance that takes place in the south in the 1960s. It's about a forbidden interracial relationship. The story deals a lot with grief. When Angela came to me after reading it, she was in tears. But it was happy tears. I think we see things in this story that we relate to. Maybe that's my niche, writing fiction that crosses over to my own realities and experiences."

"Hmm," Ellie says with a smile. "I'd love to read it one day if you'll let me."

I watch as Ellie's smile slowly grows wider. It's like she's living in a beautiful daydream. The apprehension inside me slowly melts away as I get lost in her beauty.

"Okay, I'll let you read it. I can air-drop it into your phone if you want me to."

"Really!" Ellie shrieks, digging her hands tighter around the steering wheel. "Yes, please send it to me. And what's the book called?"

"*The Tree House*."

Despite my anxious thoughts, I send her the book anyway. Being vulnerable with something I'm passionate about is not easy. If she thinks *The Tree House* is crap, it'll hurt me more than any other opinion. That story is more than my crowning achievement as a writer. It's also a story dedicated to one person and one person only: Ellie.

We make it to Springfield, Missouri a little after 8 p.m. The distance we've covered today means we should be able to easily make it to New York by tomorrow afternoon.

Ellie and I grab dinner. We sit together on the same side of the booth and we can't keep our hands off each other. My new favorite thing is when she runs her hands through my hair and tickles the back of my neck with her fingernails.

"What's your favorite thing about being a twin?" Ellie asks.

"Favorite thing? Hhmm…" I stop to ponder. I don't see Angela in that way. She's just my sister to me. "I don't think there's a favorite thing about having a twin. We're always compared with one another, like there's this internal competition. But it's not like that. I just know her, and she knows me—too well sometimes. But we know how to be real with one another. And we know when to back off and give each other space. I don't know if that's some type of special twin telepathy, but it makes it easy to get along with her. I always know where she stands on things."

"Does she know I'm with you?"

"She does. I haven't had a long conversation with her yet, but she thinks it's very risky that I brought you."

"It is. I mean, she's right," Ellie quickly agrees, looking deterred.

"Please don't worry. She would never say anything."

I watch as Ellie bites down on her bottom lip. Her hands fidget with her napkin. "What else does your sister know about me?"

"Well…pretty much everything. But I can assure you that most of what she knows is the good stuff."

"The good stuff?" Ellie asks, her tone curious.

I feel my smile come to life. "Yes, the good stuff. Angela knows how kind and giving you are. But most importantly, she knows how you believe in me. Listen to me. She knows how supportive you've been through the loss of my mom. And how you've helped me in dealing with my dad's declining health. So yeah, she may not agree with you tagging along on this trip. But I can assure you she thinks the world of you."

Ellie's eyes light up along with her smile. But there's a new ingredient in this once-in-a-lifetime look: flattery. She can't deflect my praise because she knows my words are true to her. The best parts of her. The only parts *I see*.

"You're so good to me, David. Sometimes I feel like anything good I can do or give to the world…is because of you. I don't know why you are so kind to me. But I don't take it for granted. I never will."

The first tear trickles its way down and I'm on her, hugging her with everything I have. Everything I can give. In this moment she doesn't need my lips. She needs the pressure of an inescapable hug. And I need her to feel everything I feel, including the hope beneath my chest that beats because of her.

After dinner, we took a short walk through the downtown area on our way back to our hotel. My stomach is a bundle of nerves the whole way back. Ellie's no doubt feeling the same way. But it's no surprise. It's years of sexual tension.

Once we get to the elevator doors, the sound of her phone scares us. It's the first time I've heard it ring on our trip.

"Hello, who is this? Excuse me." Ellie starts walking away. Her hand is held out, so I stay back.

I take a seat at the nearest bench, seeing Ellie's back to me. She's far enough away that there's no way I can hear her. It's hard to read her body language, but my intuition is making me feel squeamish.

All I can think about is her dad. If he found out that I brought her with me, what would he do?

It's a reality I'm not ready to face head-on. I try washing it away by mindlessly scrolling on my phone. Then Angela calls.

"Hey."

"What the fuck is going on?"

I start laughing. She's cutting right to the chase like usual.

"I'm doing good, Ang. Thanks for asking." I love taunting her when she's impatient and bitchy.

"Seriously, is everything okay?" Her question is followed by an exasperated breath.

"Yeah, we're good—more than good, actually. We made it to Springfield, Missouri a couple hours ago. Her dad thinks she's visiting her half-brother in Brooklyn…" I stop, wondering about everything I have to tell her. "You do know this was her idea to come. And as crazy as it's been so far, I don't regret it—not one bit."

"I know you don't. I just don't trust her dad. That guy always creeped me out. And if he finds out what you guys are up to, it's not like he doesn't know where you live. Who knows what he did to Ellie a couple nights ago. Have you even found out anything about what happened that night?"

Getting knocked unconscious a couple days ago now oddly feels like something that happened a long time ago. Maybe it's all the unexpected that's gone down since that night. Nevertheless, it's an event that can't be swept under the rug.

"I don't know," I admit, swallowing back the acidic taste in my throat. My mind briefly flashes back to that night. "I haven't asked her about that yet."

"Has she at least told you where she needs to go?"

"No, not really. All I know is it's somewhere in Pittsburgh."

Angela groans. "Fuck, David! Just ask her! Give her an ultimatum…or something. You deserve to be let out of the dark. Heck, even if she's unsure about what she's doing, maybe you can help her. But you need to speak up."

"I've tried. It's just…" I stop. My words float into the foggy airspace between us. Saying that I've tried doesn't feel truthful…at all. My attempts at real truth have been me always walking on eggshells, trying to be sensitive to her situation.

But I do deserve to know what's really going on—especially if she might be hiding something from me.

I let out an exasperated, shaky breath. "You're right. I'll try, Ang."

We say our goodbyes after Angela gives me a quick update on how Dad is doing. After hanging up, I reflect on our conversation. I can't shake the uneasy feeling in my gut. Then a horrifying, eerily familiar scream shrieks through the hotel, echoing off the walls. Every single person in the hotel freezes in their tracks. Every hair on my body stands up as I run to her.

"No! No! No! No!" Ellie keeps screaming. She hunches over, gasping for breath in a state of panic.

Her phone falls to the floor as my arms go around her. I try to console her, but nothing gets through. Her eyes are catatonic. Her mind is gone. She's conscious, but in a severe case of shock.

The hotel staff hovers around us, unsure of what to do. After a while, I'm able to slowly guide her up to our room. Once we're on the bed, I continue to hold her in my arms as her breathing slows and becomes less erratic.

"Ellie, Ellie, are you okay? Look at me," I beg.

Then her lips start to quiver, twitching like she's searching for the will to speak—until two dreadful words barely leave her breath.

"She's dead."

Chapter Twelve

Ellie

I only learned about the term spooning a couple of days ago. It sounded heavenly in my book. The way the man enveloped every curve and part of the heroine's body. It feels good now, but it's competing with the pain—*so much pain*!

David is so close to me, so snuggled into my back with his arms draped around me. It's heavenly, but I want more of him. He needs to be a blanket of pressure over my entire body. He needs to extract what I feel and replace it with his goodness—his hope.

I can only imagine his confusion. All David knows is someone is dead. And I can't even tell him who it is. Not yet. It hurts just to think about it, so I try to bury it.

I want to miss her, but it's hard to miss what I never truly had in my life. All I had was my father telling me how worthless she was. How we didn't need her. How it was her choice to leave us. Maybe that's the most bothersome part— never getting the chance to know her side.

David's fingers continue to glide along my skin, sprouting goosebumps everywhere he touches. It makes me want to turn around and bury my lips into his, forgetting about everything. I want him to replace my hurt with the ecstasy of deep intimacy. The kind I could bask in forever.

But I worry about how he feels and what he's thinking. He's always tending to me and my craziness. My lapses from reality, my past full of confusion—it's the definition of who I am. *Always emotional. Always lost.*

My mind continues to hover in the oddest place at the most inopportune time. All I want is to kiss him. I can't speak, but I have the willpower to kiss this beautiful man. Am I losing my mind? I mean, how crazy can a person get before they get locked up in an asylum? How could I want to do something that feels so opposite to the emotions any sane person would feel at a time like this?

"Ellie."

His whisper hits my ear with such delicate understanding. But my throat still feels paralyzed—unable to put thoughts into words.

"You can tell me what happened…when you're ready. For now, I'm just going to hold you, and tell you a story. That is…if that's okay with you?"

I gently nod my head.

"I remember one night in the shed I was telling you how my dad's Parkinson's and Dementia was getting worse. We talked about it for a long time. I told you how my sister was morbidly depressed and in a dark headspace. Angela was so terrified to know that one day she'd have no parents to speak of. Her mind obsessed over this detail. But you looked me dead in the eyes that night, saying something I'll never forget…"

David's pause extends on until I turn around to see his face. But this is not the face of David Cohen. This man is broken on the inside. Tears stream heavily down his face, yet somehow his stare into my soul is full of confidence. He's assured by something in his story, but I don't remember any of this.

"What did I say?" I whisper.

"You said the beauty of twins is how strength comes in twos. You told me to be the crutch my sister needs right now—to do anything for her. And you told me to shower her with mitzvahs and love. So…I did what *you* said. After that conversation I felt like I became a better brother to Angela."

A shiver runs up my spine as his hand glides along my arm. His candor begins to permeate into the depths of me, becoming the crutch I need. It gives me the last bit of strength I need to tell him.

It's time.

"My mom's dead. That was her sister—my aunt—the one that called me. Her name is Sariah. She lives in the northern suburbs of Pittsburgh. She said she has things to give me from my mom. And that I need to go see her…*right away*. There was so much urgency in her voice. I didn't understand why. Then she started telling me how much my mom loved me. How much she missed me. And I lost it. I uh, I don't know. Deep down I always thought I'd one day find her and get answers. But now, I'll probably never know why she left me. Or…" My voice gives out to a desperate whimper. "If she really did love me."

I stop talking, noticing how David's face has absorbed my words. He seems oddly calm. The tears he was shedding a second ago are no longer there. Instead, all I see is this beautiful, empathetic man, intent on listening for more.

"We don't have to go—"

"No! No!" David raises his voice. "We're going. Tomorrow morning. It's decided…we're going to see your aunt."

The sharp tone in his voice catches me off guard. David is always so composed, even soft-spoken. But in the last couple minutes, I've seen many different, new emotions emerging out of him.

"But what about your scholarship ceremony? What if you miss it?"

He's already shaking his head at me. "No. We need to do this. We both know there's a lot going on here. This trip was never about me the second you set foot in my car. And I'm fine with that. I want to do this. I want to help you. Besides, it's a long shot I even win the award."

"Don't say that. Look, I'm not taking your dream away from you. We can compromise. We'll go see my aunt for a couple hours, then we'll be back on the road. We'll just arrive a few hours later than expected."

"Okay, Ellie. But we're not going to rush this. There are answers at your aunt's house. You know it, and I know it, too. There's a lot going on here—so much, in fact, I think there's things you're still not telling me."

I draw a long breath in and out, feeling the accusatory nature in his tone. But he's not wrong. I sit up tall on the bed. Then I grab his hand while taking another deep breath.

"Okay. What do you want to know?" I ask.

"What happened the night the police came to your house?"

"I'll tell you what happened, or at least what my dad told me. But first I need to show you something."

I pull the note out of my backpack and hand it to David. He reads it aloud.

"Dear Leah, I received word you're not safe. I can arrange a way for me to wire you money. You and Ellie need to come be with me. We'll find her together. Please call me. -Sariah

David reads the letter aloud one more time. His whole face furrows into confusion.

"This is a letter to your mom, right?"

"Yes."

"It says we'll find her together. What does that mean?"

"I don't know."

David points to something in the letter. "It's dated back about six years ago."

"I know. My mom left me the day after receiving this letter."

"Have you called the number on here?" David asks, pointing towards the bottom of the letter.

"It's no longer in service. But it's a Pittsburgh area code. It's my aunt's old phone number."

"Why wasn't your mom safe?"

David's question feels rhetorical. But I still don't feel comfortable saying it aloud—even though we both know the answer.

"Your father?" he mutters under his breath.

I nod in agreement, still not wanting to assume what all of this could entail. All I can control is what I know so far.

"Okay, okay, um…" David sighs, running his hands slowly down the sides of his face. Then his eyes glare deep into mine. "Does this letter have anything to do with the night the police came to your house?"

"No. I mean, I don't think so. I never told my dad I found this letter. I just found it a few days ago, did some research at the library until I finally found Sariah's number, and called her a few times. But she didn't call me back until a couple of hours ago in the lobby."

I can see David's mind turning. He's trying to piece together clues. But to me, everything feels like shards of glass, infinite in number and permanently irreparable.

"What happened the night the police came to your house?" he asks again.

The events of that night send a terrifying shiver through my body. It's still hard to understand because it still feels surreal.

"I had a night terror. I woke up from it, and all I remember is how my dad was hysterical—like a completely different person. He kept screaming at me to not say that name. He kept begging me, and begging me, with tears in his eyes. He looked so pitiful and desperate. But I kept telling him I didn't know what I said. But it's like he didn't believe me. He didn't hit me, but he was squeezing my shoulders so tightly I have bruises."

I wipe my eyes, waiting for my breathing to level out. But each breath feels more like a hopeless gasp for air.

"What else?" he asks.

"Let's see…" I pause to try and slow my breathing down. "I woke up from my night terror. Then he hid me in the bathroom and told me to be quiet because he thought someone had broken into our house. He told me to not unlock it until he gets back. Then I heard a loud thud. Maybe it was two thuds. But it didn't sound right. I thought he was hurt so I peeked through the doorway for a split second. It was odd."

"What? What did you see?"

"He came back into his bedroom to grab his wallet. But he saw me peeking through the door. He shouted at me to get back in the bathroom. I knew something was going on. Then the police eventually came, and he did most of the talking. All I know is there was an intruder that got scared and ran off."

"Ellie, there was no intruder. That was me. I was coming to help you. He knocked me out cold. I'm almost sure of it."

David rotates his torso, showing the back of his head to me. His hand moves over his fluffy hair until I see the stitches and a dried-up wound.

"Oh my god!" I realize my hand is muffled over my mouth. "Oh, David. Are you okay?"

"I'm fine. It was just a few stitches. Really, Ellie. I'm okay."

He's trying to reassure me, but I know this had to be traumatic.

"Are you sure it was him?"

"It had to be your dad. I mean, I didn't see him do it. It all happened so fast. I heard you scream from my backyard. Everything else was like a reflex. I jumped the wall and tried to make my way into your house. But your screaming just became more desperate. So, I broke the glass to your back door. Eventually I made my way up your staircase. Then, I don't remember anything else after that, other than being hit in the head from behind. I woke up when the paramedics arrived. But it makes sense now."

"What makes sense?" I ask, noticing the beads of sweat on David's forehead.

"I know why your dad came back for his wallet. He was trying to make it look like he got robbed—at least, that's the story he sold to that dumbass investigator. I think he littered his own wallet a block down the street to make it look like he got robbed. Then he made it seem like I spooked this made-up person who was trying to rob you."

I'm trying to really understand everything he's telling me. But my mind is in shock. The puzzle pieces don't connect.

"But I don't get it, David. If he caught you breaking into our house, then he had you right where he wanted you. He could've gotten you in trouble. He could've pushed you further out of my life. And I know he wanted that. You know it, too. I mean, I've never seen him angrier than he was the night we got caught by my back door."

"I know. It doesn't make sense. But I'm telling you, I remember everything crystal clear from that night. Even the things you were screaming."

"What do you mean?" I ask.

His jawline tightens. His eyes glaze over as his throat goes inward. It's like he's swallowing back the bile of a horrid memory.

"You were screaming for Sasha. I heard it, Ellie. I heard the name, clear as day. I think that's what made your dad lose his shit. Then he probably panicked when I broke in there. Maybe he figured if I'm let off scot-free then he wouldn't have to deal with me fighting whatever story he was going to make up with the cops."

David seems so confident with the dots he's connecting. But my mind is only stuck on one word, one name: *Sasha*.

"Have I ever said that name before in a night terror?"

"No." David takes a long sigh, looking spent and frustrated.

"Have I ever said any names at all?"

David emphatically shakes his head. "No. I'd remember if you did. But maybe this name will make sense to your aunt."

David runs his hands through his honey-brown hair, looking towards the ceiling for an answer. It's a nervous twitch I've seen him do so many times when he's frustrated. Then his eyes peer intently into mine.

"Is your aunt married?" David asks.

"I don't know. My dad always refused to talk about family on my mom's side. I guess we'll find out tomorrow."

"What about the letter sent to your mom? Where did you find it?"

"It was folded in a book that was buried away in my dad's closet."

"Let me read it again?" David asks.

He reads the note aloud to himself in a mumbling tone. He's analyzing it word by word, just like I've already done a hundred times.

"Should I call her back?" I ask.

I feel my insides go numb. My breathing goes shallow as David winces.

"Are you sure? You don't seem up for it."

The pit in my stomach is now piercing with agony. It feels like a tumor of everything bad in my life, growing bigger with each second that passes. And I can't even articulate why I feel this way.

David leans into my side, sensing my despair. Then his arms tightly come around me.

"Hey, hey, it's okay," he softly whispers. "We don't' need to call her tonight. It's been a long day. We'll just go see her tomorrow. I'll be with you every step. For now, if you want, I can just text her for her address and let her know we're stopping by tomorrow. Are you okay if I do that?"

"Yeah, that's fine," I whisper, squeezing a tight hug around his body.

His closeness is my safety net. It's my time to just let go and feel the only thing that rids the numbness, allowing me to feel again—*his touch.*

My hands rub all over his back, feeling muscles everywhere. All I want is to pull back, lean into his lips, and drift into a world of pleasure. But I feel incapable of making that move. I need him to do it and show me how desperate he is for me.

It's the only thing that may quiet my racing mind. But all I keep hearing is my aunt's desperate voice, begging me to come see her. It's like she didn't even know I existed until today.

David pulls back from our hug. His hands go up and down my shoulders and arms. "What can I do for you?"

I'm too afraid to tell him that the only thing I want in this moment is his body and unrelenting affection. But this time I want more than just his lips.

David's phone begins vibrating. He looks at it with a frown. "It's my sister. You mind if I—"

"Yeah, of course. I'm sure you need to hear how your dad's doing."

It's a long five minutes before David steps back into the room. He walks back in and sits next to me on the edge of the bed.

"Is everything okay?" I ask.

He rubs his neck with a slight grimace. "I think so."

"Can I help you?" I ask.

"With what?"

"Your neck. I can massage it if you like?"

"No, I'll be—"

"Stop it, David. Let me take care of you. You do enough for me. Go lay down."

David hesitates at my demand. I worry if I'm being too forward. But he lays on his stomach while I grab the lotion. Then, my nerves come to life. I've never massaged anyone, let alone a cute boy. How does this even work?

"Shirt on or off?" he asks.

His question catches me off guard. What do I say? Of course I want his shirt off. But do I need a reason?

"Um, yeah," I mutter quietly, feeling breathless. "Shirt off sounds good. I mean, so I don't get any lotion on your shirt."

David sits up on his knees. His shirt slowly comes off. It's the most erotic thing I've ever seen. The way his arms extend up and his muscles flex without effort. There are ripples everywhere. Even the way he chucks his shirt off the bed while giving me a crooked smile is too much. I only wish my mind could record this moment with perfect clarity. If I could, I'd relive it a million times over while I touch myself.

His body sprawls over most of the queen-size mattress. He's always seemed like a big man. He's probably a shade over six feet tall. But I'm only a hair over five feet tall, so maybe everyone looks big compared to me.

I'm trying to focus without drooling. But his ass looks so perky, like it's begging to be squeezed. Perhaps I asked him to take off the wrong article of clothing.

"What's so funny?" he asks.

Oh no! Did I just giggle under my breath?

"Nothing. I just…I didn't realize how strong you are," I admit, feeling another flush of heat through my body.

He lets out a tiny chuckle. "Thanks."

I slowly straddle my legs over his lower back. My butt slowly leans down until I'm sitting on the crest of his ass. I'm so unsure about what comes next. But at the same time, I feel ready to let go and be free.

The second I dig my hands into his neck, it feels like I'm massaging concrete.

"Wow! You're so tight. Try and relax for me."

"I'm trying," he yelps.

"Am I squeezing too hard?" I ask, easing up a bit. "Is that better?"

"Aaahhh, right there. That feels so good. Just like that."

His subtle moan of satisfaction is more than just a turn-on. It's also cathartic to know he's letting go of the pain.

My hands, my palms, and my fingers go everywhere. His shoulders, upper back, lower back, even the waistline of his boxers. The restraint it's taking to not slide my fingers under them is unreal. It's as if every fantasy I've ever played out in my mind has succumbed to this moment. Even my heart feels like it's beating through my chest—wanting to just be feral on this hunk of a man.

"Ellie," he whispers.

"Yes."

"Can I…" he pauses to clear his throat. "Can I return the favor?"

Those five words send a rush of euphoria through my body. It makes the moment feel even more significant. This is more than just being in love with a boy. It's trusting him. It's seeing how he truly wants this version of me. The one who is forever bald. The one that's a mess on the inside. And the one that knows so little about so much but is eager to be taught, touched, and loved.

I say nothing back because I'm too awestruck. Instead, I just lay on my stomach, closing my eyes with anticipation.

I feel him rise over me. "Where does it hurt?"

The question catches me off guard. "Nothing hurts. It's just hard to catch my breath," I shyly admit.

"Flip on your back. I can take care of that."

I slowly turn around to his crooked smile. The confidence and sexiness radiating from him is overwhelming.

"Can I touch you here?" he politely asks, putting his hand over his heart.

I nod yes, still searching for my trembling breath. He lays down next to me, propping his head on his hand. The second his hand goes under my tank top, my body shivers as I let out a quiet moan.

"You, okay?"

"Yes. Please keep going," I beg.

His hand brushes over my navel. Then it grazes over the lace of my bra, barely touching my breast before resting over my heart. I want him there, but I also want him to brush over my nipples and feel my plushness with his huge hands. But instead, he just holds his hand there, patiently feeling each erratic heartbeat.

"Thank you for this," he whispers. "Are you sure this is okay?"

My emphatic nod produces another crooked smile. I can feel his eyes trace down my neckline to my breasts. Then, his fingers spread wide over my chest. The electricity ignites my insides as his fingers brush over my rock-hard nipple.

"Can I take your top off?"

I don't answer. Instead, I quickly sit up, submitting my back to him with my arms in the air. His chest leans into my back after he removes my top and bra. His large hands come around to cradle over my breasts. David's lips brush across my neck and up to the base of my ear. Each kiss along my neck and squeeze through my breasts is like a mini orgasm through my body. Even the way he's breathing in my scent is driving me crazy.

Eventually, his teasing kisses along my neck become too much. I swing around to find his lips. His weight takes me over. He falls onto me as my legs spread wide, and our bodies envelop each other.

The pleasure coursing through me is overwhelming. It's almost too perfect. The way our kissing involves more tongue. The way our hands caress every part of our bodies. But none of it compares to the best part—the way the hardness underneath his jeans grinds over my clit.

It redefines every fantasy I've ever had about being intimate with David. Because now he's *all* mine. And I *want* more of him! I *need* more of him! But when I reach down to get my hand under his jeans, his body freezes. He quickly rolls off me.

No! No! No! No!

"Ellie, wait," he says, still gasping for air.

I'm suddenly confused, trying to make sense of the pain and regret he's suddenly wearing all over his face.

"Why not?"

David goes silent, shaking his head and biting his lip as he tries to find his words. "Not yet…I mean, we can do things. But we're not having sex. It's just too fast. And believe me, I know you feel ready. I do, too. I want you so bad it hurts. It hurts in a way that kills me, Ellie."

The pain in his voice causes an ache in my chest. Time may not be on our side. There's no telling how our lives will look when this trip ends. But I don't want his logic and sound judgment. Not now. Not at this moment. It holds no place in my world anymore. All I want is the passion we share for each other. The touch we both *so* desperately need.

So, instead of slowing down, I dive back into those luscious lips while gripping onto his perky ass. We make out deeper than before, exploring new ways to taste each other's mouths. He finds what I like, and his moans tell me what he likes. We grind harder over each other's bodies, losing ourselves in the throes of passion. Eventually, the only barrier of clothing is his boxers and my soaked panties.

Having his skin lathered over mine is bliss. But I'm still desperate for more of him. Stroking the hardened outline of his boxers and grinding over his erection can only satiate me for so long.

He pulls back suddenly from my hungry lips, trying to catch his breath.

"Wow," he whispers.

My eyes trace down his hardened pecs and torso until they've locked onto the bulge beneath his boxers. I let my hand glide up and down over the fabric, feeling his warmth and hardness in my hand. I contemplate sliding my hand underneath to feel his penis until his hand grabs hold of my wrist.

Our eyes lock as he gives me a look where his green eyes are smoldering with curiosity.

"Should we…150?" he whispers.

The book! Oy vey!

I nod yes, feeling shock and excitement coarse through my veins. But at the same time, it truly hits me—what he's really asking for. And while I want to do this, I'm also nervous beyond belief.

David dashes into the bathroom to grab more lotion while I position two pillows side-by-side against the headboard. I lie back and wait for him as my hands tremble and my chest pounds in anticipation.

He walks back with his boxers hanging low to his hip muscles and a tent pitching in my direction. He grabs my hand and lies next to me. Then, he flashes a smile that leaves me breathless. But it's no ordinary smile. It's encouraging. It's patient. It understands that it's okay to be nervous and excited at the same time.

"Are you ready?" he asks.

"Yeah," I pause to swallow deeply and catch my breath. "I'm ready. Just nervous."

My eyes trace their way down his body. David unpeels his boxers to grab hold of his penis while I slide my panties down.

We're both fully exposed as we lay side-by-side with one another. I watch closely as he begins stroking himself. It's slow and methodical. The more he does it, the more the tip of his penis swells up.

Then I feel his eyes on me as I dip my fingers barely inside myself and then around my opening. The wetness at first touch sends a shock of pleasure through every nerve ending. It's so wet I can hear my finger tracing along my most sensitive parts.

I know what feels good. I do it most nights before bed, thinking of David. But being watched by him changes everything. Seeing the arousal on his face, hearing the faint moans we share—it heightens *everything!* And I've never felt my clit swell up more than it is now. It's getting me closer and closer to the finish line. It has me noticing how his balls swell up as his pace quickens.

Reading the scene in this book was such a turn-on. You had two people falling in love who refused to touch one another and commit adultery. But in their drunkenness, they found an insanely wild compromise to masturbate in front of each other. Now, we're doing just as they did in the book. However, in the book, they could only keep their hands off each other for so long. It has me wondering if I'm allowed to truly act out the final part of this scene.

"I'm getting close!" David moans.

"Me too!"

I try catching my breath, but my whole body is simmering, ready to burst at any moment. Then, a shriek explodes out of me. My entire body loses control. I cum so hard I see stars. My whole life force, my spirit, it's all basking in the longest, most intense orgasm I've ever had.

Eventually, I roll onto my side. I'm still shaking uncontrollably as I slowly catch my breath. Then, I see the look on his face.

It has me enamored. His natural beauty. His green eyes begging with want and need. He doesn't need to say another word.

"Can I try it," I beg.

His emphatic nod has my mouth hovering over his swelled-up penis. He keeps stroking as I put my mouth over the head of it. And as I suck over the tip, it only takes a few times until a warm explosion shoots into my mouth. It shocks me at first. The salty taste. The texture. And the way it keeps shooting into my mouth while his body spasms in ecstasy. But I do as my book heroine did. I keep my mouth there, sucking out every drop of his cum, swallowing it as my own.

It takes us a few minutes to catch our breath. My orgasm has taken every last bit of energy I have left. But it's also left me with the deepest feeling of contentment. Then I feel David's naked body spoon into mine. His arms drape around me tightly. The security of having him hold me means everything. And as we fall asleep, he whispers the three most perfect words I've ever heard.

I quickly turn over to see the meaning still resonating in his eyes. Then, I do what feels right and natural. I remove my wig so he can say it again—to the *real me*.

"Say it again," I beg.

His smile grows wider. His hand begins to delicately brush along the smoothness of my head. "I love you…Eliana…Merkowitz. I *always* have. And I *always* will."

Chapter Thirteen

Ellie

The light barely cracks through the shades of our hotel room. Somehow it finds my eyes, that one tiny sliver of sunlight. It's as if God is shining his ray of hope upon me.

I'm still snug in his arms. It's a place I can live in forever. My mind is busy replaying every little thing that happened last night. It still feels like a dream. But I know last night was real. More importantly, it was only the beginning. There's so much more that we'll explore together.

This is day three of our trip. We still have four days left. What happens when we get back home is what scares me the most. I don't want to imagine a David-*less* existence. It's more terrifying than seeing my aunt, and that's also weighing heavy on my mind.

Everything about the last few days has been an ebb and flow of so many emotions. My mom being dead. My aunt begging for me to visit. My father getting on a plane and not telling me where he's going. And then learning about his violent encounter with David. Now, here I am on the outskirts of Missouri with a naked boy slathered over my bare body.

And as wrong as this may be, it's the only thing that makes sense and feels right.

The Torah does not explicitly outlaw premarital sex. It's only the Rabbinic authorities in my temple that promote this teaching. And whether it's a good thing or a bad thing, we never had sex last night.

But I still wonder how? How can we experience something so beautiful, so natural, and so needed, and not want more? I no longer want to suppress my natural hormones and my need for his touch.

After all, David never said he wouldn't have sex with me. He only said to not rush things. And as much as I want him in that way right now, I'm glad we didn't. I still don't know what he likes or how he wants to be touched. And what if he doesn't enjoy it. What if it hurts? What if he's afraid to teach me what he wants? And why am I only obsessing over his needs?

Stop it, Ellie! That's the old you!

My needs and wants are equally important to his. David's made that abundantly clear to me. He wants to please me, and I most certainly want to please him.

After getting dressed and putting my wig on, David wakes up. He stretches his limbs to every corner of the bed, causing the blanket to slide down past his hips. I quickly notice how he's already hard.

"Good morning," I say, sitting at the edge of the bed. I wash my hands over his chest, feeling my insides heat up. "Can I ask you something personal?"

David's smile stretches up a little closer to his green eyes. Then he gives me a gentle nod while yawning. "Sure."

"*That*," I say, pointing to the outline of his fully engorged erection bulging beneath a thin layer of sheets. "Do you always wake up like…*that*?"

David starts laughing. "Yes…*that*…is how I always wake up. Probably how most guys wake up, too."

"How come?"

"I don't know. I can't help it. It's normal for a guy to wake up with morning wood."

"Morning wood?" I ask, giggling under my breath.

"Yeah. That's what we call it. It's not that funny. I mean, don't girls ever wake up feeling kind of…um…you know…moist?"

"Really…moist?" I couldn't hide the disdain in my tone for that word.

"Okay, wet?"

"Hhhmmm. That sounds better," I say, feeling my grin widen as I stare at this beautiful hunk of a man.

David starts laughing. I join him because his belly laugh is so infectious and adorable.

Our conversation feels fun and erotic. I need to keep it going.

"Yes. We can wake up feeling like that down there. Especially if we had good dreams…or a night like last night."

"Hhhmmm. I see." His smile goes crooked as his hand brushes along my inner thigh.

"Should we?" I ask, unable to keep my eyes from salivating over his body.

His eager nod pulls me to his lips. We fall right back into the bliss of last night. Touching, feeling, tasting, and letting go. The hunger we had last night could only satiate us for so long.

"Wait," he whispers when my hand begins stroking under his boxers. "Can I please you first?"

My body shudders at his words—said with such giving sincerity. He wants to put my satisfaction ahead of his own. And I'm more than ready, *I hope*.

I lie on my back. All I have on are my panties, which he slowly slides down my legs. When he chucks them aside, I feel a nervous excitement electrify through my body. It's all because of his eyes. *Oh my! That look!* He's looking up and down my body like he's the luckiest man on Earth.

When my legs spread wider, he trails soft kisses along my inner thighs until the warmth of his mouth hovers over my clit. The second I feel his tongue dip inside me and up to my swollen clit, I almost faint. The pleasure is so exhilarating, so satisfying, it's almost too much.

After a minute I start to settle in and relax. It's surreal. Here I am, having the boy of my dreams taste my insides. It feels so natural, and right. And it's all because I trust David.

I begin watching him. He's living in his own world of ecstasy. I wonder, could this man look sexier. The way he's reading me with his eyes to find what I like. The way his tongue brushes over my clit in circular motions. And the way he uses his plump lips to taste around my opening. It's a hunger he can't get enough of. And I could never get tired of watching his green eyes stare up at me from between my legs.

Eventually, he starts using his finger and tongue at the same time. Then one finger becomes two. It helps me find a new world of pleasure I never knew existed. And it's bringing me to the brink of losing control.

"Please don't stop!" I scream. "Right there! Right there!"

The climax hits and I lose control of my body. It shakes uncontrollably. All I hear is my own shrieking and all I see are white lights flashing in my vision. It's as if I'm no longer myself. It's only the highest pleasure and the release of a mind-altering orgasm that has my whole body, and especially my warmth below, pulsating over his wet mouth.

My eyes eventually open. All I see is his heart-warming smile and his plump lips still glowing from my insides. It's a look that keeps my orgasm alive a little bit longer as my hips start to spasm.

"How was that?" he asks, flashing a tantalizing smile.

All I can do is laugh. It's an odd response to his question. But it's the organic way my happiness comes out. After all, how do I explain the feeling of having ten orgasms combined into one?

"I'll take that as a yes," he finally says, giving me a sly smirk.

It takes a minute to catch my breath, but I know what comes next. He knows it, too. I can see it in the alluring smile he's giving me. And he doesn't need to beg for it. I want it.

"Can I try on you?" I ask.

"Please," he begs, nodding like he's possessed by my beauty.

There's so much to notice as I peel his boxers off. There's the way his chest is rising and falling at an erratic pace. The way his eyes are begging me to return the favor. And the way his penis and balls swell up, looking like the most delicious dessert I could ever dream of.

But a fear suddenly washes over me. I have no clue how to do this. What he likes. What he doesn't like. All I know is what I read. But that's not enough. I need his help because I want this to feel good for him. I want him to bask in the pleasure just like I did.

"Tell me what you like?" I whisper, my tone sensual.

He licks his lips, reminding me that his tongue was just inside my body. Then he explains what he wants with calm and confidence in his tone.

"The tip is most sensitive. But I want lots of saliva. I want to cum in your mouth. And I want you to swallow it."

He's moaning right away as my mouth swallows the tip. I bob up and down slowly, seeing my saliva spill down to his balls. Then I tease my tongue over the tip, emulating what I read in my book. And he loves it! His moaning gets louder the longer I tease. But eventually I give in, swallowing it down deeper into my mouth.

"Right there! Right there!" he begs.

David arches his hips up. His penis goes further into the back of my mouth. His balls swell up even more. Then he cums. The warm liquid comes out in heaps. His penis pulsates as I hold my mouth over his girth to swallow every bit of his cum. The whole time I watch his face melt away in satisfaction to something so perfect, so deserving, and so erotic.

David's giggle keeps drawing my attention out of my book. Then his side-glancing crooked smile does it. I swoop in for a quick smooch on his lips.

"Sorry, I know it's hard to keep your eyes on the road," I playfully tease.

"Should we find another rest stop?" he asks with a playful wink.

We told Aunt Sariah we'd get to Pittsburgh around noon. But after two longer than usual breaks at rest stops, we'll probably get there closer to two.

The rest stops were a necessity. They also weren't rest. Each break involved thirty minutes of foreplay on random back roads hidden behind trees. His back seat is small, but we make it work. I'm now on my third pair of panties today and his seat has multiple damp spots. So yeah, I'd say each break has been more than worth it.

David gives me another crooked smile as I ponder his question. It would be nice to ease the tension and take another break. The pressure on my insides is growing heavier the closer we get. But I can't delay our arrival any further.

"How close are we?" I ask.

"Less than fifteen minutes. How are you feeling?"

His hand rubs along my shoulder. It feels good to be touched. However, it can't undo all the anxiety I'm feeling.

"Hey, it'll all work out, Ellie. I'm with you every step of the way. You hear me?"

I nod my head to his smoldering look of confidence. I wish I could have his optimistic outlook. The way David sees hope in the world comes so easy to him.

The neighborhood is not what I expect when we pull in. It's a trailer park filled with all types of travel trailers and motor homes. Some are run down and dilapidated, others are more extravagant. The one on Lot 58 is Sariah's.

It's a massive white and tan travel trailer that's the length of a full-size city bus. Out front is an awning with plastic chairs and a table. The potted plants hang down from the awning, giving it a very homey and inviting look for a motor home.

"You ready?" David asks.

I close my eyes, taking a deep breath. On the exhale I squeeze out the tension into his hand. "Let's do it."

David raises his hand to knock on the door. But before he can knock, we hear the lock unlatch. A woman wearing an apron opens the door. I'm guessing she's around forty years old. She has bright blondish red hair tied up into a messy bun. There's a familiar look to her that I can't quite articulate. It's just a feeling.

"Eliana," she whispers.

A silence settles over the three of us as the woman brings her hand over her mouth. Her eyes well up as a muffled cry escapes. My throat locks up. My whole body becomes clammy. Then it happens, faster than a blink of an eye—her body careening into mine for the most desperate hug I've ever felt.

We hold each other, soaking away in each other's tears. I may know nothing of this woman. But her emotions are sincere and genuine. I feel missed. I feel needed. But most importantly, I feel loved.

I already know this woman is my aunt. I feel it in my bones. And all I know of her story is she gave up on Judaism a long time ago. It's why my father shunned her from my life, and my mother's life. He never had a kind word to say about Sariah. It brainwashed me in a way. But in this moment, none of that matters. I'm here to learn *her* story.

She leans back from our hug. Her hands rub along my shoulders as her eyes look me up and down.

"Oh my," she marvels, awestruck by something. "Just a carbon copy. You are a sight to behold…so stunning."

Sariah introduces herself to David. He steps in to shake her hand. His voice becomes deep and confident.

"I'm her friend, David Cohen. It's so nice to meet you, Sariah."

"You as well. Please, please come in," she says, gesturing for us to come inside.

We take a seat at a round table with booth style seating. I'm guessing it's their dining room. Then we take a moment exchanging pleasantries. David even tells Sariah a little bit about his ceremony in New York. I can tell Sariah is listening to David, but she's clearly distracted. Her eyes keep darting to me. She even glances down at me and David's hands, holding on tightly.

Then, an uncomfortable silence settles over the three of us. We all have questions for one another. But no one knows where to start. When I can't take it any longer, I hand her the letter she wrote to my mom.

"I uh, I found this. I need to know what this means."

I glance at David. He gives me a hopeful smile. Together, we watch Sariah read the letter. Time passes slowly as her eyes transfix on her own words. It's hard to tell if she's still reading it or if she's just lost in her own memories.

I become transfixed by her blue eyes. They slowly go from glossy to heavy tears running down her cheeks. She gets up slowly, placing her hand on the counter for balance.

"I'm sorry." Sariah's lips purse as she lets out a shivering exhale. She puts her other hand on the counter as if it's a crutch to help her stand upright. "I'm so sorry. Please give me a moment. I need to show you something."

Sariah dashes down the hall. She returns quickly with a shoebox. She opens the lid, handing me a picture.

It's two tiny babies. I'm guessing they're minutes old in a hospital bayonet. I look up from the cute little picture seeing Sariah's smile widen with delight.

"They're so adorable. Are these your children?"

"No…me and my husband, John, well…we're not able to have children. These are Leah's babies. Your mom's babies," Sariah says in an admiring tone.

Her words are clear, but they don't process in my brain. I look back at the picture and notice details. The picture seems old, but I'm not sure if it's ten years old or twenty years old. Each baby has a pink beanie. They're wrapped like burritos so there's no way to tell if it's a boy or a girl. But if color was associated to gender, I'd assume these are two girls. But wait…

No! No! That's impossible!

"Ellie," David whispers. His hand squeezes my shoulder tightly. I notice his eyes peering around to the back of the picture. "Look at the date, sweetheart."

It's the first time David's ever called me sweetheart. That singular word sends an electrical shock through my body. But it was more than just the tenderness in his tone or the sanguine look in his eyes. It's knowing that the unimaginable, can now be imagined. And the feelings deep in my soul are the missing pieces to *who I am.*

I need to flip over this picture to see the date, but it's like I suddenly know that what's staring back is in part my own reflection. *In part.*

And with my hands shaking, my lips trembling, I turn the picture over.

Sasha Shalom Merkowitz and Eliana Elizabeth Merkowitz

Born: May 6th, 2006. Phoenix, Arizona

Location: Banner Good Samaritan Hospital

"I have a sister?"

That two-syllable word barely leaves my breath as Sariah gives me a gentle nod.

"Not just any sister. It's *your*…twin sister," Sariah says, grabbing my hand with both of hers.

"Is she alive?"

"Yes! Yes! She lives with us!" she cries, sniffling away tears. "You'll never meet anyone more alive than her. I mean, she has her own challenges. But, man oh man, is she ever alive." She chuckles under her breath while shaking her head. "She should be home in about ten minutes. Would you like to meet her?"

The picture falls from my hands. I fly out of the booth so quickly I'm climbing over David to escape. Once outside, the heaves of emotion pour out of me. My knees buckle and I'm on the ground.

"Give her a minute," I hear in the background. Then I feel him—his body enveloping mine. The security, the pressure, and the way he soothes my pain with just his touch means everything. And yet, I know his soothing can only do so much. Pain like this can't be defeated.

It's overwhelming to be angry at so many people. My mother. Myself. My aunt. But all that combined rage comes nowhere close to the anger I have towards my father.

I've lived most of my life pretending my mother made the choice to not be a part of my life. It's how my father brainwashed me to believe things. She was the enemy—never him. But after seeing my aunt's tears, I know there's much more to what happened. Perhaps there's even things I'm not ready to hear. But I've come almost 2,000 miles. There's no looking back now.

After blowing my nose and taking a few deep breaths, we head back inside. I take a seat across from Sariah, feeling my own glare penetrate her.

"Please tell me what's going on. And don't hold back. I need to know everything. You hear me. *Every…damn…thing,*" I say with gritted teeth.

Sariah clasps her hands together. She leans forward a bit as I notice her eyes wilting.

"Well, I don't know the story your father fed you. And there's some things I still don't know or understand. But here's what I do know. Your mom never wanted to marry your father.

But it was arranged, and it became our father's choice—not hers. So, she performed. She was a good actor. I, on the other hand, had stopped being Orthodox for some time—for my own reasons. But that's a whole different story. Leah, on the other hand, wanted to be a good wife. And she tried. She got pregnant with you and Sasha. But halfway through her pregnancy it all became too much. And she finally spoke her truth to Joshua."

"What truth?"

"You see, your mom was never in love with Joshua. He knew that. And it was his choice to live in denial. It was also his choice to be verbally abusive. But what you also need to understand is your mom was just not attracted to men. She never was. She hinted at things when we were younger, but anytime I brought it up, she denied it. She knew it was forbidden as an Orthodox woman. It took her a while to build up the courage and tell him. But one day she finally did it. Joshua tried convincing her that it was the change in hormones from pregnancy. He even tried convincing her that she was mentally ill and needed conversion therapy."

Sariah scoffs, shaking her head in frustration. I notice her fists balling up, lightly thudding on the table.

"What is it?" I ask.

"I'm sorry. I just don't like your father. He ruined everything for Leah—my only sister—my baby sister. And I can't forgive him for the lies he's told."

"What lies?"

Her mouth opens, like she's ready to speak. But Sariah has a hard time finding her words. Then she draws in a long and strenuous breath, exhaling it slowly.

"Well, your mom had major complications at your birth. It was severe preeclampsia. She had to be induced three months early. But she fell into a coma. She almost died. When she woke up about six weeks later, your father delivered the news that you had survived, and your twin sister didn't make it."

"What! But the picture—"

"He lied, Ellie!"

Her interruption is harsh, leaving me breathless.

"He lied to everyone. Even your mom. But your mom eventually found out what he did."

"My dad lied about the birth of his own daughter." The words sound so ridiculous coming out of my mouth. I want to believe Sariah. But why? And how could he pull that off? How could someone stoop to such lows of evil? And where the hell was Sariah?

"Why didn't you help her?" I raise my voice.

"Ellie, at first, I didn't know about any of this with Sasha. I swear. After I gave up on Judaism your dad wouldn't even allow your mom to talk to me. There was a long period of time where we'd rarely talk. But about ten years after you were born, we started to reconcile. And your mom started coming to me for help. She was having these visions, Ellie. I thought she was crazy, but it's like she always knew a piece of her was missing. Then she found out about all the horrid things Joshua had done. And you have to remember during his time your mom already wasn't in a good headspace. She was a lesbian woman denying her true feelings. She was clinically depressed for years. Then she finds out Sasha is alive. Apparently, he forged your mom's paperwork and put Sasha up for adoption while your mom was in a coma. That's why your mom left you. It was only to be temporary. She needed to go find Sasha. But then it became unsafe for her to come back."

My whole body goes numb. It's all too impossible to comprehend. Yet, I have to try and believe it.

I've always known my father was not well. He was physically and verbally abused as a child. It doesn't justify a crumb of the damage he's caused our family. Nor does it justify the verbal abuse he's inflicted on me and my mom for most of our lives. It only makes him a greater coward who couldn't break the cycle of abuse.

"Ellie, Ellie," David keeps repeating my name. My mind has zoned out from reality. My name echoes like he's shouting into the abyss of a darkened well.

But David's touch slowly brings me back. He rubs his hand along my wrist as my eyes draw up to his.

"Ellie, maybe we should take a quick break and go for a—"

"No, no, no, no!" I pound my open hand on the table. "I'm not leaving until I understand what's really going on here!"

I glare at Sariah. She's accountable for some of this. After all, she's the one who's been living with *my sister*—trying to hide Sasha from me.

"I still don't understand. Why would my dad want me, but not my twin sister?" I beg, on the brink of more tears.

Sariah begins rubbing her temples. The apprehension to my question is palpable. It's like a dense, dark fog has infiltrated the room. She takes a long, deep breath before answering.

"I don't know for sure. I can only tell you what your mom believed," she says, taking another deep, arduous looking breath. "She thought your dad didn't want Sasha because she's different."

"Different? I don't get it. Is something wrong with her?"

Sariah's voice becomes stern with certitude. "No! Sasha is a *normal, beautiful, lovely girl*. She just has an extra chromosome. That's it. She's just as capable as we are."

"I don't get it. Extra chromosome?"

"Down Syndrome?" David chimes in.

Sariah nods to him. "Yes, but we don't do labels here. You'll rarely hear those words from Sasha, so me and John don't use them either."

The squeaking of brakes draws our attention to the door.

"They're here," Sariah announces, looking on edge.

"I'm not ready to meet her." The words come out of me like a reflex. I can feel the life draining out of my body. The fear is too much. Because the truth is, I want to meet her, but not like this.

"Does she even know that I exist?"

Sariah flashes a hopeful smile. "She knows."

I can't do this.

There are so many things I don't know about this other part of my life. And while the biggest unknown is having a twin sister, the other pressing concern is why she's been hidden from my life for so long. And why was it not safe for my mom to come back to me after going to find Sasha? Furthermore, how did my sister end up living with her aunt?

I hear a car door. My mind is a wreck, still swimming in a sludge of unanswered questions. I look at David, feeling the panic quickly set in. It's a mix of so many competing emotions at once. The strongest being the ache in my chest. But the more I listen to and feel the ache, the more I understand the feeling. It's not so much rooted in pain or hurt. It's yearning—a deep yearning for what I've never had but always needed. It's as if the person outside is the other half of a magnet in need of connection. But most importantly, it's my magnet. It's *my* twin sister.

Chapter Fourteen

David

"We need a few minutes," I overhear Sariah explaining to her husband John. She heads back inside to be with Ellie.

I take a seat underneath their awning. I crane my neck around looking for Sasha, but she's nowhere to be seen.

The need to go back inside and be with Ellie is unrelenting. But I offered to come out here to help distract and give them a little privacy.

"So, you're Eliana's friend?" John asks, walking up to me.

His tone was so skeptical. He crosses his arms over his puffed-out chest. He's trying to intimidate me. It's working. The guy is at least four inches taller and fifty pounds heavier than me. It's all lean muscle. And if that wasn't enough, his arms are covered in two full sleeves of tattoos that make him look like more of a badass.

I stand up tall and extend my hand. "I'm, David Cohen. Nice to meet you, sir."

His handshake almost breaks my hand, but I swallow back the pain and squeeze back with everything I've got.

"So, you're not one of Joshua's kin?"

148

"Kin?"

"Yeah, you heard me. You're not one of his prick cousins, uncles, or nephews."

I'm dumbfounded. Is he kidding?

"No."

"Show me your ID."

I laugh in John's face. It feels fake and forced. I'm uncomfortable and unsure because I don't know if he's being serious. But his scowl doesn't budge an inch.

It makes no sense. Why is he being so paranoid? There's a part of me that just wants to say, "Fuck you." But I know it'll only complicate things for Ellie. The last thing she needs is complications—especially now.

He takes a long glance from my ID to my face. The picture is barely two years old. Then he hands it back to me, looking a little less on edge.

"I know Sariah and Eliana spoke the other day, but why are you guys really here?"

"We found an old letter from your wife." I pause to clear my throat. "I mean, Ellie found the letter hidden away in her dad's closet. It was written to Ellie's mom."

John clears his throat and then hocks a massive loogie on the ground. He rubs his steel toe boots over his spit like he's putting out a cigarette.

"Okay. And what's the deal with you and Ellie?"

"Me and her. Oh, uh, we're just friends. I'm headed to New York for a scholarship ceremony. She wanted to come along to support me, but to also find you guys—at least I think that's part of the reason she came."

He's scowling at me again. "You think, huh? I don't believe you. There's no way her piece of shit father would let an Orthodox girl travel across the country with an underage boy."

"I'm eighteen, sir," I quickly correct him.

John scoffs at me.

"Of course you are." He angles his face, glaring at me. His efforts at intimidating me are starting to really piss me off.

I step up closer to him until my face is inches from his. Then his cocky, smug smirk sends me over the edge.

"I don't give a shit if you don't believe me. Everything I've told you is the god's honest truth. And you're wrong about one thing. Her dad is the worst human being on earth—way worse than a piece of shit. If it were up to me, he could fucking die in a pit of fire. And I would do anything…*any…god…damn…thing* to protect Ellie from that monster."

And just like that, in the blink of an eye, John is laughing. It's not a soft chuckle, but a deep, guttural laugh. I'm so caught off guard I don't know what to do.

"Okay, okay," he says, giving my shoulder a cracking squeeze. "You passed the test, buddy. If you're not a Merkowitz, then you're all good in my book. Welcome to my home on four wheels. Now, come on back with me. Let's go check on Sasha."

I follow John around the travel trailer. We turn the corner and I see her right away. The sight of Ellie's twin sister causes me to break out in goosebumps. She's on one knee, about thirty yards away in a pasture of open green grass. It looks like she's fixing a baseball glove.

I quickly grab John's shoulder to stop him. "Wait, John. I uh, I don't know what I'm allowed to say to her," I admit, lowering my voice.

John scoffs, looking at me like I'm a complete idiot. "Is this because she has Down Syndrome? She ain't stupid. She's got more smarts then the both of us combined."

"I didn't mean it like that. I mean, what does she know about this whole situation and having a twin sister?" I whisper.

"Don't worry about that. She'll be thrilled as fuck that Ellie's here."

"John, did you just say 'fuck' again?" Sasha shouts, turning around to walk in our direction.

"Goddammit," he mutters under his breath, reaching in his pocket.

Sasha walks up to him with her hand extended out. She has to arch her chin up to John because she's barely five feet tall, like Ellie. Her strawberry blonde bob flutters off her shoulders in the breeze. She's wearing blue overalls with a jar bulging in the chest pocket.

"That'll be two dollars, Uncle John. And don't think I didn't hear the 'goddammit' come out of your filthy mouth. By the way, who are you?" she asks me with a grimacing side glare.

I hesitate while Sasha's gaze continues to linger on me.

"Hello! Are you there?" she shouts as if I'm deaf.

I extend my hand out to her. "Sorry. My name is David...David Cohen."

The next thing I know, my hand is crunching under her grip. "Oh, shit!" I shout, pulling my hand out of her death grip.

"I did it! Pay up, David!"

I scoff at her as her eyebrows rise up in contempt.

"You heard the girl. Pay the swear jar queen," John demands. "I'll let you two get acquainted while I run in to grab some water."

I begrudgingly pull out my wallet with my hand still aching from the power of her tiny hand. Then I notice her jar. It actually has the words **"Swear Jar Queen"** on the front.

What the fuck is going on?

"Why are you here?" she asks, inspecting my dollar bill with some type of UV flashlight.

I start chuckling under my breath. Does this girl think she's a counterfeit detective?

"You know, it's a real—"

"I'll be the judge of that, thank you very much!" Sasha barks back. "Okay, it's good. Now continue."

I'm flabbergasted. I don't know whether to laugh or be annoyed.

"Are you deaf, David? Please turn up your hearing aid! Why are you here? Can you hear me?" she shouts, leaning up to my ear to mock me.

"I'm not deaf, Sasha. I'm here to find you."

"But I don't know you."

"That's not what I meant. I meant to say that we are—"

"Do you want to play catch?"

Her interruptions and lack of patience make it hard to carry on a real conversation. It's like she's bored if I don't come up with an answer or a snide remark in the blink of an eye.

"Sure, let's play catch," I concede.

The first three balls she throws at me go in and out of the mitt she gave me. To make matters worse, I'm also having a tough time throwing the ball back to her.

"You're not very good," she says with a sour look.

"Oh, really? Tell me more."

"Yeah, I can tell. You really suck at sports. You must not have an athletic gene in your body. But you do look kind of buff."

I chuckle at her honesty. "Yeah, I'm not as good as you. I'm also not used to throwing and catching a softball. It's been a while. I think the last time I played was with my twelve-year-old Little League team."

"Can I teach you?"

"Sure, why not."

I let Sasha teach me the basics of softball. Most of it I already know since the rules are identical to the sport of baseball. Nevertheless, I try to be a good sport. Sasha's very thorough as a teacher. She goes over the mechanics of throwing, fielding, footwork, and even underhand pitching.

"Do you play for Special Olympics?"

"Ha! No way. Those guys suck. I'll dominate them. But I play slow pitch with my uncle. I'm batting 350 this year."

"What grade are you in?" I ask.

"I don't know. I just do homeschool. What grade are you in?" she counters.

"I just graduated high school."

"What are you going to be when you grow up?"

"I'm not sure."

"Why?"

"Because I'm only eighteen."

"Do you have a girlfriend?"

I pause, taking a deep swallow of discomfort. "Do you always ask a hundred questions?"

"Yes. Now tell me, do you have a girlfriend?"

My insides begin stewing. "Kind of, well no, I mean—"

"You like someone. I can tell. Your cheeks are getting pink. Come on, tell me. Who is it?"

Oh fuck!

I'm biting my tongue and fighting off the need to laugh at her brute honesty. I mean, how do I respond to this? I guess I can just be honest.

"Sasha, I don't have an *official* girlfriend. I promise."

"Well, I don't have an official boyfriend, either. But I'll have one soon. He looks a lot like Zac Efron," she proclaims, fanning herself with a smile. "Anyways, you like someone—a lot. I can tell. Maybe you have an unofficial girlfriend. Or a side bitch."

"A side bitch," I repeat in a disbelieving tone. "I definitely don't have that. But you can think what you want."

There's finally a whole second long break in our conversation. I seize my opening.

"Did you always know that you have a twin sister?" I ask.

Sasha begins fidgeting with her glove. I know she heard my question.

"What do you think about meeting your sister today?"

She continues to ignore me, fidgeting away with her glove. But I patiently wait for her to give me some type of answer.

"She doesn't care about me." Sasha's words are softly spoken, but the indignation in her tone hits me like a punch to the gut.

"She didn't know about you, Sasha. I promise."

"Well, she knows about me now. And I don't see her. I know she's inside. If she wanted to meet me, she would've been out here by now."

I take a deep breath, noticing how her gaze looks away, like her mind is stuck in a very dark, desolate place.

"She's just scared, but I don't think—"

"Does she look like me?" Sasha interrupts. Her gaze intensifies. There's something about her almond-shaped blue eyes and the way they're emitting such genuine curiosity.

"Well, she has your blue eyes," I admit.

"But David...*does...she...look...like...me*?" Her seething anger lives in every word. There's so much simmering beneath the surface. And now my delay in responding is the answer she probably already knows. Anything I say in this moment could easily be the wrong thing. Maybe all I can do is be straightforward. It's how I'd speak to Ellie. So, why should I be any different with Sasha?

"Are you asking me if she has Down Syndrome? No, she doesn't have an extra chromosome. She just has her own set of differences and special abilities. The first being her beauty. But now I finally see where she gets it from."

I wink at Sasha, and her cheeks turn pink. She looks as if no one has complimented her appearance before.

"Are you sure you don't want to meet her?" I ask again.

"Well, I'll think about it. For now, I'm going to practice my pitching," Sasha says, turning to walk towards her designated pitching area.

I stand there, watching, wondering, and hoping she'll reconsider. But she keeps walking.

"Hey, Sasha!" I shout.

She looks back over her shoulder. "What?"

"Thanks for teaching me how to play softball. And for taking the time to get to know me. It was so nice to finally meet you. And good luck with Mr. Efron. He'll be one lucky guy."

Sasha giggles. The innate beauty in her smile reminds me so much of Ellie.

"David!"

I turn around to see Sariah waving me over. I quickly glance at my phone to see it's only been fifteen minutes since I came out to meet Sasha.

"How's it going?" I ask, walking to the side of the travel trailer.

"She wants to get going." Sariah stops to wipe her eyes and blow her nose. Her face is pink all over with stress.

"Don't you think they should meet while we're here?"

"Yes, I do—wholeheartedly. But she doesn't feel ready. And I'm not going to force it. But I don't blame her. This is a lot to take in all at once. Poor girl."

I nod with a hopeful smile while Sariah's lips begin to quiver. More tears begin raining down her cheeks.

"I don't want her to leave," Sariah cries, shaking her head in disgust. "I feel so bad. I should've been there for her—taken her away from that monster."

John walks up behind Sariah. "Ellie's already in the car. She's ready to go right now."

I walk away while John tries to soothe his wife with head kisses and whispering comfort in her ear.

"Hey, David!" John calls out, still hanging onto his wife. "You two are welcome back anytime. I mean that."

"Thanks. It was nice meeting you. It was nice meeting all of you."

Once I get into the car, Ellie's face looks pale and lost. Her gaze and mind are so far out the window I don't even know if she heard me get in.

My options are limited. I could talk her into staying—meeting her wonderful sister—getting to know her family. Or I can drive away to an award ceremony that now means nothing to me. Everything I want, everything I can give, I want to give to Ellie. And it's here. Right in front of us. Not in New York.

"Ellie, are you sure—"

"Just drive! Please! Just drive, David! I can't be here right now!" she cries.

Every thread of my being knows right from wrong in this contentious moment. Leaving is the wrong thing to do—especially right now. But Ellie may know more about what's going on than I do.

After starting the car, I adjust my mirror to stall things. I notice John in my rearview mirror with his arm around Sariah. They look like they are walking inside. But as I shift the car into gear, the sound of pounding metal startles the shit out of us.

"Ellie! Ellie! Ellie!" Sasha screams for her sister. But it's no ordinary scream. It's blood-curdling. It's desperate, like a sound of horror that will haunt us for eternity.

"Please! Please!" she continues to beg.

Ellie shades her hand over her face, screaming at me to drive off. There are only inches of glass separating these two. I've never felt more conflicted, more scared, and more unsure in my entire life. Staying and leaving are both wrong decisions. But I listen to Ellie, driving off as the dirt plumes over her hysterical twin sister.

The last thing I see in my mirror is Sasha collapsing onto her knees. The pain is too much. I'm not mad at Ellie. I'm mad at God. How could this shit happen to these two innocent girls? How could her dad be this evil?

"Wait! Stop! Stop! Stop!" Ellie's screams as I slam on the brakes.

Her door flies open. I get out of the car. Ellie and her sister sprint towards one another. Then they collide into each other's arms, crying uncontrollably. My vision fogs up. The emotions pour out of me. I've never felt so sad and happy at the same time. But more than anything, my heart is full. Ellie has her other half. Her missing half. *Her twin sister.*

Chapter Fifteen

Ellie

We've been talking for a couple of hours now. Well, she's doing most of the talking. I'm mainly just listening, trying to absorb everything that is *my* beautiful twin sister. I've smiled, laughed, and cried so much my cheeks are starting to hurt. But it's the best kind of hurt.

Sasha is also incredibly funny. Thoughts pop into her head and the questions just roll off her tongue. She can't relate to some of my answers because she wasn't raised in an Orthodox community like I was. But it doesn't mean we don't relate to one another on so many other levels.

She's boy crazy right now. It's something we both have in common. She's asking me every question under the sun about who I've dated, my type, and what I think of David. She knows without me saying that we like each other. But for now, I'm just referring to him as my friend.

It's surreal to have her in front of me. I want to learn more about mom and her past, but she's hesitant and quick to change the subject any time I ask.

According to Sariah, Sasha lived with many different foster families growing up. She doesn't believe that any of them were stable family environments. And when Mom found out she was alive, she traveled to where Sasha was living in Brooklyn, New York. Mom spent the next two years in and out of litigation trying to regain custody of Sasha. She eventually won, gaining full custody of Sasha when she was fourteen years old.

Sariah has yet to tell me how my mom died. All she's told me so far is that my mom dropped off Sasha at her house a couple years ago. The plan was for Sasha to stay with Sariah for the weekend while my mom went to a custody hearing in New York. However, my mom never returned to pick up Sasha. And that was the last time Sasha and Sariah saw my mother.

"Ellie!"

I realize my mind has been dazing. "Sorry, what was that?"

"So, David is just your friend, right?" Sasha asks, frowning her eyes at me.

It's now the third time she's asked me this exact same question. Each time her tone becomes more disbelieving.

"Yes, Sasha. Just a friend."

"Is he your best friend?"

"Yes."

"Aunt Sariah always says John is her best friend. She thinks the guy I marry one day will be my best friend, too."

I nod my head, feeling a flutter of happiness in my tummy.

"Do you want to kiss him?" she asks.

I try to suppress a chuckle, but I just can't. My face instantly flushes with heat. It has me thinking how it's feels like forever since we last kissed. And I'm yearning for it, every second.

"Well, I'm not sure. But if he did want to kiss me, I know David would be a gentleman about it."

"Yeah, yeah, yeah. I know. Aunt Sariah and Uncle John have taught me about consent. Uncle John says I should even tell boys my uncle will squash them like a bug if they break my heart. But I don't say that anymore. It's scared off a couple boys."

"Do they let you date boys?"

"I don't know. Most boys don't like me or even look at me. I don't have long red hair and big boobs like you do. I only have a nice butt. At least that's what one boy told me."

"Hhmm, I see." I take a deep, contentious breath. Sasha's suddenly quiet, staring only at her fidgeting hands. Her feelings are so relatable.

Before David, I never felt noticed by boys either. Losing my hair made me feel like I lost my femininity as a woman. It made me incredibly insecure and paranoid. I convinced myself that no boy would ever want to be with a girl who has no hair of their own. Nevertheless, the boys I grew up with in temple were always so awkward. They never tried talking to me or listening to me like David does. They never complimented me like he does either. And the ones that may have been attracted to me would typically stay away because their parents knew about my family history—mainly my mom abandoning the synagogue and leaving her husband. It's the greatest two sins a Jewish wife can commit.

I also had very few friends in general growing up. My dad would rarely let me leave the house unless it was a religious function. The friends I did have grew apart from me when they got phones because I was never allowed to have one. Some parents also didn't want their daughters hanging out with me when they found out about my family history with my mom.

By the time high school rolled around, I pretty much gave up on finding friends through Judaism. Instead, I mainly saw lots of David. Whether it be late night meetups in his shed or sharing notes with him across our wall. He was able to fill that void as the one constant in my life. Thinking about David in this way has me suddenly overwhelmed with gratitude.

"Do you believe in God, Sasha?"

She shrugs. "I don't know."

"Well, I do. I've been treated badly most of my life. I think you can relate. But with all the bad, there's been some really good people that have come into my life, like David. You see, the good people you let into your life will teach you to be hopeful. They'll believe in you."

I stop to rub my hand along Sasha's arm. Her eyes tilt up to mine.

"All we can do is be kind and be ourselves. If you keep doing that, you'll find the right person. It may happen tomorrow, or it may happen ten years from now. But keep being yourself. Because I've only known you for a couple hours and I'm blown away. Any boy that gets to be in a relationship with you will have won the lottery. You have to believe that, Sasha. You are so unique, and so wonderful. And I love you so much."

We embrace. The emotions spill out of us. The catharsis of this moment feels timeless. But it's the way we cling on to one another. It's so innately desperate—like we're making up for the lifetime of hugs we've lost.

Eventually, we both run out of tears and just talk. We learn more about one another. It's wonderful to be able to share this time with my sister, but my time feels constrained.

The front door squeaks open. David walks out.

"Is everything okay?" I ask.

"Yeah, everything is more than fine. Can we chat in private for a moment?"

"Sure, what's up?" I ask, walking away from Sasha.

David lowers his voice. "I think you should stay for a couple days while I go up to New York. Your aunt and uncle just offered you the guest bed."

"No way. I'm coming with you. I want to be there whether you win or lose."

"Ellie, you belong here with your family. This is more important, and you know it."

"I'm coming, David! You can't stop me. New York is important to you. You can downplay it all you want. But it's important to me, too."

"You're not leaving already. Are you?" Sasha asks, appearing from behind me with her aunt and uncle.

"We have to be in New York by tomorrow evening for his event," I explain, watching Sasha's eyes wilt. "I'm sorry. But I promise I'll be back."

"You all should at least spend the night," Sariah chimes in. "I mean, you just got here and you're already running out of daylight. Plus, if you leave early tomorrow morning, you still got plenty of time to get to New York by tomorrow afternoon. What do you think, John?"

John smiles down at Sariah, squeezing her close into his side. "Of course, babe. We'd love to have you all stay. I mean, it's a tight fit in there, but I can always set the old air mattress and tent out under the awning. It's a queen size mattress fit for two."

An awkward silence settles over the five of us. His eyes lingered upon David and I when he uttered those words, "*fit for two*." I swallow the tension in my throat, not knowing what to say as Sariah gives John a curious glance.

"I don't want them sleeping outside," Sasha whines. "But then again, I'm sure they really, really would want to sleep outside…*together*," Sasha says with a wink and a chuckle.

"Oh, no, no, no, no. I didn't mean it like that!" John raises his voice. "I just meant it's a big mattress that'll fit David. This way he'll have plenty more room than if he tried squeezing in on that little couch inside. Yeah, um, and Ellie can sleep inside with the rest of us…away from, David."

"I'm glad we got that settled. Real smooth, honey." Sariah laughs, lightly patting his chest.

"Are you worried they'll have sex?"

"Sasha Shalom!" Sariah shouts.

"What? I don't even think they've even kissed yet. But they both really want to. I can tell. I mean, just look at their faces right now," Sasha says, pointing at my face.

I will myself to not blush, but that's impossible. And the more this awkward silence carries on, the more I feel the embarrassment weighing heavy on my face.

"Oh, my." Sariah sighs, shielding her eyes. "Sweetheart, remember what I said about reading the room? Anyways, I'm going to head inside to start on dinner. Would you like to join me, Ellie?"

I eagerly nod, noticing David's beet red cheeks. If it wasn't already evident that David and I are more than friends, now it's painted on our faces.

Dinnertime provides a much-needed distraction from earlier. It starts when Sasha brings up the idea of going with us to New York for a couple days. She tries her best to persuade John and Sariah. But they don't budge. I'm disappointed she can't come, but I also understand.

It's a weird experience to just share a dinner table with family. We learn about everyone's day. Everybody listens and asks questions to show genuine interest. There are even moments where we're laughing and being silly with one another. It's everything I could've ever wanted, and it's here in my life almost eighteen years later.

My father and I never ate dinner together after my mom left. We didn't do it much when my mom was around either. The rare times I did eat with just my dad, it was always very quiet. He wouldn't ask how my day was. I'd try asking him, but he'd usually just give one-word answers. Eventually, I gave up on trying to have that kind of relationship with my dad. It was too exhausting to try and make someone happy who was eternally unhappy.

After dessert, I help with the dishes. John takes David outside to enlist his help with the tent and getting his truck jacked up so he can start replacing his brake pads. When they run out of sunlight, I notice how their conversation with one another seems tense and in closer proximity.

"What do you think they're talking about?" I ask.

Sariah smirks. "Um, I can take a guess at it. But you probably don't want me to tell you. Anyhow, I'm sure David will fill you in."

Sariah's smirk gets wider. She lets out a soft chuckle. I suddenly feel the need to change the subject.

"You know, I honestly wouldn't mind if Sasha tagged along with us for a couple days in New York."

"That's sweet of you." Sariah smiles, drying off her hands. "I honestly would love for you two to spend more time with each other. But a road trip is not going to be the best situation for her. She needs to have structure in her day. It's how we've learned to raise someone with special needs. Plus, me and John are just very protective of her safety."

Sariah puts her hand on my shoulder. Her usual, natural smile suddenly has a tinge of pain in it.

"You know, for most of our lives all we wanted was children. We tried IVF, but it didn't work. In fact, it almost bankrupted us. Then we got close to adoption, but we went into such debt with IVF we just never had the funds. We eventually just accepted the reality of having no children. Then, one day, out of the blue, you're parenting and homeschooling a special needs teenager. It was super hard at first. Poor Sasha had spent most of her life transitioning from family to family. But my oh my, is she resilient…and absolutely brilliant. And now she's a beautiful 18-year-old woman. And it could be a little while until she's mature enough to live on her own, but one day she'll get there. I'm just so happy she has you in her life now. It's a blessing."

Sariah's eyes well up. I rub my hand along her shoulder for comfort. "I'm so happy we found you guys. You two are doing such a great job raising Sasha. I mean that."

Sariah smiles, breathing in my words as if it's something she's been yearning to hear. But it's true. A girl like Sasha deserves to be loved unconditionally, not passed along from family to family. I've only known her for a few hours, but it's impossible to not fall in love with her and know that she's happy with her aunt and uncle. And more importantly, her happiness has clearly brought so much fulfillment to Sariah and John.

Later that night, I step outside to say goodnight to David. He's busy writing when I unzip his tent.

"Hey, get over here," he begs, patting his lap. He's flashing his usual adoring smile. But there's something about this smile that's insanely sexy.

Our lips are like magnets once I snuggle into his lap. The way he pulls me so tight into his body makes all the pain and worry drift away. It's everything I've been starving for since we got here. Those juicy lips. The way his tongue lightly glides along the inside of my mouth. It has me fantasizing about spending the night in his tent.

I break away from a long kiss, gasping for breath as we star gaze into each other's eyes.

"Oh my," I whisper.

He deftly glides the tips of his fingers along my cheeks. His smile stretches across his face with effortless beauty. "God I've missed this. How are you?"

"I'm pretty good. I just asked if Sasha could come with us to New York. They said no. But I kind of knew that would be their answer."

"Are you sure you don't want to stay back for a couple days?"

I taste his lips again, slowly lifting off. "I'm sure of it. Tomorrow's a big day and I'm going to be there to support you. It would also be hard if Sasha came with us…you know…" My words trail off while my insides simmer for more of his touch.

"I guess it'll be nice to get our privacy back," David admits, squeezing his hands along my hips. He lets out a nervous chuckle.

"What's so funny?"

"Oh, I was just thinking. Your uncle gave me a bit of a speech after we finished up the tent. He told me there'll be no sneaking in or out of the tent tonight." He laughs.

"Really?"

"Yeah, really. Just when I thought I've been mortified enough by Sasha. But he's a good guy. He means well. I guess we'll just have to wait on snuggling again until tomorrow."

Tomorrow feels like too long to wait. Then an idea pops into my head.

"Why are you giving me that sexy smirk?" he asks.

"I had an idea. I noticed John has one of those CPAP machines like your dad does. You've always told me how loud those things are. Maybe he wouldn't hear me if I snuck out for a bit in the middle of the night…right?"

David's smile illuminates. "Yes. And I wouldn't be breaking his rule because if you came out to say hi at say…12:01, it would technically be tomorrow."

Sasha hollers for me to come inside. We're both laughing with giddy excitement.

"Sweet dreams. I'll see you first thing tomorrow." I wink. Then I give him a quick peck on his forehead. I'm still chuckling with excitement as I step out of the tent.

My entire body feels lighter knowing that I'll see David in a couple of hours. The risk of being with him in the middle of the night and in a tent only heightens my arousal. Because all I want is him. But this time, I want all of him. And I'm ready to share all of me.

Chapter Sixteen

David

The screams of panic have me wide awake, gasping for air. It feels so close and desperate. But that's not the worst part. The worst part is knowing that scream.

My pants are barely pulled up as I crawl out of the tent. The lights to the RV next door flicker on, but the commotion is coming from John and Sariah's travel trailer.

Once inside, Sasha is screaming with her hands over her ears. John is trying to soothe her while Sariah has Ellie cornered by the table. The closer I get to Ellie, the quicker I realize what's going on.

"It's a night terror! It's a night terror! She's not awake! Just give her a little space!" I yell at Sariah, holding my hand out to stay back. "John! Get Sasha out of here!"

John and Sasha head outside. Sariah steps back as Ellie begins pacing the tight hallway. I flick on the lights to see Ellie's catatonic face living in a different world.

Ellie's arms hug tight around her chest. I walk with her, rubbing her shoulders and trying to soothe her with my words.

But she's not snapping out of it. She keeps mumbling gibberish I don't understand.

"How can I help?" Sariah asks.

I guide Ellie to the couch to sit down. Then I turn to Sariah. "Music. Anything classical. It brings her back quicker. And just stay calm. The calmer we can be, the quicker she'll snap out of it. Trust me."

Sariah has a classical station playing on her Bluetooth speaker in seconds. The moment it comes on, the tears pour out of Ellie as she frantically shakes her head. Then she starts repeating words I can finally understand.

"No accident. No accident. She tried, David. She tried, David."

Her words have my body covered in goosebumps. It was more than just the begging cadence in her voice. It's the way she said *my name* that has me frozen in fear. It's not the usual Ellie way of saying Dav*ee*d. It felt more like a different voice than her own was speaking to me.

"She tried, David."

Our hands cling so tightly together I can see the whites of our knuckles. Then I realize her wig is not fully on. I try to adjust it, but it's hard when she's having trouble sitting still.

"Here, let me try." Sariah steps in and fixes the wig like she's done it a million times.

I look on in astonishment. "Do you—"

"Her mom had alopecia," she calmly interrupts, making a couple more minor adjustments to Ellie's wig. "Her wig sure hides it well. But I knew right away. She didn't need to tell me. Besides, we all have our own little secrets."

I glance back at Ellie. She's still stuck in her nightmare, but I can tell she's closer to snapping out of it. Meanwhile, Ellie's aunt looks troubled by more than what she's witnessing in Ellie. Her words from a moment ago begin replaying in my head. This time they carry an unbearable weight.

"We all have our own little secrets."

I can't hold back. I need to know for Ellie's sake.

"What happened to her mom?" I demand.

"Um…I don't know," she barely mutters.

"What? How do you not know?"

Sariah's face wilts. Her lips quiver. "I, I uh, I tried giving Ellie the journal. But she didn't want to read it. I never had the courage to read it either."

"What journal?"

"Her mother's journal." Sariah suctions her hand over mouth. She's trying to hold it in, but it's no use. Her body begins shaking uncontrollably. Then she quickly gets up and runs to the bathroom. The second the door shuts, I hear her groaning in pain.

"David!" Ellie calls for me.

Her blue eyes are dilating. I lean in inches from her face to make sure she's finally back. "Ellie, are you okay?"

She nods then slowly sits up, sliding to the edge of the couch to take a couple deep breaths. "How long?" she asks, looking at her feet.

"About fifteen minutes. It scared Sasha. She's out front with John. Your aunt's in the bathroom. But you're okay."

The commotion out front distracts us both. Sariah comes out of the bathroom as John and Sasha rush in.

"Code Blue! Code blue, Sariah!" John panics.

Sasha rushes into the back room, coming out quickly with a duffel bag.

"I'll be outside waiting," she says, rushing out the front door like she's done this routine before. All Ellie and I can do is look on in shock.

"The neighbors told me they called them. My police scanner has them less than five minutes away. They'll pull up any second now. I don't know what to do. The truck is jacked up with no tires or brakes."

John's words came out in a frantic, machine gun's pace. Then I feel the piercing pressure in my arm. Sariah's nails are digging into my skin as she leans her face inches from mine.

"Take her. Please take Sasha with you guys," she begs.

Sariah keeps begging me with such sorrowful desperation until John steps in between us. "No! Are you crazy? She's staying with us! We'll run on foot if we have too!"

I step backwards, yanking my arm out of Sariah's grip. "What the fuck is going on?"

Sariah ignores my question like I don't exist. Then, she puts her trembling hands on John's cheeks. Tears pour down her face as her voice becomes feeble. "As long as they don't find her, that's all that matters. We'll find them later. Please, John. It's the only way to keep her safe and you know it."

Ellie's hand grabs tightly onto mine. Our eyes fixate on her aunt and uncle. They look like different people. It's as if this moment, this decision, is life or death to them. But the worst part is the hopeless look in their eyes. It's as if they're losing Sasha forever.

"Fine," John concedes, bowing his head to the ground.

"What's going on?" Ellie demands.

Neither of them gives a response. Instead, Sariah quickly leans down by their bookcase. Her arm reaches towards the back, pulling out a small blue book. She shoves it into my chest. "Just take it. You both need to know. Now go!"

"Go where? We need to know what's going on!" I shout back, refusing to leave with no explanation.

John steps in front of Sariah, still looking lost in panic as he speaks quickly. "Look, when the police get here, they're going to take Sasha away from us for a long time. It's on you guys to keep her safe for a couple of days. Sasha has a burner phone in her bag. Make sure you guys turn it on. You'll get a call from an unknown number in a day or two. Then we'll hopefully be able to meet up."

"But where do we take her?" Ellie begs.

"It doesn't matter!" John screams, pounding his fist on the table. "Anywhere as long as it's away from here—away from us. Just keep going to New York. Pretend this whole conversation never happened in case you run into trouble. You hear me? Play dumb if you need to. But please go. I'm sorry, it was never our intention to get you guys involved."

I'm still not satisfied with their explanation. But Ellie is pulling me towards the door. We spend barely a few seconds grabbing our luggage as her aunt and uncle practically push us down the front steps of their trailer.

Once we're both in my car, we look on to a conversation we can't hear. But I'm glad we can't hear it. If we did, it would hurt even more.

Sasha keeps shaking her head. Her aunt and uncle keep showering her with hugs and kisses to soothe her. Everything is done with such finality and immense sadness. But the worst part is they're rushed, unable to bask in a true goodbye.

A couple of neighbors look on as a screaming Sasha is forced into our car. The door shuts and Sasha is beyond hysterical, screaming for them to come. We drive away just as two cop cars turn onto their block.

Once we pass them, Ellie jumps in the back. I glance in my mirror to see Ellie cradling her twin sister in her arms. Her comforting does little to stop her desperate pleas to not leave. The helplessness and begging in Sasha's voice is too much to bear.

We hop on the interstate as things slowly start to settle down in the backseat. There's still the occasional whimper or cry, but at least they have each other. It's in this exact moment I think about my sister—*my twin sister*. I can't imagine eighteen years of absence because she's always been in my life and in my corner.

I take another couple glances in the mirror. This time all I can see, and feel, is the determined look on Ellie's face. She *will* protect Sasha at all costs. It lives in every kiss on Sasha's head. And I can feel it in every soothing word she whispers.

Chapter Seventeen

Ellie

"Is she asleep?" David whispers over his shoulder.

"Yeah. She's been out for about an hour now."

I put down the blue book Sariah gave me. I need a break to calm my nerves. My focus goes to my breathing. I'm trying to process certain parts of my mom's journal. But some of it doesn't make sense.

"Why don't you come sit—"

David stops talking because I've already read his mind. We share a smile after I finished climbing into the front seat. Our hands interlock. The sheer touch of his skin is the instant catharsis I need.

"How's Sasha?"

"Not good," I admit, lowering my voice. "She'll barely talk to me. She spent close to three hours just looking at that phone—waiting for their call. I don't know what to do. I mean, what if they don't ever call us?"

I watch as David's jaw clenches. He rubs his hand along the side of his neck, letting out a loud sigh. "I don't know. I don't even know why we're going to New York anymore."

"We're doing it because they said it's the only way to keep her safe. Remember, we just play dumb and keep going on our trip."

"But Ellie," David pauses to lower his voice even more. "Safe from what? What's the danger? And why was Sasha prepared to run away?"

My stomach aches to his question. His eyes begin lingering on me more than on the road.

"What do you know, Ellie?"

"Pull over."

He pulls into the first gas station. I glance in the backseat to make sure Sasha is still sound asleep.

"I've been reading the blue book that Sariah gave me. It's my mom's journal. I've skipped around a bit. But I've read the last forty pages in there, including her last journal entry. But…"

My throat locks up. The panic sets in, building like an unbearable weight in my chest. I feel like I'm going to lose it until his other hand grabs hold of mine. I look up, seeing my own reflection through the tenderness in those green eyes. Then I realize, I have no choice. David *wants* to be involved. He *wants* to help me.

"David, my mom spent years trying to regain custody of Sasha. She even tried suing my dad for what he did to her. But she never had the money or enough evidence to see it through. But…she didn't stop trying. She was determined to do whatever it took."

"What do you mean?"

"Sasha was never adopted. Sariah and John lied to us. Probably to protect us from knowing something illegal. But it's all written in her journal. My mom took her from a broken foster home."

"Took her?" David repeats my words in a disbelieving tone.

"Yes. My mom kidnapped her. But Sasha was always rightfully hers. Apparently, Sariah and John were able to obtain fake identification for the two of them. You know, licenses, passports, birth certificates, Social Security cards."

"What?"

"I checked, David. In Sasha's duffel bag is a passport with her picture and the name Theresa Hunt. It's the same name written in my mom's journal. And my mom's name was changed to Samantha Hunt. They were worried my dad would find them. She writes a lot in her journal about feeling like she was being chased or followed."

"What else did she write?"

"Her last couple of journals were about meeting with a custody lawyer in New York. His name was Richard Stein. She seemed excited to meet this lawyer because he claimed to have incriminating evidence against my dad. But there's nothing after that. And there's nothing in my mom's journal about giving custody to Sariah and John, or even wanting to do such a thing. She only wrote about dropping Sasha off with them so she could attend the meeting on her own. She left the journal with them in case something happened. And I guess something happened because she never came back."

"Something feels off," David mutters. "Sariah couldn't tell me what happened to your mom when I asked her. Did she say anything else to you."

"No."

We stop talking when we hear shuffling around in the back seat. "Where are we?" Sasha yawns.

"We just crossed the state lines into New York about an hour ago. We're almost at the hotel," David tells her.

"Did they call yet?" Sasha asks.

"No, remember we may not get a call until tomorrow."

Sasha's been told this quite a few times. It's either she doesn't believe me, or she's still holding out hope that they'll call us sooner.

"Can I tell you about the awards ceremony?" I ask, needing to change the subject.

Sasha's mute to my question. I notice David giving me a concerned look. I ignore it.

"Sure," Sasha finally mutters.

I spend the next few minutes hyping up the screenplay David's written. I tell her how the winner receives a full tuition scholarship to any college in the country. Then I tell her how there's even a chance his script could be purchased by a major film studio.

Sasha becomes surprisingly intrigued. She begins asking questions about his story. She even starts equating the ceremony to an event like the Oscars. I tell her I'm unsure about a red carpet, but I know people will be dressed fancy. Then I threw out the idea of going dress shopping after we check into the hotel.

The words left my mouth like I'm some kind of fashion expert. It has Sasha legitimately excited. But I'm no expert on fashion, or anything when it comes to looking fancy. All I know is shopping for modest-looking plain dresses.

I want to share Sasha's excitement. I want things to feel normal, or even a crumb of normalcy will do. But it feels unrealistic to live in a fake reality even though I'm faking it on the outside. After all, if everything I'm learning is true, it means my mom kidnapped Sasha. She committed a very serious crime according to the letter of the law. But is it against the law when your baby was given away without your knowledge or consent? There must be a precedence where the egregious wrongs committed by my father can be undone.

Luckily, Sasha starts asking David about his story. They get to talking which gives my mind a break. But it also sends my thoughts down a new rabbit hole.

There's only one person who knows about the mysteries of my mom. And she's right here in the back seat of this car. I tried asking questions yesterday. I got nowhere quickly. But maybe I can find a creative way to get her to open up. Sasha may be my only hope.

The hotel we check in to is much nicer than I would have ever expected. The lobby has massive chandeliers scattered along every section of the ceiling. The marble flooring glistens and makes me feel like we're walking on glass. It's even got a massive red carpet that leads its way towards the elevators and the first floor of rooms.

"Are you sure I don't owe you any money for this?" I ask David again.

"I'm sure. It's all paid for by the people running this event. They even sent me a stipend to pay for the flight."

"Why didn't you fly?"

"Me and Scotty always wanted to do a cross country road trip. Besides, I'm glad we didn't fly. This trip would've been much shorter with you. I mean, I know things are weird right now, but I'm still glad I'm here with you. That part I wouldn't change for the world."

David's smile perks up for the first time today. I envy his optimism in light of so much unknown.

Sasha walks back from the gift shop. "When can we go dress shopping?"

I pause for a moment. David clears his throat before speaking. "I don't think—"

"Twenty minutes," I interrupt David.

He shoots me a glare I'm pretending to not notice. We both know dress shopping is at the very bottom of our priorities. But I need a little time alone with Sasha. She may be more likely to open up with David not around.

Together, Sasha and I quickly hash out a plan to put our stuff up in our room, grab a snack, and then head out to find dresses. David wants to say something, but he also sees how excited Sasha is to go dress shopping with me.

I'm glancing at my phone when I hear the elevator ding. Then I hear the shock in David's voice.

"Angela! What the fuck!"

Everyone's mouths drop to the floor—except for Sasha. "That'll be one dollar!" she beams. Her hand is held out while the awkward encounter debilitates my ability to produce a coherent thought, or word.

"Pay up, David. Come on," Sasha begs, sounding more impatient.

David's sister awkwardly steps around some strangers to get through the elevator doors. But her eyes are only on one person. And it's not myself or David.

"Are you…her?" Angela asks, looking confused.

"Who are you?" Sasha retorts.

Angela chuckles nervously, clearly at a loss.

"This is my twin sister," David chimes in.

"Right, and this is my twin sister," I say, putting my arm around Sasha. "We met for the first time yesterday. Maybe you and David should go chat. He can get you up to speed. We were going to head out to buy dresses for tonight."

I try to scurry away, but Angela grabs my shoulder. "Wait, wait, wait. What's going on here?"

David lightly places his hand on Angela's shoulder. "It's okay, Ang. Ellie's right. Let's go take a seat and chat."

We start walking away until Angela gets our attention. "Wait! Are you two ladies…okay?"

Angela's words catch me off guard. I barely know her. And she doesn't even know who my sister is, let alone her name. Yet, she's looking at us with such concern.

Then, out of nowhere, she lunges towards me. My whole-body spasms to her touch. It's the most unexpected, yet welcome gesture. Her hug over my body is like a blanket of empathy. It coats my soul with the warmth and security I desperately need—and all from the person I'd least expect.

I doubt David's told her much about the last twenty-four hours. Especially since doing so would involve her in knowing something illegal. But she clearly knows this trip has not gone to plan. She should be caring about him—not me. But here she is, hugging me. And all I can do, all I can feel, is the need to hold on and hug her tighter.

"Thanks," I whisper as she steps back.

She looks down at Sasha. "Pardon my manners. I'm Angela. David's twin sister. You must be *Sasha*."

My whole body is suddenly tingling with adrenalin. It was the sound of my sister's name—said as if Angela and Sasha have known each other for years. I look at David, seeing his mouth drop to the floor and his face go pale. Even his eyes are bugging out. It's then I realize something impossible. Something nonsensical. His sister somehow, some way, already knows about Sasha.

"Nice to meet you, Angela. Now…" Sasha pauses to give another fake clearing of her throat. "Can you have your brother pay his debts to me? He owes me a dollar for his dirty mouth."

Angela chuckles. "You heard the lady, David. Pay up. You pay this beautiful young woman her money."

Sasha blushes while David hands over his dollar. "Let's all meet back in our room in a couple hours," David suggests with a nod to his sister. "Me and Angela need to talk in private."

Sasha and I head up to our room. She's having a conversation with me, but I can barely follow. I'm at a loss over so many things. The first being why Angela's here. Secondly, why was she looking at me and Sasha like she knew we were in danger? And most importantly, how did she know my sister's name?

Chapter Eighteen

David

"I'm sorry, Ang. I can't tell you. It's for your own safety."

"If you're not safe, then I don't care. Come on, please," Angela begs.

I shake my head while Angela gives me a look of exasperation.

"I think I know what's going on, David. Can you at least tell me without…you know…telling me."

Angela scoots closer to me. Her arm comes around me. She huddles her head down to mine as we sit on the edge of the bed.

"David, is that really Ellie's sister?"

I give a gentle nod yes.

"Okay. Then it makes sense," she says with a look of certainty.

"What makes sense?"

"Look what I found." Angela hands over a red notebook from her purse.

"What is this?" I ask.

"It's Mom's journal. Dad had me clean out the attic the other day. There are things written in there that you and Ellie need to know about."

"What?"

"David, I haven't read it all, but it turns out that Mom was very close friends with Leah Merkowitz. There's quite a bit written about how mom helped Leah with her depression. It sounded really bad. Leah was having hallucinations and—"

"Wait a second!" I interrupt. "You said Ellie's mom was hallucinating. What do you mean?"

"Well, you can read it all in the journal. But Leah kept dreaming about a little girl. Sometimes Mom would be with her, and she'd tell her about seeing this girl in her mind. Then, one day, Leah told mom she found birth records for another daughter. A girl named Sasha. There aren't many journal entries after that. Her last journal entry was really close to the time when Mom…you know…"

Angela's thoughts trail off to Mom's passing. My mind joins her. I interlock my hands behind my head. Every thought floating around is a bad one.

"David, how does Ellie's mom not know she has a daughter for so long? And how does Ellie not know she has a sister?"

Angela's question hangs stagnantly in the air. We're at an impasse because there's still things I don't fully understand. And she can't know about the illegal things going on.

"Fine." Angela huffs out a raspy breath of frustration. "Don't tell me. I'll just go ask—"

"Stop!" I shout while grabbing her wrist. "You're not going up there. Give them some time together. They just met yesterday. Let them build trust with each other. Maybe Ellie can learn things from Sasha. Besides, we both know her dad is the culprit in all of this. And I don't know all the details. But I'm not making you an accomplice by knowing about something illegal. It only complicates things. Just trust me."

"Then let me help you," she pleads. "Even if it's something small. What can I do?"

The begging tone in her voice was so desperate and loving.
I look into her eyes seeing the heartache. The weight behind
my eyes suddenly feels unbearable. My throat closes up. I can
barely whimper out the words.

"I…don't…know."

Angela's hug swallows me whole. She's clinging onto me
as I cry the weight of the world out of me. She tells me it's
going to be okay. The more she says it, the more I will my
heart to believe it. But it's so hard. It's hard because I love
Ellie more than I love myself. That, I know without
equivocation. I think about her pain, feel her sadness, and it
somehow becomes mine to drudge in. And I can no longer
suppress these feelings, especially as my sister squeezes them
out of me.

Then I feel it, the wetness on my shirt collar. It's Angela's
tears, bearing the weight of my emotions. My hopeless
thoughts suddenly become succinct.

My sister is feeling the deepest levels of my pain. But it's
the way love works. We share the hurt. Because while she may
not know everything, she knows enough. She knows I'm
hurting, *badly*. And while neither of us has an answer, at least
we've had each other since birth. It's a blessing I can't ever
take for granted. And it's a blessing that was deprived of Sasha
and Ellie.

Angela and I spend the next couple hours in her hotel room.
We comb through Mom's journal by reading it aloud to each
other. We're blown away by how often Leah Merkowitz is
mentioned in her writing. There's genuine concern for her
welfare.

It's heartwarming to read how their friendship blossomed
over the years. But reading about Mom's giving nature
towards Leah is no surprise to us. As a mom she was always
attentive to our needs. She loved showering us with affection
and showing us true kindness. It could be a kiss on the head,
lending a helping hand to a stranger, a smile showing how
proud she was, or a hug that felt like it could break your ribs.

We didn't get near enough time with her. It's why reading her journal feels like a part of her is still living on.

The journal covers the last two years of Mom's life. It would take hours to go through all of it. And only some of it has anything to do with Leah Merkowitz, but there's enough on Ellie's mom that makes us wonder about their friendship.

We learn how they both struggled with their Jewish identity. Leah even struggled with her own sexual identity and felt comfortable enough to confide in mom. There's also a lot written about how Leah dealt with so much verbal abuse from Joshua. Mom encouraged her to leave but recounts how Leah felt trapped.

Eventually, we read about the dreams and hallucinations that Leah told Mom about. She had visions of a young girl that we now know is Sasha. I'm intrigued by what she writes even though it doesn't sound anything like the night terrors Ellie experiences. And Mom, being the hippie she always was, writes about supporting Leah. It would have been easy for her to think that Leah was going crazy or losing her mind. But she encouraged Leah to embrace her visions and write about her dreams—not bury them away and deny their validity. She wanted Leah to see it as trusting her intuition. Her hope was that it would one day give her friend the courage to leave Joshua for good.

The final two journal entries recall the day Leah showed mom the birth records for a girl named Sasha Shalom Merkowitz. Mom encouraged Leah to go find her. And the next day Leah was gone. In her last journal entry Mom wrote about how sad she was that Leah left, but she was also happy for her. Two days later, our mom, Maya Cohen, was killed in a car accident.

"But I don't get it. Why would she leave Ellie with that monster for a dad?" Angela asks.

"I don't know. Her mom didn't sound like a bad person. Maybe she thought taking Ellie with her would put her in danger."

"There's more going on, David," Angela says, her brow furrowing with concern.

"What do you mean?"

"Joshua put their house up for sale yesterday. Why would he do that? And does Ellie even know he was trying to sell their home?"

"No—I mean, I don't think so. I don't even think they've talked once since we left Phoenix. The day she got in the car with me is the same day he flew somewhere. But she doesn't even know where he went. He wouldn't tell her."

I want to tell her more, but I hesitate. She can't know what just went down with the aunt and uncle. Then the alarm on Angela's phone goes off.

"What's that for?" I ask.

"I need to get ready. What? Why are you looking at me like that?" she asks with an annoying tone.

All I can do is shake my head and groan. "I don't want to go anymore. This scholarship ceremony just feels less and less important."

"Don't say that, David! The day you were nominated, me and Dad booked two surprise plane tickets. Way before all this shit with Ellie and her family. I want to be there whether you win or lose. *The Tree House* means a lot to me," Angela pauses, placing her hand over her heart. "It means a lot to you, too. It would mean the most to Ellie if you ever let her read it. Besides, we both know that book is written for her. And I know you wouldn't mind seeing Ellie in a lavish dress tonight. Come on now, who's it going to hurt if we all get dressed up and watch you walk across that stage a winner?"

I mockingly chuckle at her confidence. Then a thought occurs to me. "Wait, did you say you and Dad had a plane ticket. Did Dad come?"

"No. He's just not well enough. But when I reminded him this morning about your ceremony, he wrote this note for you."

Angela hands over a white envelope. I look at her, feeling confused. "Should I open it now, or later?"

"He didn't say. But I don't see the harm in opening it now. But scram. I need to get ready. And so do you. You look like shit," she says with a taunting crooked smile.

I'm about to shut her door when she calls out. "Wait, David!"

"What's up?"

"Are you and Ellie, like, um…how do I say this?" Angela pauses to bite down on her bottom lip.

"What? Just say it."

"What are you and Ellie? I mean…when this trip is over. Have you two talked about it?"

I don't have an answer. The truth is I'm just trying to get through today.

"I don't know," I finally admit. "All I know is she's the one I want to be with. And I know I'm too young to know. But right now…I just know. And I don't see that changing…*ever*."

"What does she like?"

"Poems."

Angela's smile becomes full. "Aaahhh! You've written her poems?"

"Yeah, just one. But I'm going to get going."

I head back to my room, smiling on the inside at my sister's reaction. She was so touched.

It's funny how that word left my mouth like a reflex. "*Poems.*" I didn't even have to think about it. The look in Ellie's eyes when she read my poem at Cadillac Ranch is the kind of awestruck look that'll never leave my memory. She's never looked as happy as she was in that moment.

I get back to my room, realizing I don't have a key. All I hear is commotion and cackling. I'm surprised they sound so happy-go-lucky given everything that's gone down in the last twenty-four hours. Nevertheless, I'm relieved Ellie and Sasha are enjoying each other's company.

I knock twice. Sasha pokes only part of her head out. I can tell her hair is being done up.

"What? Can't you see we're a couple princesses getting ready for the ball?" she jokes in a playful tone.

"I uh, I just need my bag so I can get ready downstairs. It's a black duffel bag."

"Wait right there." The door stays cracked open as Sasha gets my bag. Then it goes flying through the door and into the adjacent wall like it was shot out of a cannon. The door shuts as Ellie hollers, "Thirty more minutes!"

While heading down to the hotel lobby bathroom, I feel the heavy weight of my father's note in my pocket. I was going to read it later tonight, but Angela said I could read it whenever.

I open it up seeing a short Post-it note from my dad that's stuck to an old, wilted-looking envelope.

You'll do great tonight. Don't forget that I'm proud of you no matter what. And I love you so much! By the way, Angela said that I found this letter the other day. I don't remember finding it, but it's written for you. Enjoy!

Love,
Dad

The envelope under the Post-it note has my name written on it. The handwriting is identical to my mom's penmanship.

Dear my sweetest David,

Today you were born into the world a five-pound, seven-ounce, healthy baby boy. I've never felt more grateful to be alive than I am today. Seeing you and your sister come into this world is a true miracle. It's also the inspiration behind this letter. It may seem odd that I'm writing a letter to you and your sister on the day you were born. But it's something my mom did and it's a tradition I want to continue. I don't know yet when I'll share this letter with you, but when the time is right, my hope is this letter finds you.

Your name is that of the hero that defeated Goliath. It's fitting given the courage you've already shown me. You see, today it took you almost two minutes to find your first breath of life. Your sister was already taken into another room, crying up a storm. But you joined my world in complete silence. It was the longest, scariest, 120 seconds of my life. You see, my breath stopped with yours. All I could faintly hear was the work of doctors and nurses trying to resuscitate you. Then, you finally cried the most beautiful sound a parent could ever dream of. And it was in that exact moment I knew you had a different kind of fight in you.

Your greatest gift to this world will be the perseverance in your mind. You will become a mentally strong man full of compassion for everyone. You'll live a long life full of doing kindness and good in the world.

I'm crying as I write this letter because I can already see it so vividly in my mind. Your beauty. Your brightness. A doting brother to Angela. A son that makes us proud, shining his natural light into the world. This is YOU! And you'll never give up on anything. You'll do what you discovered on the day you were born—to find your next breath—and keep on breathing. Everything else will be guided by God's grace and my love. Because a mom's love for her baby boy never dies. Not for a second. It breathes on forever. Remember that. Breathe on my love.

Love always,
Mom

Chapter Nineteen

Ellie

"Don't cry. Don't cry. Please don't cry." I keep quietly pleading the words to my reflection.

The panic sets in. The tears well up to the edge. I don't know how to properly reapply my makeup if my eyes become a waterfall. And ever since I heard David come into our room, it has felt inevitable. To make matters worse, I can only hide in the bathroom for so long.

Not recognizing my own reflection is hard. It's still me staring back. I know that. But the lavish red dress with the slight V cut near my breasts is not me. The ruffled design on the hem of my skirt that stops an inch above my knees to show off my legs is also not me. But then again…*who am I*?

I take a couple more deep breaths to try and really see the person staring back at me in the mirror. My breasts are lush, full, and extra perky despite my wiry bra being so uncomfortable. Even my legs look long and shapely on my five-foot-tall body. There may be bits of cellulite and thickness in areas I'm not fond of. But they're being shown for the first time. And in this dress, with these heels, I don't look too bad.

It's odd to feel this way again. My mind ebbs and flows from feeling deeply insecure and then to feeling beautiful again. There's never an in between. It was always a daydream to wonder what I'd look like in overly revealing clothes. Now I'm wearing heels, makeup, styled hair, and an outfit that I can't fully recognize myself in.

"Are you coming out?" Sasha hollers for the second time. "Ellie! You okay in there?"

My floundering emotions have my throat locked up. Then I hear David and her talking. They're concerned. I shouldn't be surprised. I've been in here questioning my life choices for the past fifteen minutes as I hopelessly try to suck in the tears.

It's just odd to feel this way. Everything going on in my world and with my family should be the crux of my emotions. But it's a couple hours of dress shopping and worrying about my looks that has me falling apart. It makes me feel so irrational.

There's another couple knocks on the door. These were quieter. "Ellie, let me in," Sasha demands with a loud whisper.

I unlock the door and quickly shut it when Sasha walks in.

"You okay, sis?"

Sis!

Oh my! I love the way Sasha says that one word. It's like an instant bright light of hope to my darkness. She says it with such proudness and admiration. She's been calling me sis ever since we went dress shopping. The word is wonderful to hear, but it still puts a bit of ache in my own smile.

There it is again, that mix of happiness and profound sadness. But there's justification in my ebbing and flowing emotions. After all, I've been deprived of a mother and a sister for most of my life.

Sasha's concerned look drags on as she waits for me to say something. But now I'm shocked by something else. I can't believe how stunning she looks in her purple apron dress.

I blot under my eyes as the tears slowly spill over. "I'm sorry. I just really like when you call me that. And you look so…*absolutely…gorgeous*!"

"I know," she replies with sassy confidence.

I giggle while blotting my eyes once more. "I'm sorry. I'm not used to wearing these types of clothes. It's forbidden in my culture. I mean, I look pretty in the mirror. But I want to feel pretty, too. It's like impostor syndrome, you know, not knowing who you are. Does that make sense?"

Sasha's eyes glaze over. She seems completely lost in her own thoughts. Then it hits me like a ton of bricks. *Theresa Hunt!*

"Yeah, I uh…I know exactly what you mean," she finally admits.

I want to dig into her for more details about this other part of her life. But as I watch her eyes go deeper into the mirror, my chest starts to ache. I know the look she's giving her reflection because I was just there, drowning in my own insecurities. I've *lived* in that reflection for a good part of my life—especially after losing my hair.

"You look amazing, Sasha. This outfit. Your hair. You are a stunning young woman."

I run my hand along her upper back, but she's a statue—unmoved by my compliments—numb to my touch. There may only be one way to get through to her.

My gaze goes to the mirror as I slowly undo my wig. When it comes off, I hug it to my chest and slowly take in Sasha's response.

I watch as the first tear rolls down Sasha's cheek. Then her hand caresses my cheek until it slowly glides up to the top of my head. She glides her hand along my bare skin with a look of wonderment.

"Just like Mom," she whispers.

"Really?"

"Yeah. Mom said the last of her hair fell out shortly after leaving you. She talked about you all the time. She missed you so much, Ellie. We both missed you."

My throat locks up. The tears pour out of me. I can barely speak the next words. "I love you…*soooo much!*"

We share a long hug. The kind that feels like it can go on forever. It's the most important hug of my life. The relief of knowing that my mother suffered because she missed me strikes a chord in the deepest parts of me. It was always my hope that she missed me. But more than anything, I wanted her to just love me. And now, with Sasha's words still resonating in my chest, I know that it was more than just missing me. My mom truly loved me.

We eventually walk out of the bathroom because David's ceremony is starting soon. I feel so much lighter on the inside. David's adjusting his tie in the mirror. It looks like he's having trouble, so I head over to help him.

I start adjusting his tie but it's hard to concentrate. He looks so delicious in this navy-blue suit. Furthermore, I feel his lustful stare blanketing over every part of me. The moment is pure intimacy without words.

I want to tell him how handsome he looks. How I appreciate him not saying anything about my dress—letting his eyes do all the complimenting. But I don't know how to verbalize anything after my moment with Sasha.

Angela walks in while I'm putting the finishing touches on his tie and picking off the last bits of lint from his blazer. After paying us all compliments, she offers to take Sasha down to the lobby while we finish up.

The second the door shuts, I'm on his lips. The harmony and rhythm of the kiss is every perfect feeling we've been starving for.

"What are you thinking about?" he asks, his lips still inches from mine.

My stomach flutters to his question. Every perfect memory comes rushing into me at once as I softly whisper four words. *"Last night. The tent."*

"Me, too." His mouth goes to my neck, trailing kisses up and down. I feel his warm breath breathing in my scent as I moan. Then I trail my lips along his neck with soft, wet kisses—just the way he likes it. I desperately want to relive last night. But we need to get going.

I'm getting ready to head out the door when David grabs my hand.

"Wait, Ellie."

I sit next to him on the edge of the bed. His whole demeanor quickly becomes reticent.

"How was dress shopping?"

He's asking me about dress shopping, but I know there's a deeper meaning to his question.

"It was good, but kind of hard, too," I admit. "But Sasha made it fun. She's so interesting."

"Interesting?"

"Yeah. She's like me with her emotions being a roller coaster. One second, she's talking my ear off and giving me fashion advice. The next second, she's quiet and mumbling one-word answers. And when I tried asking about mom or Sariah and John, she gave me nothing. But I can't blame her. She's understandably fragile right now. But maybe she'll open up when she's ready."

"I'm just glad you guys have each other. I was thinking earlier how hard it would be to not have Angela in my life. I just don't know how you're navigating all of this. But just know I'm here for you," David says, reaching for my hand.

His gentle squeeze and the way his other hand glides along my wrist helps me relax a little.

"Hey, I need to tell you something." David clears his throat, scooting closer to my side. "Angela told me that your dad put your house up for sale. Did you have any idea he was thinking of doing that?"

"What?"

"Yeah, she said the for-sale sign went up yesterday. Have you even heard from your dad since you last saw him at the airport?"

"No. And I'm not calling him. I'm not going home either. I don't care if I have to emancipate myself. I mean, I'm an adult now. It's my choice to live where I want to live, right? I just don't want to see him…*ever again*."

David's expression becomes stoic and unmoved by my words. "I know, Ellie. I won't allow you to be near that man. And I'm not leaving your side. We're in this together. And I will always keep you safe from him…no matter what."

David's eyes light up with a fiery intensity. Then his hands cradle my cheeks. He leans his lips down to the top of my forehead. He holds his lips there, kissing me over and over again.

I whimper a little when he takes his last kiss and leans back to star gaze into my eyes. The gleam in his green eyes is almost hypnotic. He has so many emotions circulating behind those eyes. But it's the stress in his face that gets to me. Here he is at his final destination, being honored for his passion in writing. This is his moment. But all he's worried about is me.

"Hey, can we just enjoy tonight?" I say, trying to put on a brave face. "This is your special day. We'll figure out the rest as we go. What do you say?"

He gives me a half smile. "I'll try," he says with a tentative nod.

The event is much more lavish than I ever thought. It takes place in a grand ballroom with hundreds of priceless chandeliers and large murals full of exquisite contemporary art. It has me relieved that we went dress shopping. Otherwise, I would've stuck out like a sore thumb.

The ceremony kicks off shortly after I walk David to the stage and give him a goodbye kiss. He takes a seat next to the nine other nominees as the ceremony begins.

David's name is the second one to be announced. We cheer loudly even though it's just the three of us. The excitement from Angela quickly turns into tears. The way she looks at her twin brother with such adoration has me crying happy tears as well.

The feelings of elation are short-lived. I suddenly feel nails digging into my forearm. I look at Sasha, seeing the deer in headlights look on her face. She's terrified by something.

"Sasha, are you okay? Sasha!" I shake her shoulder to try and snap her out of it. But she's a statue.

I glance over to where her eyes are taking her. It's an exit near the front right of the stage. It's at the opposite end of the ballroom. I can't see what's freaking her out.

"Is she okay?" Angela whispers over my shoulder.

"I don't know."

I grab her cheeks to try and pull her eyes closer to mine. But she's still catatonic.

"What is it, sis?" I beg.

Her lips start to quiver. "That's…him…That's…him," she keeps repeating the words, looking lost in her own terror.

"Who? Who?" I let out a huff of frustration because I'm getting nowhere. I turn to Angela. "We'll be right back."

Angela insists on coming, but I let her know we'll only be gone a couple of minutes. We shuffle our way up the aisle to the exit. My hand is draped around her as we bypass the main women's restroom for the private family bathroom.

When the door shuts behind me, she's still mumbling the same words.

"That's him."

"Who? What? Tell me something!" I shout, shaking her shoulders.

She flinches, letting out a raspy gasp for air. Her eyes finally peer intently into mine. Then she says something even more terrifying.

"The man that wants to hurt Mom. The man with white strings."

My body feels paralyzed. Her words keep echoing in my head. But the echo slowly fades to a loud, inescapable ringing noise. I look towards the ceiling, feeling helpless as everything in the bathroom begins to spin. All I feel is the panic in Sasha's face and the haunting terror in her words.

"That's him. That's him," she mutters again, looking even more lifeless behind those blue eyes.

I can't take it anymore. I grab Sasha's shoulders, shaking her violently. "Stop it! Stop saying that! You're scaring me! Please! Stop it!"

The door behind me squeaks open. Sasha's eyes widen with fear. "No!" she screams with blood-curdling terror.

I try turning around, but my whole body is swallowed from behind. Large arms strangle over me like a straitjacket. I try to squirm free as a cloth goes over my mouth. All I hear is Sasha's helpless screams until my limbs go limp.

The last thing I see is a man lunging at Sasha. He's wearing a blue uniform with a Greek symbol on it. Then I slowly fall backwards. My world goes quiet. My body feels weightless as my vision fades from fluorescent lights to darkness.

Chapter Twenty

David

The pressure in my chest builds. Each passing second makes my hands clammier. Even my stomach is nauseous.

I try hugging my arms around myself to fight through the dark cloud of anxiety. But it's no hope. The feeling of something being seriously wrong is inescapable. And I'm stuck on this stupid stage.

They'd be back by now if it were just a trip to the bathroom. I saw the panic in Ellie and Sasha, and I even felt it.

Angela's waving her hands in the crowd to get my attention. But it still feels like my world is spinning. The keynote speaker is talking on stage, but at this point, the background noise is deafening. Meanwhile, I'm trying so hard to focus on Angela's lips.

Everything's okay. Be right back.

She keeps mouthing the words *be right back.* Then, she hastily makes her way up the aisle and out of the ballroom. I know she's going to check on them. But I feel the desperate need to go with her. The speaker continues to give brief bios on the other nominees. Then he pauses for applause. But he speaks slowly. *Oh fuck!* Why does it feel like he's talking in slow motion? Announce the fucking winner already!

My eyes begin to fixate on only two things: the large digital clock on the back wall and the exit doors below it. These are the same doors all three ladies went out of, only to not return. But the clock moves at an agonizing pace, and the doors refuse to open back up.

There are only two people left for this jackass to introduce. Then he'll announce the winner. *I can do this. I can wait a little bit longer.* It's words I keep repeating in my head. But I don't believe them—not one bit.

The need to trust my intuition becomes everything. This moment is something my sister and Ellie wouldn't miss. It means just as much to them as it does to me. But to me, all that matters is those three girls. Their welfare is everything. They are *my purpose.*

Do it now!

I quickly rush off stage, going through the side exit. As the door closes behind me, I hear the speaker announce: "And the winner is…"

I make my way around to the back exit doors. But I don't see anyone in this section of the lobby. Then I notice the closest women's bathroom. I rush in, but there's not a single soul. On my way out, I see the family bathroom across from me. I bust through the door, and my heart sinks.

My sister is lying face down in a pool of blood. I frantically rush to her side. Blood trickles down her face as she tries to get up.

"Ang! Ang! You okay?"

She shakes her head while blinking rapidly. Then she grabs my shirt collar, pulling me violently into her face. "I saw them! I saw them! They were wearing blue uniforms!" she shrieks.

"What! Who?"

Angela shakes her head, trying to catch her breath between words. "The ones who took…Ellie and Sasha…They had them on stretchers—" Angela is out of breath, hacking up a lung as she tries to find her words.

I try to encourage her. "You're okay. Just breathe."

I watch as her breathing slows. Then her eyes grow wider. It's a fear I've never seen in her before.

"They're not EMTs! They're not EMTs!" she screams.

I rip off my dress shirt and press it into the side of her head. Angela keeps pleading to me that they're not EMTs. All I can do is nod. The meaning in her words isn't processing.

The idea of someone disguising themselves as EMTs and taking the people I love is insanity. But Angela wouldn't make this up.

Then, I slowly start to feel it. My insides simmer with volatility. It's something so volcanic with rage. But it's morphing into an even stronger emotion: *revenge!*

It's unlike anything I've ever felt because it has me paralyzed. I'm completely numb—unsure of what to do, and how to unleash the madness I feel.

Angela's shaking me violently. "David! Are you hearing me? You need to do something!"

She's trying to get up but is writhing in pain. I notice the large black and blue bruise on her knee.

"Can you walk?"

"No. They hit me with a tire iron," Angela cries.

Pull your shit together, David!

My eyes and hands begin assessing Angela. She has a single gash above her temple and a large bruise on her knee that's already swelling up. She's hurt badly, but I slowly realize she'll be okay.

I dial 911 and give my location. Then I hand the phone to Angela as I pull her arm around my shoulder. I drag her out of the bathroom and sit her up on the closest bench.

"I have to go, Ang. Are you sure you're okay?"

"Yes! I'll be fine! Go!" she shouts, then goes back to talking to the 911 operator.

I sprint out the nearest exit and find myself frantically searching for something. But there's nothing. Only a parking lot full of cars and a few people living in their own peaceful worlds. There's no sign of the girls and no men in blue uniforms or an ambulance of any kind.

I circle my gaze around the parking lot so many times I'm stumbling from dizziness. Nothing looks out of the ordinary. Then, my tunnel vision narrows onto a large white van. It's driving slowly as it merges onto the main road several hundred yards away. The windows have an extra dark tint. It looks big enough to hold stretchers in the back.

There's no time to second guess. I sprint to my car. The second my keys go into the ignition, I feel a cold metal firmly press into the back of my head. I freeze, remembering only one time what the tip of a gun feels like against my head.

"Don't fucking move," the eerily calm, deep-sounding voice demands.

My hands instinctively go in the air. I glance at where my rear-view mirror should be. It's been torn off, leaving me blind to the man holding a gun to my head. All I feel is the gun digging harder into my skin. Then it clicks. My eyes squint shut, and I wait for everything to end.

Seconds pass, and I'm still waiting to die. All I feel is utter despair. My life is full of so much unsaid. My future is full of so much yet to be done. Only one thought becomes succinct in my mind. It's a voice, sounding like my mom, sending tingles up my spine—telling me as she did in my letter: *Breathe on, my love.*

"Drive, sheygetz," the voice demands in a cold tone. "One wrong move, and I blow your fucking brains out."

I hesitate for a moment, knowing only one person in this world who's ever called me sheygetz. Then, the gun slams into the side of my face. "Fucking drive! Now!" the man screams.

I pull out blindly, already feeling the blood trickle down the side of my head. I follow his directions to merge onto the interstate. Then I notice the first cop car and ambulance driving past me.

The tip of his gun stays firmly pressed on the back of my head. All I hear next is the coldness in his voice.

"I have sheygetz…" he pauses, listening to the person on the other line. "After exit twelve. Okay. Be there in a few."

I still don't know where we're heading. I'm too afraid to ask and get pistol-whipped a second time. All I know is we're heading out of the city. But the longer we drive, the more I wonder if I should try talking to this guy. Besides, he's not going to shoot me or hit me while I'm driving and risk a fiery crash.

"Where are we going?"

No response. The gun digs deeper into my head. But I no longer give a fuck.

"You're not going to shoot me."

"Perhaps…not yet, at least." I feel him leaning closer to my ear. "But it's coming," he whispers.

"Where's Ellie and Sasha?"

"Just drive, sheygetz!" he demands.

"Why are you calling me that?"

He doesn't respond. It's not Ellie's father. I know that much. But why would he use a word only her father has ever called me?

All I know is his accent is thick. Furthermore, he pronounces the word sheygetz with an eerily similar Israeli accent to Ellie's father.

"Turn here," he barks.

"Where?"

"Dirt road, sheygetz!" he screams.

I slam on the brakes and fishtail down a dirt road. His gun comes off my head, and for a split second, I glance behind me, seeing a medical mask over his face and a blue uniform. Then, his gun strikes across my face. My foot slams into the brake as we come to a grinding halt.

I take another pistol whip to the head. And then another one causes white spots in my vision. The blood pours down my face like an open faucet. I'm dazed, but I don't lose consciousness. All I know is my vision is completely gone in one eye.

I feel his body reach across my face. That's when my one good eye notices something. It's the collection of strings hanging at his waistband. They briefly brush across the side of my face as he puts the car in park.

"Fuck! Fuck! Fuck!" he keeps shouting. "You had one job, sheygetz!"

He grabs a large clump of my hair and slams my face into the steering wheel, pinning the tip of his gun into the side of my head. The pressure digs into my scalp. I hear the gun click again—like a loud echo to the last sound I'll ever hear. And I wait for the end…again.

The sound of his phone startles us. "What!" he pauses with a huff of frustration. "I know, I'm here. I'm just a mile up the dirt road. But I'm done with this motherfucker. I don't trust him to get me there in one piece."

There's a long pause. I can hear the person on the phone raising their voice. Then my captor lets out a loud grunt. "Fine!" he shouts.

"Do it, pussy!"

"Nope. Not yet. You're lucky, sheygetz." I feel the warmth of his breath on my ear as he whispers, "He wants to do the honors."

"Who?"

"You know who."

The gun lifts off my head. It quickly collides into my skull, sending me back into the darkness.

Chapter Twenty-One

David

The desperate screams awaken me to an inescapable blindness. My entire body feels bound. My hands, knees, and ankles have me squirming like a fish out of water. But the worst part is the blindfold over my eyes. It makes me helpless to distant screams echoing from a place that feels far and out of reach.

I try screaming for help, but I can't. Instead, I'm coughing uncontrollably. My mouth spews a grotesque mix of what feels like saliva, dirt, and blood.

The screams for *help* grow louder until I hear a door shut, drowning out the noise.

"Ellie! Sasha!" I scream back, hoping they'll hear me.

Footsteps approach as I try to catch my breath. Then I feel it knock all the air out of me. A kick so hard to the gut I hear my ribs snapping like thin twigs. I roll away from the person, writhing in agony. I keep rolling over my body until my back slams into something hard. It feels like a huge rock, maybe even a boulder. My hands feel along it in search of a sharp edge or something that will allow me to get free.

The footsteps approach as the panic sets in. I'm rubbing into the boulder, trying desperately to find a sharp spot, but my progress feels hopeless.

Dirt is kicked into my face.

"Show me your face! You fucking coward!" I scream, hearing my voice echo.

"As you wish," the familiar voice whispers.

A large hand grabs a clump of my hair, pulling me up until I sit against the boulder. This time, my hands are shimmied underneath the rock, giving me a bit of leverage to pull up and try to break what feel like thick zip ties.

Every ounce of strength in my body goes to my arms. I try sliding along the rock for friction. I try pulling up to snap it. But everything further strangles my wrists, sapping away what bits of energy I have left.

My blindfold is ripped off. Everything is blurry, and I can't see anything from my right eye. I keep blinking until what's left of my vision slowly clears up.

Standing before me is a forest of endless trees. I feel distant from civilization. A large white van to my left is stopped on a deep downslope that leads into a body of water. I crane my head to the right, seeing my car. Then, a figure steps around me.

The man has a towering presence over my hunched-over, battered body. His blue uniform is identical to the man who kidnapped me. But his thick salt and pepper beard sprouting out from behind his medical mask gives him away.

He slowly pulls off his mask, flashing a smirk and insidious glare that has my insides raging. It's Ellie's father. He looks the same with his large, almond-shaped, brown eyes. But knowing what I know of him now, I can only see the evil that he *is*. This is a man with no regard for human life. It's a man so deeply troubled that the roots of his evil reach a level of Hell I only hope he visits one day.

"What did I tell you, David?" Joshua asks, taking a step closer to me. Then he leans down onto one knee.

"Fuck you!"

His maniacal giggle sets me off. I spit on him like it's a reflex. My bloody saliva sprays over his entire face, triggering his fist to crack right across my jaw.

My vision becomes a spattering of white dots. The ringing noise in my ear slowly fades. I feel my chin slumping onto my collarbone as his hand tilts my chin up to meet his eyes.

Inches in front of me is the blurry face of Ellie's father, still lathered in my bloody mucous. He leans closer to whisper in my ear.

"Like I said, if you have anything to do with Ellie, I'd hurt you. But now you've done worse. You've both done worse. And I'm going to kill you. You and that pathetic retard excuse of a daughter. But first, I'll have you watch. I want you to suffer…*like I have.*"

He stands up, smirking down at me, before spitting on my face. Then I watch as he walks over to the other man in a blue uniform. He's still wearing his medical mask. It makes it almost impossible to hear what they're saying.

All I can do is observe. They're both armed with guns. The one Joshua has is at his hip in a holster. The other man still has his gun in his hand. His finger lies over the trigger as I notice how his gun still has my blood on it from the multiple pistol whips.

My arms continue to press, pull, and rub against the underlip of the rock. But it feels like I'm getting nowhere other than cutting off my blood supply. It makes me want to give up. After all, even if I break free, they'll shoot me. A gunshot to the head may be the quickest way to go. But it would also save me from watching the people I love die before my very eyes.

Then, I hear my mother's voice. It's like an echo bouncing out of a well. But this time, her words feel more desperate, repeating in my head as if she were whispering the words inches from my ears.

"Bloody strings. Keep pulling."

My eyes narrow in on the person talking to Joshua, and that's when I notice his waistband. But what I notice most is the tzitzit that hangs off his uniform. These little strings of fabric stained red from my blood transfix me.

My mom's voice gets louder in my head. *"Bloody strings! Keep pulling!"*

A shot of adrenalin courses through my body as it hits me. This is no ordinary collection of words. It's suddenly familiar. I've heard it before, but in a different voice—Ellie's voice—from a night terror a few days ago.

I shimmy my body into the rock, finding a new spot to pull on the zip ties bound to my wrist—every bit of strength in my body multiplies. The slack begins to loosen until it quietly pops. For a split second, my hands fly out from under the rock. Joshua glances over his shoulder as I quickly shove them back under the boulder. His stare lingers a bit longer. I'm pretending to be bound, but I'm free, or at least my hands are. My legs are still bound at my knees and ankles by thick zip ties.

Despite the freedom in my arms, I still feel defenseless. My only hope is lunging at them in close range. That will likely get me nowhere, but I have no choice. Time is running out.

I try taunting them. "Come on, you pussies! Come over here and fucking kill me!"

Joshua chuckles under his breath. "Go do it." He gives the other man a nod. Then Joshua starts walking in my direction.

I continue to egg him on. "That's it. Come on, you pussy!"

"Do it, Elias!" Joshua shouts as he crouches at my side. *Fuck!* His gun is holstered on the side furthest from my reach.

Joshua grabs a thick wad of my hair. Then he yanks my line of vision towards the van. The man who must be Elias opens the back doors and my heart crumbles.

Ellie and Sasha are bound to their gurneys, lying on their backs with gags in their mouths. They're trying to squirm free, but their ankles and wrists are cuffed to the metal railing. There are even straps over their chest and hips to make their escape even more impossible.

The worst part is now they can both see me. I'm bloodied and battered in ways I could only imagine, judging by their panicked faces.

"I hope they're good swimmers. You ready to…*watch*," Joshua whispers.

His words are like a thousand stab wounds in my chest. I wonder how a man, a father, and a human being could be so horrid. And he wants me to take the brunt of the suffering, watching Ellie and her sister drown in shackles while I wait for my turn to die. It's like living through a slow-suffering death three times over, but infinitely worse.

"Why?" I mutter hopelessly under my breath.

His hand digs tighter into my scalp, turning my head to see the crazed look on his face. It's void of any remorse. I only see one thing in those bulging brown eyes: *insanity!*

"It started with your bitch of a mother," he says, gritting his teeth. "She befriended Leah and turned her into some rebellious lesbian—a lesbian cunt who couldn't even bear me a normal child. And when Leah found out about Sasha, she told your mom and left me no choice. I had to deal with her in case she had a loudmouth. You're lucky your dad has no memory."

My body convulses. I vomit a mix of bile and blood, gagging to try and breathe. Each breath I find is cut short by the panic, the anger, and the pain I want to inflict on Joshua.

"Joshua! Someone's coming!" Elias shouts, jogging over to hunch down by us.

"Who?"

"I don't know. It's a black SUV. Could it be—"

"No!" Joshua tersely interrupts. "Just get down!"

I try craning my head around to see the approaching car until Joshua grabs me by the back of my neck. He slams the side of my face into the dirt, using his knee to pin me down. The two of them hunch down closer to me, using the boulder for cover with their guns drawn.

I'm still able to keep my hands bound behind my back and underneath the rock. But now I'm feeling different parts underneath the rock. Specifically, it's the smoothness of a round rock impaled into the ground with a jagged edge. I feel around the rock as my mom's voice returns to me.

"Keep digging. Swing when you see strings. Keep digging. Swing when you see strings."

I do as the voice tells me. My nails dig vigorously around the rock until I feel it coming loose from the dirt. It may only be one rock, but it's no longer just *a* rock. It's *my mom's rock*.

Slowly but surely, the rock comes loose from the dirt. My hand palms tightly around it, feeling the heavy girth and sharp indentations. Then I hear what sounds like squeaking brakes. The hum of an engine stays idle while I wait for my opening.

"Who the fuck is this? The windows are too dark," Elias whispers.

The car shuts off. A door squeaks open. Their guns click. Then I watch, feeling mesmerized by what I'm seeing. The strings saturated in my blood hang down from their waistbands—floating inches above my eyes.

The exploding gunshot has Joshua on his back and blood splattering into my eyes. He quickly gets up, running towards the van while Elias opens fire. I see my opening, swinging my rock into the side of Elias's head. The crack between my rock and his skull has him flat on his back. I army crawl to him as he lies motionless, groaning with blood pouring out of his ear. Then I rise to my knees, raise my rock in the air, and pound it repeatedly into his face.

I'm no longer myself amidst the gunfire ringing in my ears. I keep striking him. The blood spatters everywhere with each dent I put in his face. And I can't stop. I won't stop. This is my moment that's bigger than validation or rage. It's the unequivocal need for *revenge*.

Eventually, I collapse from exhaustion, unable to catch my breath. My body rolls on its side right next to his dead, mangled-looking face. The gunfire that's been nonstop comes to a sudden halt.

"Sasha! Ellie!" a voice screams. I don't recognize the voice. I only know that it sounds like a woman.

I carefully peer over the large boulder that's still shielding me. I see a woman wearing all black with bleach-blonde hair past her shoulders. She has a gun at her side as she's breathing heavily against the rear bumper of her black SUV. I have no clue who she is, why she's here, or how she knows Sasha and Ellie. All I know is her vehicle is littered with bullets and broken glass. And she's groaning in pain while her bloodied hand is held over her collarbone.

"Sasha! Ellie! I'm coming, sweethearts!" she yells, coming around the car with her gun pointing at the van.

"They're in the back! Don't shoot! Don't shoot!" I plead.

She quickly turns her gun on me. My hands go up in a panic. "I'm with Ellie and Sasha! I swear! Please don't shoot!"

The woman's face morphs into confusion. Her eyes squint. "Are you…Dav*ee*d? Dav*ee*d…Cohen?"

My heart stops at the sound of my name. The long "e" pronunciation sounds so familiar: "Dav*ee*d." It's the Ellie way of saying my name. But this woman is not Ellie, even though everything about her face is suddenly a carbon copy of Ellie. The oceanic blue eyes. The plump lips. Round face. Even the expression of confusion and how her eyebrows furrow is 100 percent her, like a mirror to *my* Eliana Merkowitz.

I nod slowly, shocked by everything I don't understand. This woman knows my name. She knows Ellie and Sasha. And she's alive, in front of me, gun drawn, and sacrificing her life for these two people.

A thud by the van snaps me back to reality. My heart stops as the van slowly rolls into the water at a forty-five-degree angle.

My eyes turn towards Elias's dead body. I frantically search his pockets, finding a set of keys and a Swiss army knife. I quickly cut through the zip ties at my knees and ankles.

Then I grab his gun and sprint to the van as it quickly fills with water. The whole hood and most of the front seat are already submerged.

The blonde-haired woman frantically tries to pry the back doors open as I pull up to her side. The water rushes up to my knees as I help her. But it won't budge. Then I try the keys, but nothing works.

"Get back!" the woman shouts, firing round after round at the door handle until she's out of bullets.

Together, we pry the doors open as the water fills inside. Ellie is no longer moving. Sasha is frantic, screaming through her gagged mouth with terror. She's closest to me, so I quickly pull out the keys. The first two keys don't work. Then, the third and final key clicks, releasing the restraints on her wrist. I make quick work of the cuffs on her ankles and undo the straps.

"Give me the keys!" the woman screams as the water rises to my waist.

I toss them to her so she can undo Ellie. Then, I remove the rubber ball gagged in Sasha's mouth. But the second I do it, her eyes widen.

"Behind you!"

My world goes black in an instant. The will to live floats out of me. All that remains is a cold wetness over my body and the taste of metal. I feel my spirit drifting further away into a deeper darkness with no way out. And all I know, all I feel, is my worst fear—*my death.*

Chapter Twenty-Two

Ellie

I'm floating above my own self, watching the water rush in. It's helpless from this perspective—looking down on my lifeless body, chained to a gurney, waiting to die. My sister hopelessly flails her body, but there's no escaping.

Sasha must have more fight in her than I do. She didn't hyperventilate and pass out like me. Maybe she believes in some type of superhero miracle. But miracles are not reality— at least not this one. The evil of drowning alive is the only thing real in this moment.

The loud pops go off. One after the other, creating bullet sized holes of light. The back door slowly opens with a burst of brightness. It's a blonde-haired woman and my superhero. *My David!*

The sensation and sound of my heart pounding in my head amplifies. I look down upon my dying self as the water rises, wanting to scream but I can't find my voice.

Why am I letting myself drown? Wake up, Ellie!

David's trying to free Sasha until his keys finally work. He tosses the keys to the blonde woman. That's when I see her face for the first time. The hair I don't recognize, but the face I know.

I watch on in astonishment, still not believing the woman is real. She frantically works to undo my cuffs as the water rises to my body. The moment the water touches my skin, I can feel it tingling through me from above.

Then, a perilous figure slowly rises out of the water. I scream from above, but no one hears me. There's no time to react. David is knocked out from behind with a large metal object. His unconscious body slumps into the water. He looks dead. He's not fully submerged yet, but the water is rising quickly to his chest.

The beating in my head gets louder. It's blocking out the screams as I watch my father. He holds the tire iron up, ready to swing at the woman in blonde hair. She's frantically pulling me up by my armpits, trying to shield me as my father wades towards both of us.

Wake up! Wake up! Wake up!

The woman retreats backwards, clinging to my unconscious body until there's nowhere left to go. The water reaches our chins. She cradles me in her arms, shielding me from evil as she whispers her final words into my ear: *"My baby girl."*

The tire iron swings at her head, colliding right as the bang goes off. Then another three shots fire off into my father's back. He collapses. The smoke lifts off the gun and blows into Sasha's face. She's frozen with her gun still drawn at the floating corpse that *was* her father.

There's so much to see from above the chaos. My sister looking like a statue, catatonic in her stupor as three bodies float around her. But the only thing more surprising than death are the two wigs floating side by side. My eyes are mesmerized by the touching of these wigs amidst the mayhem of so much death. One is red and the other is blonde with bits of blood mixed in. They stay floating next to each other as the water rises to the ceiling.

Then my vision flashes like a bolt of lightning. Hands grab hold of me, pulling me out of the wet darkness. I'm suddenly coughing up water, gasping for air.

"Ellie, we have to go!" Sasha screams, pulling me towards the crack of light in the back of the van. But I can't leave yet.

I watch two bodies floating next to each other. One is David, the boy I will forever love and die for. The other is the woman who shielded her body in front of mine. She was struck in the head, knocking her blonde wig off right as my dad got shot. She sacrificed her life for mine in a way that suddenly feels maternal. But it's more than just a feeling. It's the truth I witnessed with my own eyes. The truth I heard with my own ears. But more than anything, it's the feeling of knowing. It was my mom, shielding me—*her baby girl.*

It's a helpless decision. I can't drag both bodies out of the water, so I follow my instincts and grab David. The second I lift his chin up, he starts coughing up water and blood. He's barely alive, moaning in agony. I hook my arm underneath his armpits and begin treading my way out. Sasha stays close at my side. The closer we get to the rear exit doors, the stronger the current of water hits us. I'm lagging behind. It's sucking me back into the van until Sasha pushes me and David out. I use every last bit of energy to tread my way out of the van as we swim into the light.

The three of us barely make it to dry land as I collapse from exhaustion. I look back as the roof of the van completely disappears underwater. After catching my breath, it hits me. The two people remaining in the van are my parents.

My father deserved the bullets in his back and the desolate darkness of drowning. But my mom deserves none of this. And the woman in the blonde wig is undoubtedly my mom. The intuition in my gut is no longer just a feeling. And it's the reason I must do something drastic.

I head back into the water, my feet slowly sloshing forward. I turn to Sasha once I'm knee deep. "Run! And don't stop! Keep running until you find help! Go!"

Sasha staggers to her feet and does as she's told—already screaming for help as she makes a mad sprint down a dirt road. I turn back to the water, noticing how dark and murky it looks. It's foreboding the way the water ripples outward without a sound. Meanwhile, my thoughts are screaming at me to stay back.

Let her go.

I never felt like I had my real mom growing up. But by the time I came into this world, my father had already stolen her from me. Perhaps when she found out about Sasha's existence, she also found a piece of herself. The piece she'd been missing.

My teeth chatter uncontrollably as the doubt creeps in. I turn around to look at David. He's flat on his back, but I can tell he's breathing. I don't know if he's fully conscious. If he was, I wonder what he'd tell me.

He might say I'm being reckless to think about going in for her. But would he mean it? Deep down I know what he'd do if this was his mom buried in the lake. He'd dive in without blinking an eye. That's because he knows the pain of growing up without a mom. And he knows if he had the chance to save her, even a small one, *he would*. Because at the end of the day, courage is selfless.

David didn't have to bring me with him and help me find my family. He didn't have to help me through years of night terrors. But he did all those things, and more. And just as he's shown me courage, so has my mom.

It's in this moment I realize that courage, true courage, has always been close to me. Even on days when I couldn't see it or feel it. But it's more than just a closeness—it's *within me*.

My gaze goes back to the water. I barely nod my head, feeling a swell of emotion ignite my insides. But it's no longer fear. It's strength. I feel it in my lungs, expanding to calmer breaths. Then my throat opens up. I take a long suck in for air, and dive into the darkness.

The cold shocks me at first, but the adrenalin keeps me going. I swim deeper into the blindness, unable to see a thing. I have a sliver of hope that I can get to her. Then an even smaller sliver of hope that I'm strong enough to pull her out.

My fingers jam into metal. I feel around until I find the small opening to swim inside. My arms flail in every direction, trying to feel for anything. But nothing I touch feels like her. The panic sets in. The need to breathe has my chest aching. It's not until I touch the baldness of her head that I know I've found her.

I desperately swim my way out, towing the lifeless body of my mom. My heart aches, compressing on my lungs with immense pressure. The need for air is life or death as I make my way through the back door. My vision lights up for a brief second until her body tugs, almost slipping from my grasp. Using what little strength is left in my body, I pull on my mom. But she's stuck on something, and it feels immoveable.

The strength melts away as I hopelessly tug on her dead body. My tugs become weaker. My vision becomes a spattering of white dots. The need to breathe wins. My clenching mouth floods with water, choking me into convulsions.

I should've known. This was a suicide mission the second I dove in. But as I drift from the living, I feel one last bit of hope—an unforeseen hand gripping over mine.

Chapter Twenty-Three

David

The French doors swing open. I'm instantly blinded by the flash of lights. My body floats weightlessly as doors keep opening—one after the other. Each time the light intensifies, overwhelming my senses. .

Then I suddenly stop floating. My vision becomes crystal clear. I'm behind two women on rocking chairs. Their hair shimmers in the sun as a light breeze kicks up. I'm mesmerized by the way their hair flutters into one another. It creates a mosaic mix of blonde and honey brown.

They're holding hands as they look onto a sunset of cotton candy clouds. It's a sight to see amongst the thousands of Palo Verde blossoms. They float around them like little flakes of desert snow.

I know this place!

The women are conversing, but I can't hear anything. Then their faces turn towards each other at the same time, flashing illuminating smiles. The weight of the world sinks beneath my chest.

I know them!

It's the smiling faces of Leah Merkowitz and my mom, Maya Cohen. I can't decide what's more mesmerizing. Is it seeing my mom look so young and vibrant? Is it the happiness on their faces? The occasional laughs they share. Or is it just the way their hands intertwine so effortlessly?

I watch as my mom's fingers keep tracing along the outer part of Leah's hand. Leah squeezes back with little pulses of affection I feel deep in my belly.

I want to get closer. I want to hear what they're saying—to see more of their faces and better understand their shared happiness. But I'm stuck in this spiritual hypnosis, observing them from behind as they live in an aura of contentment.

Then my vision flashes to more blinding light. I feel myself floating away faster than before. But it's more than the wind in my face and the speed I feel. There's a turbulence jolting my body around until I feel my head snap back.

I'm suddenly in the back seat of our old car. I feel the speed kick up with my mom looking frantic behind the steering wheel. The rain is pelting the car so hard I can't hear anything, let alone see through our windshield. All I can feel is the panic in my mom's chest. The clamminess in her hands. I can even feel her strangle hold over the steering wheel. Everything in this moment is utter terror.

The sound of a honking horn draws my attention out the window. A blue Ford Expedition pulls even with us, driving erratically and almost side swiping us. The passenger window comes down on the Expedition, but I can barely hear or see anything because of the rain. The only instinct I have is to escape. I need to get out of this car *now*! But I'm stuck, unable to move an inch of my own body as both cars speed up.

Amongst the chaos, I suddenly notice my mother's eyes. The fear in them is terrifying. But the fear I see is much more than being chased. The greater fear I see, and feel, is being found.

Her hazel eyes are mesmerizing until I realize they're still staring directly at me through the mirror. Time feels frozen.

The realization hits. I know where I am. It's the moment I've feared most. My mom, Maya Cohen, is at the impasse in her life—the last moments amongst the living.

The Expedition side swipes us. Our car barely clips the guardrail and goes airborne. The limbs connected to my mom flail every direction like a rag doll. As for me, I'm suddenly impenetrable—unmoved, unharmed, and only an observer to a world where gravity no longer exists.

It's like living in a swirling kaleidoscope of horror. I watch on in the irony of silence. The car keeps rolling over itself. Her body repeatedly pummels off the steel frame as it crunches into her. Then tree limbs crash through the windows and the car comes to a grinding halt. It takes a moment for the smoke to clear. Then my eyes see the nightmare firsthand.

There's mangled and twisted metal around my mom. The car is a sea of glass. I can only see part of her head, but the parts I see have turned her honey brown hair into red. I watch on in despair as the blood seeps out of her lifeless body, dripping like an open faucet out of her head.

Then I'm floating again until I find myself in the front seat of the car. Her face is sandwiched into the dashboard. She's facing me, but she already looks so pale and lifeless. It makes me relieved that her death was likely quick, until her eyes suddenly flash open.

She's alive!

The breath barely passes through her lips. It's straining, like she's suffocating. The more she fights for each breath, the more it evolves into a desperate wheeze. It's clear she only has a few extra breaths, a few extra beats, and a few extra seconds of living.

I wonder if she can see me. If she could, she'd know I'm screaming on the inside for her to fight harder, live a little bit longer—or at least talk to me. I'm desperate for the goodbye I never got. But my voice is rendered useless. Instead, I watch the life slowly drain out of her face.

It's not her fault. She doesn't know how hard it'll be. Nor does she understand how quickly Dad's health will decline. Or how Angela will be in a dark place for such a long time. And mostly, how we'll never truly heal from her death—especially me.

I want to be strong, but I'm scared. I'm also confused. Why would God put me here? Have I not lived through enough suffering? Is there a reason I must watch my mother suffer through her last breaths? There can't be any rational justification.

But then, out of nowhere, I see it. Her lips twitch the slightest bit. It feels different—like she's no longer searching for final breaths. She's finding her final words.

"Find breath...Swim to them...Save them."

Mom's faintly spoken words fade to deafening silence. I watch her entire body become still. Her eyes stay open, but her spirit has left her. She's gone.

I stare at her lifeless face. The despair I feel somehow hurts more than the twelve-year-old boy learning of his mom's death.

My mind begins to wonder. There's something about these final words. She's telling me to swim to them, but I don't know how. What can I do if I'm already dead.

Am I dead?

The sound of crunching glass startles me. Someone's approaching the car.

"Ow, fuck!" a man's voice groans.

I watch as a long arm reaches into the car. It comes through an opening no bigger than a sewer gutter. It's the only way in as the rest of the steel frame has crunched into itself.

The hand is bloody. It feels around the car, searching. Then the person wedges the side of their body further into the vehicle. I still can't see their face—only the top of their shoulder and down to their waist is visible.

It's clearly a man's body. But something seems so odd. If it were a good Samaritan, they'd probably call out to the person. They'd talk to them to try and keep them conscious.

Then the hand touches my mom's face, feeling around until it rests over her neck. Two fingers trace slowly up the neck until it comes to a stop.

For a moment, I feel a glimmer of hope. They're checking for a pulse. Maybe this person can pull her out and revive her. But it's a hopeless thought. After all, this isn't how the story goes. The police officer said my mom wasn't found until hours later, and by then there was nothing that could be done.

Then my hope fades in an instant. It's the white strings visible by the person's waistband. I watch the tzitzit turn red from the pool of blood they're now soaking in. But it's not this person's own blood, it's my mom's blood.

This individual is not making sure my mom is alive. He's making sure she's dead. And I know who this person is—without a shred of doubt.

White light blinds me again. My body shoots up to a sitting position as I'm gasping for air and coughing up a lung. After vomiting, I pull my battered body up to stand. I'm barely able to balance on my own legs. There's no one around the lake and the van is gone. It's eerily quiet until I hear the voice come back to me.

"Find breath…Swim to them…Save them."

The echo in my head gets louder. My mom keeps repeating the same seven words. But I'm too hurt—too weak. I can barely even breathe.

Her voice never relents. It keeps coming back. But the more I hear her voice, the more I feel the transformation inside my body—like a spiritual awakening. It's as if her words are now a part of *me*, willing the strength back into me.

A tingling sensation slowly spreads over my body—until I feel it all over, living inside me as the pain distinguishes itself. Then her voice becomes desperate, whimpering a final plea.

"Find breath. Swim to them. Save the ones we both love."

I dive into the murky water, swimming blindly. My world gets darker, but I'm not alone. I feel Mom with me, guiding me all the way.

Chapter Twenty-Four

Ellie

One Week Later

"It's okay. It's okay." I keep whispering the same words to David. All I hear back is the melody of beeping noises.

Those beeping sounds have been the soundtrack to my life lately. Ever since arriving at this hospital and receiving treatment, I've been making my rounds from room to room. Each one has their distinct rhythm of noises and different nurses. Even the smells have their own unique mix of cleaning products and antiseptics.

My mom is still in a coma. I haven't been with her as often because Sasha's been keeping her company. It's still looking very bleak for her. Her brain was deprived of oxygen for almost ten minutes while she was under water.

Sasha told me everything that happened after I went back in to save my mom. Shortly after running to find help, she found two good Samaritans in a matter of minutes. They called 911 and drove back to where the van rolled into the lake. Upon arriving, David had just pulled me out of the lake and was doing CPR on me. After I coughed up water, he went back in again.

I don't ever remember waking up by the lake. But Sasha said David went back in without any hesitation or a second thought. Then he came out of the water a minute later with our mom.

The good Samaritans began performing CPR on my mom as David collapsed. Apparently, it was more than just exhaustion. He fell unconscious from what's being called a brain aneurysm. This was the result of the severe head trauma and blood loss inflicted by my father and his accomplice. He hasn't woken up since collapsing by the lake.

I look around David's hospital room noticing so many things. It's like a spider web of wires, tubes, IVs, and medical equipment. He's like a bionic man that's been put back together.

Today he's been squirming around every few minutes. It gives me hope every time I see him move. Even his closed eyelids have been shaking ever so slightly, like he's lost in a dream world.

It's been a full week now since the incident. Along with the aneurysm, the doctors have classified his injury with the acronym TBI. It stands for Traumatic Brain Injury. They weren't sure he'd make it early on, but with each new day the reports are more and more promising.

The main piece of good news is they've dramatically reduced the swelling in his brain. His vitals have stabilized and improved with each new day. And they're noticing brain activity that they weren't seeing early on. But until he wakes up, no one knows what kind of shape he'll truly be in.

The doctors have been very apprehensive to my questions. And I get it. They don't want to get my hopes up because they can't make any promises. But the way I see it, there's no option. David must wake up. He *will* come back to me.

The soft knocking sound startles me. "Hey," Angela whispers.

"Come on in. Do you need any help?"

"No, I got it." Angela drags a chair over to sit next to me. It takes a bit longer than usual because she has a huge brace on her knee. Then I cringe a little seeing the wound by her temple as she takes a seat next to me.

She gives me a funny look. "Are you comfortable like that?"

"Um, I'm fine. Why?"

"Your poor back?"

I realize my posture is hunched against the bed railing. It's the only way I can reach over from a seated position to grab hold of his hand. I've been holding on to him for every second I've been allowed to be with him. It's the only antidote to the pain and guilt that keeps gnawing at me.

"He needs my touch. I know it's helping," I say, gliding my hand up and down his arm.

"What about you?"

"What about me?"

"We all need touch, Ellie."

Angela's smile perks up on one side. She slowly gets up to walk behind me. I start to get up until she pushes me down by my shoulders.

"Stay."

Her hands dig into my upper back. My first thought is telling her she doesn't have to do this. But I can't. The tension inside is finally melting away.

"Thank you." I take a loud sigh of relief, realizing how exhausted I truly am.

I've been internalizing this tension for a whole week now. I can't help it. I want to be strong for everyone. I want to maintain the belief that everyone will be okay. But sometimes, I can't do it. My mind imagines a life without David and my mom. Then everything inside me becomes numb and lifeless, again. It's a dark depressing cycle that I can't shake away.

"Can I tell you a story about David?" Angela asks.

"Sure."

I hear Angela take a deep breath. On the exhale I can sense the strain and tension.

"When our mom passed, he took care of me and Dad."

"How so?"

"He did…well…he did…*everything*." Angela stops massaging. I hear a sniffle.

I turn around as she's wiping her eyes. She tries forcing a hopeful smile across her face, but it only makes the pressure in my chest even more suffocating.

"I'm so sorry, Angela. For this situation. For everything."

"You don't need to be sorry. You've done so much for David over the years. More than you'll ever know. And the things you did, well…they trickled down to me."

"What do you mean?"

"I'm going to tell you a story," Angela says, sitting down and sliding closer to me. Her eyes gaze deep into mine. The intensity and conviction in those hazel eyes have me already tearing up as she grabs my hand.

"Ellie, Aprils have always been the hardest month. It's the anniversary when Mom died. And one day, about four years ago, I remember I couldn't even get out of bed. I was so sad. And David came up to my room. At first, he just sat down next to me…for hours, not saying a word—just being close to me. After a while he grabbed my hand and said something I'll never forget. He said…" Angela pauses, closing her eyes like she's searching for the memory. "He said 'it's okay to be sad today. Because tomorrow I'll still be here. And tomorrow means new hopes and possibilities.' He said you told him that one time. He was repeating your beautiful words."

I throw my body into Angela, hugging her with every bit of strength I have left in me. Then we cry together for a long time.

Our lasting embrace makes me feel like we've known each other our whole lives. But we haven't, and that hurts. I'm sad my father deprived me of friendships like this. Yet, the more I think about it, I know Angela well. David's been singing his sister's praises since the first day I met him. And now we're holding on to each other next to his hospital bed. And the tighter she squeezes, the tighter I squeeze back.

"I need to tell you something else," Angela says, sniffling as she slowly pulls out of our hug. I don't want to let go, but when I do, I notice her demeanor shift.

"What? What is it?"

"In case something happens, there's something else you need to know about David. A couple years ago he told me what really happened the night you two first met."

Angela takes a long pause, looking unsure if she should continue. But I don't understand her reticence. I remember the night we met, or at least I remember most of it.

I stare into my lap as I recall what happened. "He said I had a night terror. He brought me into his shed for the first time. I eventually woke up. And once I calmed down, we talked a little, and he walked me back to my house. He was real sweet to me. I think that was it."

I bring my gaze up to Angela, feeling confident in what I remember. But as I stare at her longer, I get a funny feeling fluttering around in my stomach.

"There's more," she whispers.

"What do you mean?"

Angela's face wilts. Her voice becomes faint and lifeless as she speaks. "You were like an angel that night. Ellie…he was two seconds away…*only two…God damn…seconds.*"

"What? I don't—"

"He was about to kill himself." Her eyes widen with disbelief. She holds her hand against her chest. I watch her throat go inward, like she's searching for her voice. But she still can't even believe her own words. And neither can I.

"I don't understand."

"Ellie, he told me he was two seconds away from pulling the trigger. He didn't want to live without Mom anymore. He was going to kill himself. But you showed up out of nowhere that night. He thinks…” Angela sighs. “I mean, he believes that our mom sent you that night…*to save his life.*”

My breath stops. My mouth falls open. The goosebumps tingle through every nerve ending in my body.

“But why?”

“You said something that night in the shed—during your night terror. That’s probably why you don’t remember it. It was something only me and David would know. You see, our nickname for our mom growing up was a mix of Hebrew and English. We called her Ima Bear—you know, like mama bear. And on that first night, in the middle of your night terror, in our shed, you kept saying… *‘Ima Bear sent me’*. David says you repeated those words at least a hundred times. Don’t you see, Ellie?” Angela’s voice fades away to a whimper. “You saved him…I mean, you and my mom together, *saved…my brother’s…life.*”

Angela swallows my body with another hug. I try matching her strength, but I can’t. I’m still processing what she just said. It’s so nonsensical, and yet, how else would I know to use those words if it wasn’t his mom speaking *through me*?

I tightly squeeze down on my eyelids, wishing they’d permanently stay shut. But it’s no use. The tears flow right out of me.

I’m trying. I’m trying so hard to keep it together and understand the enormity of what I’ve just learned. But I can’t. Because all I truly want is to trade places with David—give up my life for his. David’s life feels much more important than mine. And it’s killing me that he won’t wake up.

I feel Angela’s hot breath and lips pushing up to my ear. “That boy loves you. He loves you *hard.*”

Then, I feel Angela rising over me. I want to open my eyes, but seeing the heartbreak on her face would be too much. Until I feel it. The warmth of her lips gently pressing into the top of my forehead. And she holds the kiss in the most profound spot.

It's déjà vu to my first night in the hotel with David. The night he kissed me without my wig.

Chapter Twenty-Five

Ellie

One Week Later

I arrive back at the hospital in David's car. My mind is still in a daze. The steering wheel becomes a temporary pillow for my forehead. I close my eyes, needing a minute to collect myself before heading back in to be with David.

My meeting with Investigator Hollins was supposed to be a quick update on our legal situation. However, after an hour of what felt like interrogation and another hour of learning about more of my family's crazy, I'm emotionally spent.

The good news is I didn't buckle on certain parts of my story. I did as my aunt and uncle told me. I played dumb.

The story of visiting them in Pittsburgh and then bringing Sasha with me to the ceremony in New York is all Investigator Hollins knows as my reason for visiting them. Whether it was the right or wrong thing to do, I don't know. After all, they did lie to me about my mom being dead, or at least I think they did. They also lied to me about adopting Sasha from my mom.

But I think they did these things to keep me in the dark about anything illegal and to keep Sasha safe.

I learned many troubling things from that two-hour meeting. For one, the investigator told me more about Sasha's life growing up. She lived with seven different foster families. Never once was she with a family for more than two years. She was between families and living in a group home in many instances.

As for the foster parents my mom took her from, well, they were terrible people. They never even reported Sasha as missing, and now they're both in prison for fraud and racketeering. It only became a missing person's case when Child Protective Services did a routine wellness check to discover that Sasha was gone. At the time, Sasha was fourteen. I don't think she understood the enormity of it all. Perhaps she was just excited to be reunited with her real mom. I can only assume these things because I honestly don't know. She still refuses to disclose details about this period of her life, and I don't know what she's disclosed thus far to the investigator.

Investigator Hollins also informed me that he recently received a large package of incriminating evidence against my father. It came from an anonymous person. The evidence ties my dad to forged birth records and multiple instances of death threats made on my mom over a long period of time. Nothing can be proven at this point because my dad is dead, and my mom is in a coma. However, it further shines a light on how evil my dad was to my mom.

My dad's accomplice was also just identified. His name is Elias Kauffman. Apparently, he's my dad's cousin. Elias *was* a licensed Private Investigator. He lost his license about four years ago after my mom filed a suit against him for criminal threats, trespassing, aggravated assault, and stalking. He was never formally prosecuted but was fired from his job. Investigator Hollins believes my father continued to use him to keep tabs on my mom for years. He also believes my dad used his cousin's services to ensure my mom would never come back for me.

Neither myself or the investigator knows how everything came to a head a week ago at the lake. We may never know with Elias and my dad being dead. But one thing stands out amongst the troubling things I've learned today. I learned today that David was the person that killed Elias.

I know he only did it to save our lives, but I'm wondering how he'll be able to live with the trauma if he ever wakes up. I've already seen how it's affected Sasha. She can talk to me a little, but it's typically meaningless small talk.

The social workers assigned to her case at the hospital have been holding at least two counseling sessions a day with her. I don't know if she's opened up to them yet. I can only hope. Either way, it's going to be a long road for her.

A few days ago, the social worker told me that creating routines for her, even in the hospital, would be best for her. I've taken the advice by eating lunch with Sasha every day at the same time. We also go on short walks every day in the late morning and early afternoon. However, most of our time together is spent in silence. Sasha's still in no place to open up to me about how she's feeling or anything resembling what she's been through.

When Sasha and I aren't together, I'm with David, and she's at Mom's bedside. Sasha has this unwavering belief that Mom will wake up anytime now. I want to tell her she may never wake up, but she seems convinced otherwise.

The elevator doors slowly open as I make my routine walk down to David's room. The closer I get, the more I hear a new mix of voices. I slowly peek in to see Angela and Scotty chatting at David's bedside. Angela had told me he'd be flying in today. It makes me happy that David's best friend is here. And even though he's still unconscious, I like the idea of David hearing a new, familiar voice in his room.

I decide to let them be and go see my mom for now. The elevator up to the eighth floor has my stomach racing a little quicker than usual. I walk past the usual nurses and staff at the front desk. They're usually cordial, but for some reason I don't even get a hi. Then, I notice two nurses staring at me with their hands over their mouths. After turning into my mom's room, I freeze at the doorway. Two sets of eyes are glancing back at me from inside the room.

My heart stops. I can't breathe. Nor can I move any part of my body. What I'm seeing cannot be real. It's my mom. But not the same unconscious person I've been visiting for the past few days.

"She's awake!" Sasha exclaims, smiling up at me with glistening eyes.

My hands grab hold of the doorway but slip from my grasp. All I see next are the lights on the ceiling, followed by a loud thud in my head.

The clamminess and chills take a couple of minutes to go away. The nurse gives me more Gatorade and crackers.

"You okay, sweetie?" the nurse asks.

I nod my head. My eyes gaze down the long hallway of hospital rooms. I'm trying to get my bearings. After a deep swallow, I find my voice.

"I'm sorry. I'm not feeling like myself."

"Well, you just fainted. That's all. Give yourself a minute to collect yourself. Other than some low blood pressure and dehydration, you're doing fine."

Her smile lifts higher on her face. She glides her hands along both of my shoulders. The comfort it provides is so needed given my hallucination and complete lapse from reality.

I start laughing for no good reason.

"What's so funny?" the nurse asks, looking befuddled.

"I'm uh, I'm just a mess," I tell her shaking my head. "I'm hallucinating again. But I swear I just saw my mom smiling at me. She looked good as new, minus the bandage on her head. I don't know what's going on with me." I bow my head down, shaking it in defeat.

The nurse's hands grab hold of my cheeks. Her eyes widen as her stare penetrates me.

"Hun, your mom is awake. She woke up about an hour ago. We've been trying to reach you. She's awake and talking to us. It's a miracle. You didn't imagine this. She's right around the corner here. When you're ready, you can head on in there."

I glance at the doorway. It looks so familiar, like the one I was just standing in and staring at Sasha and Mom. But that was a dream. I'm sure of it.

"Excuse me?"

"She's awake," the nurse persists.

"So I can—"

"Ellie!" Sasha impatiently shouts. "Get your ass in here and love up on your mom!"

I start laughing. Or am I crying? The conflicting emotions make no sense as they pour out of me.

The nurse helps me stand. I shuffle my feet into the doorway. Once I peer inside, I see Sasha standing up—her hand clings to Mom as their smiles light up the room. There are no words for this moment. They just look at me as though they've won a grand prize. But the prize is not me. It's *them*. It's always been these two souls in my life. One I never knew existed. The other was supposed to never come back into my life. But they're here. And as I put my arms around them both, I finally feel it. The love of a family. A real family. *My family!*

Chapter Twenty-Six

Ellie

Sasha's hand glides along my back. It's so soothing to feel her touch. We take a short break from questions to just stare at each other. There's nothing we can say that isn't already showing in the gratitude of our smiles.

Mom needs a couple of minutes to catch her breath. The last twenty minutes have been spent bombarding her with questions—well, to be fair, it's mainly been Sasha. I'm eager to get my turn and ask more substantive questions, but perhaps those questions will come in due time.

Mom's nurses begin retaking her vitals. Then, a third neurologist walks into the room. His words are a carbon copy of the previous two neurologists that spoke to her. They all throw the word miracle around because they have no other explanation for how she's recovered in the blink of an eye.

Sasha and I listen intently as her memory goes through another battery of tests and questions. There continue to be no issues with her cognitive functioning. The only challenge for her is her energy level.

It truly is a miracle. No one expected this. The last conversation I had with her doctor was yesterday. He talked about the prospects of her waking up in a vegetative state or never waking up at all. *"No brain activity."* Those were the words of two doctors only twenty-four hours ago.

Eventually, the hospital staff gives Mom a break. Once the last nurse leaves the room, Mom starts asking her own questions.

"How's the boy?" Her lips perk up into a hopeful smile. "The boy?"

"Yes, David Cohen? I saw him. Did he make it out?"

The ache in my chest is a reminder that David is still unconscious. It's also been over four hours since I was last at his bedside. It's the longest I've gone since being here.

"Um, he made it out, but he's hurt pretty bad. We're, uh, we're still waiting for him to wake up."

"But how? How did we make it out?"

I turn my head to look at Sasha. I'm on edge because of the haunting memories. But to my surprise, Sasha seems undeterred. And more than anything, she looks courageous.

I take my gaze back to Mom, feeling a stir of emotions in my chest. But what I see most are Mom's hazel eyes. They're like staring into a priceless painting where everything is immaculate—not a single flaw, just the perfect mix of honey and green.

"Sasha saved us. She saved your life. She saved all of our lives. She's the hero."

"No," Sasha chimes in. She leans her shoulder into me, resting her head against me. "We all saved your life, Mom. David, too."

Mom's eyes start to glisten with tears. We watch as they spill down her cheeks. I take a tissue and begin to wipe it away until she flinches.

"Please, don't. I want to feel my tears. I've spent too much of my life not feeling—or at least not knowing how to feel— not understanding why I am the way I am or why so many things were taken from me. But now I have you girls. And these tears…seeing you two together…these are the feelings I could only dream of ever having. If only Maya could be here.”

“Whose Maya?” Sasha asks.

The tears pour out a little faster after Sasha’s question. Mom closes her eyes like she’s lost in painful memories. Then she breathes out a shaky exhale as her eyes open back up.

“Sasha, sweetheart. When we have time, I’ll tell you all about her. But first, I need a moment with just Ellie. Can you give us a minute?”

Sasha hesitates. Then she nods and heads out of the room. When the door closes, I lean in to be closer to Mom. Her hand caresses along my cheek.

“Mom, I’m so—”

“Stop. Before you say anything, you need to hear me, Ellie.” She pauses for a moment to clear her throat. Then her head leans closer to me until our faces are just inches apart. “*I…am…so…sorry.*”

I lower my voice to match the tenderness in her tone. “It’s okay. You’re here now. That’s all that matters.”

“No. Listen to me. You need to know why I left. It was never my plan to be gone for six years. I mean, I know I wasn’t well for most of your life. And I’m so sorry for that. But when I found out Sasha existed, it woke something inside me—like a spark ignited.”

Mom begins telling her story. It’s everything my father spent years hiding from me. It was a long, arduous journey when she left to find Sasha. She always intended to come back for me once Sasha was found. However, she believes my dad was so ashamed of losing his wife and worried that all would be uncovered with his secret daughter that he completely lost his mind.

It also didn’t help that he had bipolar disorder. Mom recalls how he used to take medication to manage his erratic emotions. However, 12 years ago, she had a miscarriage. The miscarriage is when he stopped taking his medication regularly and became the disturbed, verbally abusive father I've always known.

When my mom left, she never once believed he'd be capable of the atrocities that would follow. The first thing he did was hire Elias to stalk my mom. The goal was to make sure Sasha always remained a secret and to keep my mom from ever coming back. If she did, my dad swore to her that he'd kill everyone.

She didn't believe him at first. But then she discovered in a threatening phone call one day that Maya Cohen, her neighbor, was killed in a car accident. My father admitted over the phone to causing that crash.

The threats from my father and Elias never relented. Mom even recalls one time being physically assaulted by Elias. She reported these things to the authorities but was not taken seriously. Apparently, her lifetime record of mental health issues led the authorities to not believe her. Instead, shortly after being assaulted, she recalls having a nervous breakdown. The nervous breakdown was partly due to running out of money and having no leads on where Sasha was living.

Mom stayed in a psychiatric hospital for the next two years. She believes my dad and Elias were responsible for keeping her there against her own will. She only got out because she escaped.

It was at this time she went to her sister for help. Sariah and John helped her obtain fake identification as well as a fake death certificate. She knew it would be the only way to find Sasha without our father ever finding out. And when she did find Sasha, she was living in a broken foster home. She didn't have time to see if she could adopt her because her living situation was so bad. That's why she was left with no choice but to take her and go on the run.

She lived with Sasha under the aliases Theresa and Samantha Hunt for the next two years. Life was never normal for them. My mom wore a blonde wig. She wore it as a form of disguise and because her hair was falling out due to the extreme stress she was under at the time. They never stayed in one place for longer than three months. They were always worried they'd be found. Mom also worried every single day for my well-being. And she worried that if Dad ever found out she was alive and living with Sasha, he or Elias would come for them and kill all of us.

So, instead of risking everyone's life, she secretly built a case against my father. She studied up on the law and gathered up years' worth of threatening text messages, voicemails, pictures of forged birth records, and any form of evidence that would indite my father. Her over-arching hope was if Leah Merkowitz couldn't convict my father for all the crimes he committed, then maybe Theresa Hunt could.

"But, wait. What about Aunt Sariah? She told me you were gone…*forever*. Those were her words. I thought you were dead. Why would she do that?"

"She was just following my orders because she hadn't heard from me in a while. You see, Joshua eventually found out what I was doing. He was coming for me and Sasha. That's why I left Sasha with her aunt and uncle for as long as I did. I knew they could keep her safe. And I needed more time to save up money and finish building my case against him. But then I received word from Sariah that they got arrested and that Sasha was headed to New York with you. And I knew with Elias's connections in law enforcement that they'd find you guys. But luckily, I got to you guys just in time."

My mind feels like it's living in a daze. Everything she's told me about her life sounds certifiably insane. But as I look into my mom's eyes, it's like staring into an entirely different person. This is not the withdrawn, depressed, heavily medicated parent I grew up with. This is a determined woman who found purpose. But there's still so much that makes no sense.

"But why did he hurt David's mom? Are you sure it was Dad?"

"Yes. Your dad hated Maya for many reasons. The fact that I told her about Sasha's existence just sent him over the edge. But it's not what he hated most about her. He hated that I fell in love with Maya. And I never would have left Maya if I knew she was in danger. I just didn't think he would ever try to hurt anyone."

I take in more of Mom's story. I learned how she and Maya started as neighbors who became close friends. Eventually, they fell in love over the years. She tells me how Maya Cohen always believed in her journey and how she never expected them to fall in love. It just slowly happened shortly after David's father began losing his memory.

It's ironic to hear about this part of my mom's life. After all, it's like our lives coalesced with the Cohen family at different times. We both fell deeply in love. But the woman she fell in love with can never be hers. All because of my father.

"Is David really going to be okay?" Mom asks.

I swallow the acidity in my throat to find my voice. "It's a Traumatic Brain Injury. They still don't know. But he's been improving over the last few days."

"That's good. And you like this boy?"

I emphatically nod while my eyes become a waterfall of tears. Mom wipes them away with her thumb and starts caressing my cheek.

"It's okay. He's going to be okay. I can feel it, sweetie."

She gives me a hopeful smile. I try raising my cheeks to smile back, but I can't. It feels like too many miracles to ask for in one day.

Eventually, Mom and I become too tired from all the digging up of memories. She invites me into her bed. The second I snuggle into her side, we're both out like a light.

"Ellie! Ellie!"

Sasha's words rattle around in my brain until I feel my body quickly sit up. Sasha's bobbing up and down at the doorway while I rub the grogginess out of my eyes.

"What is it?"

"He's awake! He's talking to his sister right now! It's David! Come on! I'll stay here with Mom! Go!"

I crawl out of the hospital bed and sprint to his room. My body feels like a live wire of electricity the whole way there. Then I pause right outside his door.

Angela's getting up from his bedside as I take one tentative step into the room. She moves out of the way so that David's unbandaged eye finds me. My entire body freezes at the sight of David's conscious body.

Angela walks up to me and puts her hand on my shoulder. "He's okay. It's just hard for him to talk." She pauses for a moment to lean closer to my ear. "He said something about a letter. But I don't know what he's talking about."

I'm still in shock but I'm able to barely nod my head. Angela gives my shoulder one last squeeze before giving us the room.

My walk to David's bedside feels like slow motion. Then I reach for his hand. The second we touch, I feel his strength go through me as he speaks slowly. "You…o-kay?"

"Yes, I'm fine. Everyone's fine," I say, feeling out of breath as I clear my throat. "My mom just woke up. You woke up. Two miracles in one day. Things couldn't be any better."

David nods and gives me a half smile. I wipe away the tears that just flood right back out of me.

"I read *The Tree House*. It was beautiful. I didn't know you wrote it for me."

David's mouth slowly lifts into a half smile. "Always…meant…for you."

I squeeze tighter through his hand. The harder I squeeze, the more I feel my heart becoming full again.

"Letter," he mutters.

"What letter?"

"First…night, ah!" His face morphs into a grimace of pain. I feel bad, but I don't know what he's talking about.

Then it hits me. My memory flashes back like a bolt of lightning to the first night in the hotel. The moment he wanted to tell me how beautiful I looked, but I wouldn't let him. I never read his letter.

After frantically digging the letter from my backpack, I hold the purple envelope up to his face. He nods to show his approval.

"You…need…to know." David pauses to clear the raspiness from his throat. "Read it…out loud."

"Okay."

My heart feels like an ignited stick of dynamite, ready to explode. I tear open the envelope and begin reading his letter aloud:

"Dear Ellie,

Today, you wore a dress for me. But maybe you didn't do it for me, or because it was my birthday. I hope you did it for your own reasons. Because you matter. You matter to me. And I see you. <u>I've always seen you!</u>

You see, your beauty has always felt the same to me. Wig or no wig. None of that matters to me. That's because beauty does not exist like we are trained to believe. You taught me that by just being your own kind and authentic self. And I believe we find people in our lives who redefine beauty so that it's no longer just a word. It becomes a feeling of need. And you, Ellie Merkowitz, are the person I need. I felt it on that first night in the shed. It's grown stronger with each day I've known you. And while life for both of us is full of uncertain tomorrows, I will, forever and always, CHOOSE YOU!

Forever yours,
David Cohen."

I stare in awe at his letter. That moment in the hotel room plays back in my mind as if I just lived it. I *felt feminine* for the first time since losing my hair that evening. I had just put on that pink and white floral dress. Then I walked out of the bathroom feeling like a different person—completely unsure of myself. But his green eyes were magnetic on me the whole time. He made me feel truly beautiful without ever uttering a single compliment.

In that moment, I remember wanting to recognize myself—*so badly!* I wanted to revel in the beauty and newfound femininity I felt because I couldn't believe it was me. And David wasn't allowed to say a word, but he shared his true feelings in this letter—*choosing me*!

The thought of everything he's done for me overtakes my emotions. I lean over the bed railing to hug him and fall apart in tears. His hands rub along my back, pulling me tighter against him. Then, I slowly tilt my eyes up to see his face. His lips twitch as he slowly utters four words I'll never forget.

"I…love…you…Ellie."

Epilogue

Ellie

Five Years Later

The wheels touch down, and my chest floods with relief. It's a weird feeling. The mix of jet lag, horniness, and elation to be back in Phoenix has me over the moon with excitement. The only challenge now is waiting at the back of the plane to be one of the last ones off.

I've just returned from my backpacking trip through Europe. Over the course of 10 days, I visited ten sites, including my favorite stops in Venice and Prague. It was always a dream of mine to explore the world after graduating from college, and I can't believe I just did it.

The slow-moving herd exiting the plane gives me time to reflect. These last five years have been full of ups and downs. But having David in my life has helped stabilize my foundation. We've been living together for the past three years. It was an adjustment initially, but now it's like living in the perfect dream. We still share late-night talks just like we

240

did in his shed. On other nights, we'll stay up late binge-watching TV shows and eating junk food. And most nights, we make love. But the best part is the blessing of falling asleep every single night in the arms of my best friend.

The other constant in my life is now I have a *real* family around me. Healing from everything I've been through would not be possible without their unwavering support. That's because my healing journey may always be an ongoing process. Every day is an ebb and flow of emotions that I'm still learning to circumnavigate. But having David in my life and my family close by gives me the hope that better tomorrows are always on the horizon.

As far as religious horizons go, I still don't know if my Jewish faith will be a part of my future. A part of me wants to rekindle that spiritual connection. David's even open to the idea of joining a less stringent reform temple. However, I'm still unsure. My father took so much away from that experience. It left scars in me that still feel years away from healing. But in spite of it all, I won't give up hope. Deep down I know, one day I'll find my *own* Jewish identity again.

Another significant change in my life is I no longer have night terrors. I haven't had one since that night at my aunt's house. I don't know why that is, but my theory is that having my mom back in my life and my father out of it has brought a sense of newfound peace. My other theory is that David's mom has something to do with it. Even though I have no memory of her existing in my dreams, her spirit has always felt close to me.

When I finally step into the aisle, I feel the butterflies coming back to life. I take a quick moment to glance at my phone to check my appearance. There's not a whole lot that needs adjusting. I typically only wear a small amount of makeup, if any at all. As for wigs, I'll typically only wear them on special occasions like tonight.

For now, I'm just my bald self. I've come to enjoy the freedom of existing in the world this way. I still get stares, but usually, it's just pity stares because people think I have cancer. But I'm nowhere near the realm of dying. How I feel is every bit the opposite of that word because I'm doing more than just living. I'm *thriving*.

It's taken a long time to get used to living this way, but now it's like blinking or breathing. This is just me. I am a bald woman with Alopecia. And if I'm not proudly showing it to the world, I'm wearing a cute bandanna or headscarf. However, having the freedom to be bald in public and private started only because of David. He says it's when I'm at my most beautiful and vulnerable. And it's bigger than David liking me in this way. It's become my way of showing how much I love my true self and the person I've become.

Once I'm out of the jetway, I make a mad sprint to the TSA line. The first thing I see is not his exquisitely gorgeous face, chiseled cheekbones, and smile that ignites my soul. It's the couple dozen white roses he's cradling into his chest with at least a half-dozen balloons. It makes me giggle how all of it silhouettes around his perfectly symmetrical jawline as his eyes search for me like a lost puppy. Then he sees me, and his body is mine again.

There are hugs we give to the people we love and hugs for the people we've missed. But it's the first embrace in an airport that encompasses every perfect feeling into one. And *this*, this hug, is everything I've been missing in my life.

I lean back through blurry, tear-filled eyes to see David's eyes glossing up as well. Then, time freezes all at once as our lips meld together in blissful harmony.

Our hands cling to one another in the center console. But my eyes are busy obsessing over the bulge in his jeans. It's his residual hard-on from the ten minutes we spent making out in the airport parking garage.

My eyes obsess over the part of him I want inside me. I can't help it. Ten days is the longest we've ever gone, and I know it's the only thing on his mind right now. And the longer my eyes linger and my mouth salivates, the more I realize I physically can't wait until we get home to our apartment.

I love every part of this man. Especially how he keeps flashing that smirk while batting his eyes at me; it's incredibly sexy. It's also the invitation I need as my hand slowly creeps up his thigh.

"Contain yourself, my love," he says with a taunting smile.

"I don't think I can."

"Really? We're only twenty minutes from home." He shoots me a couple of side-eyed looks as his smile perks up higher and higher. It's effortless the way that smile sends my hormones to the point of no return.

My hands go to the zipper of his jeans. I don't care if we're still on the freeway. The second the zipper is down, I've already pulled out his girth and swallowed him whole. His moans are loud and guttural. I'm so thankful to taste him as I've fantasized about this moment for the last 14 hours. But I'm more grateful for the illegal dark tint he recently put on the windows of his Yukon for this exact reason.

Our sex life has slowly become more adventurous over the years. It helps that we've both learned how to communicate our needs, desires, and fantasies. It didn't come easy to me at first, but I'm no longer afraid to let David know how I want to be touched. And he reciprocates the same to me with the utmost respect.

When the car clicks into park, I pull my drooling mouth off his cock to taste his lips.

"Take your panties off! Now!"

His demanding tone has my insides dripping with desire. I glance around, seeing nothing but overhanging branches from the tree we're now under. I decide just to remove all my clothes, and he follows suit. I want every last bit of his closeness.

The second I straddle his hips, I feel the warmth of his cock stretching my insides. I slowly ride deeper into him while cradling his face in my hands and getting lost in the desire in his eyes.

I love being on top and in control. When it starts feeling too good, I slow down a little to tease him. Then I pull up so the tip of his cock barely teases along my lips and wet bundle of nerves. His eyes are now begging to fill my insides as I rub my fingers along my clit. And then I can't wait any longer. I sink down fully onto him and ride him hard until his cum fills up my insides.

I'm not there yet, so I arch my hips in the way I need to reach my own finish line. It doesn't take long until I find the right spot. Then, I ride over his girth until I find myself spasming into the most mind-altering orgasm.

My body collapses into David's arms while he stays inside of me. I can't move. My breath can barely catch up to my still-racing heart. This moment was more than just the dire need for intimacy. It was the reigniting of our connection. The love we share becomes more profound with each new day.

A long time ago, he told me in a letter that he had chosen me. But the reality is we've chosen each other. That's the way it always has been and always will be. The next step is marriage and maybe children when we're ready. But those things don't feel like a priority. What feels important is to be young and free and bask in this perfect time of our lives. After all, this is just the beginning of *our forever*.

I make the final adjustments to my wig so it fits correctly on my head. Then, I apply my last bits of makeup. My reflection in the mirror shocks me with how beautiful the wavy red hair looks on my wig after my mom spent an hour styling it for me.

The knock on the door gets my attention. "Can I come in?" Mom shouts.

"Of course!"

Mom enters the room in her elegant purple Versace halterneck mini dress. It's not just stunning. It's a dress emblematic of the confidence and beauty that defines her new self.

"Wow, Mom!"

"No, no, no," she quickly replies with her hand coming up to her mouth. "Look at you, sweetheart. Oh my!"

I look down at my purple halter dress as I stand up in front of my mom and spin around. The ruffles on the dress land just above my knee and it fits tightly onto my skin to show off my curves. Initially, I thought it was a little too much, but David told me it's the sexiest dress he's ever seen me in. And after seeing him smile at me the way he did that day, the decision on my dress was made.

My mom and I chat as we had fifteen minutes to kill before things started. We spent most of the time talking about my backpacking trip through Europe. I showed her pictures from all the famous landmarks and museums I visited. She tells me how courageous I was to take the trip alone. Then she showers me with more praise since I'm a recent college graduate.

It was only two months ago that I graduated with my master's degree in social work. The degree helped me land my first real job as an art therapist for children who have experienced trauma. I'm nervous to start this next stage of my life. However, the excitement to fulfill my life's purpose by giving hope to children who have lived through trauma means everything.

As for my mom, she graduated six months ago and now works as a preschool teacher. Getting her teaching credentials was a long process because it took two years to go through the court system to get everything expunged from her record. She also just started dating a new woman named Tara in the last few months. Everyone loves her like family already. I just love that she accepts and loves my mom for who she is.

My mom has become her own person over the last few years. She regularly attends therapy and has even joined support groups for people recovering from post-traumatic stress. The resilience and resolve to keep living after everything she's been through is inspiring. But of all the things she's found in life, the biggest is finding her *own* happiness.

It also helps that she lives with Sariah and John. Their support has been monumental. And their lives have turned around just as much as Mom's. They recently got off probation for the identity crimes they committed. Now, John works as a truck driver, and Sariah is a stay-at-home mom. They also finally got pregnant through IVF, and their five-month-old Eric is the shining light in their world.

"Is Tara here yet?" I ask as we head outside for the start of the festivities.

"Yeah, she's talking to David and Angela by the bar."

My eyes go to where she's pointing. Angela gives me a quick wave while flashing a smile. She recently got accepted into a program where she'll work to get her doctorate in physical therapy. We're all excited for her but sad to know she'll be moving to Boston in a couple weeks. I'm sad because we've grown so close over the last few years. Angela is much more than a sister to the man I love. More than anything, she's become my best friend.

I put my arm around my mom and rest my head on her shoulder. We're both staring in awe at our significant others. I lift my head off her shoulder to see her expression. It's clear she feels just like I do—overwhelmed with gratitude and love.

David couldn't come with me on my backpacking trip through Europe because he's having his screenplay, *The Tree House,* adapted into a film. The night everything in our lives almost ended was the same night that David won his prestigious scholarship for the story he wrote. And now that he's graduated from film school, he's already begun working for the same film studio that bought the rights to his story.

David's living his dream, and I couldn't be prouder of him. I tell him every day. And every day I say those words, I mean it somehow more than the day before. It's bigger than the fact that he saved my life on that day by the lake. To me, it's about his resilience in the light of so much terrible trauma. He showed it to me by making a full recovery from a Traumatic Brain Injury. And through all the trauma he's endured, and the tough days that still lie ahead, he stays committed to us. He sets the appointments for all our counseling and therapy sessions. And he supports me even when I'm feeling at my lowest.

The reality is we'll never fully recover from what we've been through. Not Sasha. Not me. Not David. Not my mom. Not even Angela. But we all have each other and support one another through good days and bad. And all this shared love has my heart feeling so full on a special day like today.

We stand on opposite sides in front of the small crowd of seated guests. I'm already crying up a storm as I stare at David, Zach, and his brothers. They're all best men patiently waiting for the woman of the hour.

It's only fitting that Sasha would be marrying a boy named Zach. She met him through Special Olympics three years ago and still swears to me that he's closely related to Zac Efron.

He's a beautiful soul like Sasha. And together, they're ready to share their lives and spread positivity in the world. I'm happy for them, but more so proud. The two of them live independently. They both work full-time to support themselves. But more than anything, they look out for each other and support one another emotionally.

In the last few months, I haven't been living next door to Sasha and seeing her every day. It's been hard because prior to her moving in with Zach, we had been either roommates or neighbors for over four years. But as Mom told me a few months back, she's been ready. And now she's marrying the love of her life. It's everything she's always dreamed of. And now she's living out that dream as she makes her way down the aisle.

"Canon in D" begins playing as everyone rises. The tears flow heavily from both families. It's a small gathering of people, but the people here know our family's journey and how fortunate we all are to be in this moment.

After they say their "I do's," everyone erupts so loud I can't even hear the officiant say kiss the bride. But my god, do Zach and Sasha share a first kiss that will be remembered? It keeps going…*and going…and going*. It lasts so long David pretends to look at a watch on his wrist. The crowd gets louder the longer it goes, but no one cares. This is their shining moment. And all I can do is cry away to my heart's content.

Later that night, David and I hold each other on the dance floor. It's the last slow song of the night, and we're swaying under a full moon, and a sky lit up full of stars. When the music plays its final melodies, I lean back to stare into the eyes of my one and only. The glossy moisture in his eyes has an unforgettable sparkle tonight. His smile shows me the most natural feeling of happiness. Everything about this man's face fills me with a profound sense of gratitude. And yet, in all his natural beauty, I still sense a profound, hidden emotion in his face. It's the sadness for what's missing tonight.

"Why are you crying again?" he asks.

His words only make the tears pour out faster. But I can't help where my mind has gone. I know he misses his dad—we all do. But my mind is crying for only one person right now.

"It's hard to say," I finally admit.

David wipes my eyes with the sleeve of his dress shirt. "Are you sure you're okay?"

"I'll be okay. I'm just grateful you chose me. And I'm not sure that would've ever happened unless I was sent into your backyard that night. And that makes me sad. Because I have my mom, and you don't. I'm so sorry."

I wipe my eyes while sniffling. It's hard to get my emotions in check when the sadness suddenly overwhelms me. Then, his hand tilts my chin up. His eyes burn into mine with a look I've never seen before. It's as if our minds can share in the hurt and somehow channel it into a greater love for one another.

"Don't be sorry, Ellie Merkowitz. I chose you a long time ago. But first, it was my mom choosing you. She knows a beautiful soul when she sees one. And you let her inside you. You saved me, Ellie. You are everything good I can ever want in this life. That's because you are my life. You're a part of me...*forever*."

We kiss as the last note plays. Then I fall into his chest, whispering the exact words that have been living inside my head—because I know they'll find a way into David's heart.

"Thank you, Ima Bear. Love you forever."

The End

Thank you for reading my story. If you are interested in checking out my other work please continue reading for a sneak peek at my other book, *The Tree House*.

A Message from the Author

Thank you for reading my story. I'd greatly appreciate your support by leaving a review on Amazon and Goodreads. For new authors like me, it helps us grow our readership and improve as writers.

Writing is my passion and I'm truly honored to share it with the world. If you'd like to learn more about my author journey and upcoming book releases, please subscribe to my mailing list by visiting www.timothykylebooks.com.

If you're interested in checking out my other work, please continue reading; on the next page you'll find a sneak peek at my other book, *The Tree House*. It's available on Kindle and in paperback.

The Tree House

PROLOGUE

Benny

1956

Don't say kiss her!

Don't say kiss her!

"And one other thing..." Marcus pauses, already cringing. "You'll need to kiss her...on the lips."

I shake my head emphatically. I'd do anything for my best friend. But kissing his seven-year-old sister is crazy. She's two years younger than me, annoying as fuck, and the worst of it is she's already in love with me.

The plan was simple at first. I put on the tux. Then I put the plastic ring on her finger, say "I do," and give her a hug. That was the plan I begrudgingly agreed to.

"No, Marcus!" I shout, seeing Penny's expression wilt out of the corner of my eye.

"Come on, Benny. She needs this. Please do it," he begs.

The first tear runs down the cheek of Penny Jones. Then comes the droopy, puppy dog eyes. Her dark skin can't blush like mine, but this poor girl sure knows how to cry when she needs attention.

"Fine," I sigh, feeling suddenly nervous because I've never kissed anyone.

It's one thing to play pretend games in my red treehouse. But this is no ordinary treehouse. It's a safe haven for my neighbors.

Marcus and Penny Jones come up here most nights to escape the rage of their mother. My grandparents gave them a key to our back gate a couple years ago. They also gave them a key to our house, but they prefer the treehouse most days. Perhaps part of the reason is black kids don't just walk into a white person's house. Maybe it happens in other places, but not in Birmingham, Alabama.

I turn to face Penny. The first thing I notice is one of her eyes is still slightly swollen from her mother's latest attack. But I know the pain she feels on the inside is the worst part. It's the reason I'm up here doing a pretend wedding.

"Here's your vows, Benny," Penny says, handing me a sheet of paper.

I read it in my head, but even doing that makes me want to vomit.

"I can't say this –"

"Just do it," Marcus interrupts, gritting his teeth with a glare.

I let out a loud exhale. "Fine."

Marcus hands me the ring. I glance at Penny, whose sad face has quickly morphed into one of a giddy woman on her wedding day.

I still don't get it. She's just a kid. She may be cute, like how I'd describe most puppies. But she's looking at me like this feels real to her.

Marcus starts giving his sermon. I zone out by staring at my dress shoes. Eventually my gaze comes up to meet Penny's brown eyes. I notice how they've started to fill with tears. But she's not gearing up for her usual cry. These are about to be happy tears.

For a brief moment I have a funny feeling in my chest and tummy. It's hard to understand what I'm feeling. All I know is it feels heavy and warm. But it also feels oddly comfortable, and good for a change. Maybe it's okay that I don't understand it. All I do know is it feels really good to make Penny happy. Happiness is typically something only Marcus can bring out of her.

Marcus gives a forced clearing of his throat. "Hello. Um, guys. Can you hear me. Now you can read your vows," he says, looking at us like we're deaf.

I guess we didn't hear him the first time. It's like our eyes were caught in some type of trance with one another.

"You can go first," Marcus says, nodding to Penny.

"Dear, Benny. Thank you for marrying me and for having children with me. I want three boys and one girl. That's all. Love, Penny."

My throat locks up. I was not expecting her to demand children. I want to laugh at her, but I also don't want her crying again. Besides, she seemed dead serious and overly confident with her demands. Does she still think babies come from a stork?

"Your turn, Benny. And remember to first put the ring on her," Marcus says.

My hands starts shaking. Then I slowly slide the ring up her finger. Her eyes widen once the ring is on. The smile on her face is an illumination of happiness like I've never seen.

I pull out my vows, taking a deep breath. "Dear, Penny. You are the only girl I will ever love. I promise to love you to the moon and back. And to the moon and back again. Love, Benny."

I want to breathe out a sigh of relief, but the next part is the most nerve-wracking.

"You may kiss the bride," Marcus says. "On the lips."

I take a step towards her. Penny closes her eyes and puckers her lips. Then I lean down for my first-ever kiss.

CHAPTER ONE

Benny

Two Years Later

"Kindness, hmm," Grandpa sighs, taking a long swig of his coffee.

His stare goes over my head, to a place in another time. His eyes are already glossy with remembering, like he's wanting to freeze so many moments of his past all at once.

"Okay, here it is," Grandpa says, shooting his glare down to me. "True kindness…is willingness."

"Willingness?"

"Yes, Benny. It's the willingness to want to do good without recognition or praise. It's doing it because your heart is overflowing with love. And remember, it's the giver of kindness who gets the most out of it."

Grandpa smiles at Grammy as she walks in. "I've only known one person on this earth who did it better than anyone else. Isn't that right, Honey?"

Grammy doesn't blush or bat an eye. She just smiles at Grandpa. She gets compliments like these every day. Then he grabs her hand, pulling her onto his lap. They share a long smooch that makes me want to vomit.

"Yuck," I complain, looking away.

"Well, I think the best form of kindness is the one born from courage. Are you courageous, Benny McClain?" Grammy asks.

How does an 11-year-old boy know if he's courageous or not?

I guess.

"Sure, I think so."

Grandpa softly chuckles. "Oh Benny boy, it's already within you. It's always going to be there, no matter what. You're a McClain. Look, here's how I know. Take your hand and place it over your heart. You feel that?"

I do as Grandpa says, feeling the rhythmic thud beneath my chest. "So, what? It's beating. It's no different than anyone else," I explain, feeling confused.

"Ah!" Grandpa raises one finger in the air. "That's where you're wrong. Your heart doesn't just beat. It speaks to you!" he raises his voice as his glare intensifies. "You just have to learn how to hear it. Now close your eyes. Tell me, Benny. What is your heart telling you right now?"

I close my eyes as the thunder roars outside. I can't help but sigh in frustration at my grandpa's lesson. It's a lesson I get every year on my birthday. This year is no different than the rest.

Most grandparents shower their grandchildren with gifts or money. Not mine. I get the yearly Grandpa McClain life lesson.

The loud footsteps and panicked breathing suddenly break my concentration. I open my eyes as my younger brother wraps his arms around me, grasping for dear life. He digs his face into my chest. His noise cancelling headphones lightly bump into my jaw every time he bobs his head. My arms go tighter around him because it's the only way to calm him down.

"You're okay, Jimmy. I'm here. You're okay."

"Oh, Jimmy. Your big brother loves you so much," Grandpa says, smiling with admiration. "Now Benny, let's try this again. Close your eyes and put your hand over your heart."

I slowly let Jimmy go. He stays seated on the edge of my chair while I do as Grandpa says.

"Ah, ah, Benny. Your brother is here, too. Help him out."

"Sorry, Grandpa."

Jimmy may be different. But my grandparents have always been adamant that he gets the same opportunities as anyone else: "No differences and no excuses." It's what I've been hearing for every day of my waking life.

When I can't get Jimmy to hold his shaking hand over his heart, I settle on pulling it over my chest as our hands interweave.

"Okay. Now close your eyes, boys."

I try my best to concentrate on the sound of my heart. It's a little less frenetic. Perhaps it's because I have my brother's closeness at my side.

I try hearing through the pain and noise in my head. If only it could go away for a second. If only I could will people back from the dead. If only I could console my brother and help him find his words.

That's it!

My eyes flash open, and hope courses through my veins. I take a deep breath, feeling like I understand the meaning of life.

"So…?" Grandpa asks.

"I know the meaning of kindness, Grandpa. I'm going to change the world," I proclaim, taking my gaze from Grandpa to my brother. "I mean, we're going to change the world, together, me and Jimmy."

I hug my brother closer into my side, smiling wide at my grandpa. His eyes squint. His hand itches the grey and white stubble on his chin.

"How?" he challenges.

How? How? How?

The word pinballs around in my head, adding to the noise and fog in my brain.

I think I have an idea. But how does someone change the world? I mean, I'm only a kid. I'm not an expert on anything. My abilities in the classroom are average at best. The only thing I've known since a young age is running like a cheetah and throwing the football like Bart Starr.

That's it!

"I'm going to be the best there ever was, Grandpa. I'll win National Championships. I'll win Super Bowls. Then I'll start a charity for people like Jimmy," I declare, puffing my chest with pride.

Jimmy's hand grasps tighter around mine. His smile slowly forms across his face with the usual bit of underlying tension.

"That's great you want to be a champion and start a charity, but dig deeper, Benny. What do you really want to do?"

I glance at Jimmy as he looks away from me. I pull his hand back into my chest. Then his eyes come back to mine. His smile is gone. His thoughts on the inside feel like a broken puzzle. It makes me want to piece him together from the inside. Or maybe just understand what's going on inside his head. But I don't have superpowers like Penny.

Then Jimmy pulls my hand into his chest. The emotions on his face are still hidden. The only thing I notice is his eyes looking the slightest bit glossy. He stares into my eyes with new intentions.

It's at that moment I know. The answer to my grandpa's question is right in front of me, broken puzzle pieces and all.

"I get it, Grandpa. I'm going to be the most devoted big brother for Jimmy. I'm going to make other people see the true him. I'm going to help him be heard. And I'm always going to protect him, no matter what."

Grandpa just nods his head smiling. Then the doorbell rings. I groan right away, knowing who it is.

"Come on, Benny. A promise is a promise," Grandpa scolds. "Be nice to her."

It's almost 8 a.m. on a school day. It could only be one person—my next-door neighbor, Penny Jones.

My grandparents have been providing free daycare to Penny for the last few years. But it's become much more regular ever since her brother Marcus, my best friend, died about a year ago.

Another big reason is Penny's mom. She's been an off-and-on alcoholic for as long as I can remember. However, now that her son is gone, her alcoholism has been the definition of who she is. She loves her whiskey more than her only living child.

The story of Penny's dad is more of a mystery. All I know is he left her when she was about four years old. The only somewhat dependable parental figure she has is her Aunt Mary. She does her best to look after her, but she's always working, and she has her own family to tend to.

The doorbell rings again. I huff out another long sigh as I make my way to the front door.

A promise is a promise.

"Hi, Benny!"

She marches past me like she owns the place. I roll my eyes at her flirting grin.

"Jimmy!" she screams, running into the kitchen. She tackles Jimmy with a hug that almost knocks the air out of him.

"Penny! Penny! Penny!" Jimmy keeps shouting with an ear-to-ear grin.

My brother typically doesn't talk much at all. But around Penny, he's able to find his words more easily.

We all settle in at the kitchen table for a light breakfast.

"No, no, no, Jimmy. You have to use the fork," Penny instructs, guiding his hand to the handle of his fork.

Jimmy usually knows how to use his fork. He just loves having Penny's doting attention.

Grammy walks into the kitchen, giving me a glare I can't ignore.

"What?"

She leans down into my ear.

"Did you not hear your grandpa. It's willingness, Benny. Take a lesson here from Penny," she says, smiling her direction. "Penny has willingness."

"But Grammy, Jimmy does just fine eating with his hands."

"Manners, Benny!" Grammy's eyebrows raise up. "Last I checked, you're the big brother. And everything you're capable of, so is Jimmy. Besides, we're not savages."

I exhale, thinking of the million things I already do for Jimmy on a daily basis. It's gotten easier now that he's nine years old and doing most of his daily tasks on his own. The only challenge for him is processing the emotions around him and learning how to communicate.

"It's okay, Mrs. McClain. Me and Jimmy are best friends for life. I don't mind helping him out. Besides, one day he'll be my brother-in-law," Penny says, flashing a bright smile my way.

I can't help myself as I start making gagging noises. "You're nine, for god's sake! And I'm not going to marry you, Penny Jones. I'm sorry."

"Manners, Benny," Grammy demands, pinching my shoulder. "And Penny, please call me Grammy. You're family, Sweetheart."

"I was just kidding, Benny," Penny mutters, looking embarrassed.

Penny Jones was not kidding. She declared her love for me the first time Marcus and I invited her up into my treehouse. At the time she was five and I was only seven years old. Then a couple years later I mistakenly agreed to a fake wedding that I should have never shown up for.

Maybe it was the peer pressure from her brother that day. Marcus wanted to do something to cheer her up. She'd been crying all day because her mama abandoned her for the thousandth time. Either way she loves reminding me every single day of our treehouse wedding.

I still wish I had just said no that day. It's not that I don't care for her or know how much the McClain family means to her. But I don't like her like that. I only see her as an annoying younger sister.

Besides, Penny's been through enough in life. She lives in a town where people hurl insults at her just because her skin is black. She also watched her brother Marcus die suddenly from a rare form of bone cancer. But the worst part is never having a real mother or father figure in her life. The closest thing she has to a parent are my grandparents. And the closest thing she has to a brother is Jimmy and me. And I promised Marcus I'd look after Penny like a brother. It's a promise I'll no doubt take to the grave with me.

I watch Penny as she walks back to the table with a glass of water for herself and Jimmy. She helps him dish up seconds on his scrambled eggs. Then she whispers something in his ear that makes him giggle.

Grammy and Grandpa think that Penny will one day become a teacher to the differently abled. I could see it. She's more patient with Jimmy than my grandparents and me combined.

Jimmy is just a different person around Penny. His smile typically has a bit of confusion in it. But around Penny, his smile is wider and more natural looking. I'm a bit jealous that I can't always bring that side out of him, but I know he loves me regardless.

"Ah Penny, you're an angel darling. Thank you," Grandpa compliments her.

"Thanks, Penny," I barely mumble the words.

I do my best to pay her as little compliments as possible. Whenever I say something nice to her, she takes it as an opportunity to unapologetically swoon and give me googly eyes. Today feels no different. She keeps flashing crooked smiles at me from across the table.

"So, Benny. What did you get for your birthday?" Penny asks.

"Nothing," I mutter, rolling my eyes.

Penny's face wilts with empathy.

"We don't give presents, Honey. We made an exception for you the last couple years – you know, with all you've been through. But Benny doesn't need anything. He's got the love of his family, the roof over his head, oxygen to breathe and food in his belly," Grammy boasts with pride.

"And he's got my eleventh life lesson on kindness. A lesson Penny just performed perfectly. Here it is for the record, Benny. Now go file it with the rest of them," Grandpa says, handing over a single sheet of paper.

I read it again, rolling my eyes.

Happy 11th Birthday, Benny. And remember, true kindness is willingness.

"Thanks, Grandpa."

I head upstairs to grab my backpack, cleats, and helmet for football practice. I file my grandpa's note in my birthday folder. Then I quickly flip through all 11 of his notes, smiling and laughing at my grandpa's one-liners. Each sheet is identical in form, a single sheet of paper with only one or two sentences. But each message is unique to my grandpa's lesson on that specific birthday.

Maybe one day I'll understand his point. Besides, I already know that I'm a good person. I take on more responsibility than any one 11-year-old kid in this town. And if I complain or act ungrateful on occasion – oh well.

"You're going to be late for school!" Grammy shouts.

I put my birthday folder away and rush downstairs. "You ready, Penny?"

The question is rhetorical because she's never ready to walk to school with me. Penny loves doing long goodbyes. But I don't blame her. She knows how sad Jimmy gets each day we go to school.

It's the loneliness that gets to me. He stays home to learn things with Grammy and Grandpa, but it's not the same social experience. It hurts seeing him so isolated from others. It's too bad our hillbilly town doesn't offer educational opportunities for people like Jimmy. Instead, the people of this town look down on him like he's some pariah that should be institutionalized. Little do they know that Jimmy is academically smarter than most of them.

In some ways it's no different than the treatment of black people here in Birmingham. We're probably the most segregated city in America. There's only a handful of schools like the one me and Penny go to that are desegregated.

"Hey, wait up!" Penny yells as I rush out the door.

"Hurry up, slow poke."

It only takes a few steps out the door until I hear the thud. It's heavy and unlike anything I've ever heard in my life. I quickly turn around as I hear Penny's blood curdling scream. Then Jimmy shrills out a terrifying scream of his own.

I rush into the house as Grandpa is huddled over Grammy, holding her head in his lap. He keeps screaming her name, begging for her to wake up. Meanwhile, my body is frozen. My eyes can't look away from the pool of red beneath her head.

Acknowledgments

I'd like to first say I'm humbled and eternally grateful to you, the reader, for wanting to give my book a chance. My heart and soul live in every single word I've put on these pages. And while no book is ever going to be perfect, I'm so proud of what I've created with *The Girl in the Red Wig*. This story has suffering, but also the message of everlasting hope. And no matter what you're suffering from, because we all have our demons, I hope you never lose hope. Remember, you are *loved*, you are *seen*, and WE ALL MATTER!

The journey to the finish line with this book took a team of people. I'd like to first thank Beautiful Book Covers by Ivy for creating a one-of-a-kind cover that captures my story perfectly. To my arc and street team, thank you for giving my book a chance and hyping it up on social media. I want to specifically recognize my PA, Nicole. Thank you for your leadership and guidance in helping me promote my book. And to my beta readers, thank you for telling me when my shit (aka the bad parts of my book) was in fact shit. Your encouragement and belief in my story meant the world to me. I am eternally grateful to all seven of you: KR, Avery, Keri, Kathi, Natasha, Ambrosia, and Kelsey.

The other integral part to this team were my editors: Megan Harris, Robrt Pela, and Cassie Rabbitt. Thank you for your time and diligence in making my writing look like I know what I'm doing. Your attention to detail and hours put into making this book a finished product means so much to me.

Now, a message for my three daughters. You can NEVER, EVER read this book! But I hope you know that your inner beauty is the inspiration for this story. As your father, I worry every single day that I'm doing the best job in raising three independent, strong-willed, confident, and courageous women. But the truth is, you are all of those things and *more*. I love you three so much, my bones hurt!

And lastly to my wife, Emmy. Your support has been unwavering. You've seen the highs and lows as I pursue my author dreams and never once questioned or doubted what I'm capable of. You are my everything in this world. I'm so grateful to grow old with you and fall deeper in love with you every single day.

About the Author

Timothy Kyle is a longtime native of Phoenix, Arizona. He's a proud husband and father to three rambunctious pre-teen girls. When he's not writing or making ridiculous social media content, he's pursuing his other passion in life as a tennis coach.

Timothy received his master's degree in exercise science in 2009. He worked for the next decade in the non-profit and education sectors that support individuals with *special* abilities. He's a proud advocate of the special needs community and of women's rights.

The Girl in the Red Wig is his second book. His other book is *The Tree House*. If you enjoy his writing, he'd love for you to visit www.timothykylebooks.com and subscribe to his mailing list, so he can keep you in-the-know on his next projects.

Trigger Warnings

The Girl in the Red Wig contains the below content that some readers may find disturbing.

Suicide

Depression/Mental Illness

Violence/Physical Assault

Murder

Verbal Abuse

Child Abandonment/Neglect

Religious Slurs

Graphic Sex

Brief Mentions of Miscarriage

Hair Loss

Religious Extremism: The author has written a fictitious story where Judaism is a major theme in the book. However, the author never intended to offend anyone who follows the Jewish faith. If you are sensitive to reading a story that includes any form of religious extremism, please consider that before reading this book.